C000279000

A short time before sunset he got out his wings, had an awkward job with the harness, which was not easy to fit singlehanded. The tiny propulsor drove him to the top of the wall, where he strolled along its broad flat crest with pinions folded and gleaming.

The toothy ones in the jungle snarled and gibbered in anger at the unearthly sight.

At a point near the corner where the wall right-angled northward a local objector waddled out of its hiding place, came right to the base of the impassable rampart and stood directly below him. Staring upward with red eyes that burned beneath projecting brows, it drummed resoundingly upon its chest, made deep grunting sounds and drooled saliva.

Its attitude was challenging, an unmistakable invitation to come down and settle once for all the question of who was the superior life-form. Edham answered it by pausing in his walk, giving glare for glare and laughing inside of himself until the creature foamed with fury.

At the b̲ ̲ ̲ ̲ ̲ he calmly spr̲ ad his wings, glided wi̲t̲hin̲ ̲ ̲ ̲ ̲ ̲ ̲ ̲ ̲ ̲ ̲ ̲ ̲ ght.

Contents

Deep Space

First Person Singular

1.

New Planet

THE NEW PLANET COULD BE SEEN AS A DARK DISC SUR-
rounded by a glowing nimbus. Its halo was created
by the small red sun burning far behind it. There
were other spheres in this same locality, some with
many satellites and one—a glorious sight—with multi-colored
rings. Sensed by the instruments although not from this angle
evident to the eyes, was a dangerous belt of rocks rushing aim-
lessly through the void and forming the reef of the stars.

Quivering and red-tailed, the long particle-scarred space-
ship had tilted high above the reef and was now heading for
the nimbus. There was another smaller paler halo close to the
objective, sharing its orbit, indicative of an almost airless moon.

Seated behind the bow observation port, Captain Rafel
twisted around as Edham came into the cabin. He said, "I
summoned you forward, thinking you might like first view.
It has just expanded sufficiently for straight vision." He
pointed into the sparkling darkness. "There it is."

Taking a seat beside the commander, Selected Granor Edham looked at the thin circle shining upon the backdrop of
creation. The picture was unsatisfactory in that it told little.
All the same it meant enough. It was a dim, ghostly lamp
marking the end of his trail.

It represented the purpose for which he had been chosen
and, for all he knew, the specific function for which he had
been conceived and born. That faraway light, pale, wan and
beckoning, surrounded the hidden fact of fate. It marked the
site of death or glory. It was the cradle—or the grave.

His young, strong and decidedly stubborn features did
not change expression while his gaze remained leveled forward. Rafel was watching him and he was aware of the scru-

tiny but this had nothing to do with his grim phlegmaticism. Either he was peculiarly insensitive or had superb control of his emotions, for he gave Rafel nothing to go by. His face remained set, just a little cold, a little forbidding, and his eyes were steady, unwinking.

Rafel said quietly, "We'll be there in about two hundred tempors by the clock." He waited for comment, watching, watching. There was no remark, not even the quirk of an eyebrow. The other's countenance might have been carved in rock. Rafel went on, his manner verging upon the paternal, "You speak but seldom. Once I saw you smile and that I shall always remember. I have never heard you laugh."

"I do my laughing inside myself."

"But not often," pursued Rafel. "Not as frequently as others do."

"Not all are the same," Edham observed.

"Of course not. There are differences. So long as we can lay claim to be individuals there must be differences. Therefore some laugh and some weep."

In the same even unaccentuated tones, Edham asked, "Have you wept?"

Rafel leaned back in his air-cushioned seat and eyed the stars. He had thin aquiline features and the large luminous optics of the highly intelligent. The eyes were upon the stars without seeing them.

"Six times or perhaps seven. Please do not ask me when, where or why."

"I have not the slightest desire to do so. One cannot seize part of another man's heart." For the first time Edham showed hint of expression, no more than a narrowing of the eyes, a slight hardening of the jaw muscles. "But if ever the time comes to weep for me it would be well to remember something."

"Such as?"

"I shall be laughing."

Rafel said soberly, "I hope you will, I hope you will." He hesitated, continued, "No one sees himself truly pictured in the mirror of another's mind. Sometimes one is given to wonder how one looks.

"Has one the faults and virtues of which he is conscious

or do his fellows see some faults as virtues, some virtues as faults? Do others see additional faculties not apparent to their possessor? I am the captain of my ship but what sort of a captain am I to my crew—good, bad or indifferent?"

"It is of little consequence. The shape is set."

"Bear with me. I am leading up to something. Do you mind if I put a personal question?"

"I mind nothing," said Edham. "Would I be where I am, going where I'm going, if I had cares, susceptibilities?"

"You are treading my conversational path a little ahead of me," Rafel told him. "What I would like to ask you is this—have you ever suspected yourself of unsociability?"

"I do not suspect it—I know it." Edham turned his head, looked straight at him. "During and since childhood I have not mixed quite as others have mixed and such mixing as I have done has been done self-consciously. Sometimes I have wondered whether it is an inferiority complex or sheer unsociability.

"I console myself with the thought that I am not antisocial. I like and enjoy my fellows—providing there are not too many at one time. I have never liked crowds." His dark gray orbs studied Rafel. "Why do you ask?"

The other gave him a slow smile. "You console yourself because you think your character at fault or suspect that others consider it faulty. Is it a true flaw?" He waved his hand at the enveloping cosmos. "In the big cities, perhaps. Out here, no! Out here it is a virtue."

Edham said nothing.

"You are a Selected Granor," Rafel pointed out. "A chosen son born under the sun called Di. Selection is not based on idle whims. It is a careful sifting from the mass of Di's children, a sorting out of the hardy pioneering types, the ones who may be restless, out-of-place, unsocial in the cities.

"But on the loneliest frontiers—*ah!*" He spread expressive hands. "There, they come into their own. They are independent, self-reliant, they do not mourn for the comfort of the crowd."

Edham offered no remark.

"In the College of Granors is a great obelisk bearing eighteen hundred honored names," Rafel mused reminiscently.

"I have read them as doubtless you have read them. Every man-jack was much like you."

"That is gratifying." Edham offered it with glum humor as if he were laughing inside of himself. His gray eyes met Rafel's again. "Because every man-jack is dead."

The nimbus had grown to sky-filling size and had resolved itself to an atmosphere heavily clouded. There was a blaze of crimson light and an awful roaring and a frantic scattering of thunderheads as the space-ship came cautiously through the blanket. A huge saucer-like object, flat in its center, thin at the edge, the ship lowered amid a spume of fire.

Jungle below sent up trunks and fronds and greenly reaching arms. Steam came from it and vegetable warmth and cloying odors mingled with the stench of noisome things rotting in the dark. Living shapes came up with the vapor and the smells, flying, fluttering, flapping away, some dexterously, some with the ungainly awkwardness of creations ill-conceived, some with shrill screechings or harsh cries.

Other entities that could not fly, landbound and raging, slunk or blundered through the undergrowth and howled their hatred at each other and at the monster in the air.

For a little while the vessel hung half a mile above hell, uncountable miles below heaven. The superheated clouds it had thrust aside had now swung back together, closing the gap and sending down a torrent of warm rain.

The downpour made an angry rattle on the space-ship's topside and venturis bellowed and the jungle screamed. More clouds in the distance, black and bloated, were drifting to the aid of their fellows, rumbling from time to time and casting vivid shafts across the sky.

Planetary Surveyor Jolin was in the underbelly blister when Edham joined him. Together they looked down upon the wetness and the tangled green.

"You can blame me for this," said Jolin. "I pronounced it possible. Every time I declare a planet to be possible the decision fidgets within my conscience."

"That is natural," Edham soothed. "Since you will not live long enough to see the end result you must feel the weight of uncertainty. But why worry? No man can do more than his best."

"I have seen failures," Jolin observed moodily. "That is the curse of it. Failures can and do become apparent swiftly enough to damn my judgment. The successes are long-term ones, so long that they will be known only to my grandsons' grandsons."

"It is frustrating," agreed Edham. "What a pity that we have never achieved that time-travel which Kalteniel is so fond of depicting in his visi-scrolls. You could then go forward many centuries and see precisely where you have done well, where you have erred."

"Kalteniel irks me now and again." Jolin shook his head in mild condemnation. "Take his supposedly more plausible stories of space-travel. He dumps people here, dumps them there, keeps them alive in spite of every adverse circumstance, makes them perform all sorts of antics as if the fundamental problem of existence were no problem at all. Life isn't so resilient. It's precarious. It is balanced by margins incredibly fine. If it were otherwise you and I would have different jobs."

Edham offered no comment.

"We are life-forms delicately held within ten million tiny and elusive circumstances," Jolin went on. "One small item, one seemingly insignificant feature, can create the bias that kills. On one otherwise innocent world it is the existence in its atmosphere of an exceedingly minute trace of gas with accumulative properties.

"On another it is an unsuspected undetected virus in the water." He glanced at the other. "A few Di-born plants grew erratically but clung to life on Theta Ten. Far more would not. They lacked only a vague trace of copper in the soil."

"Who can measure the unknown?" said Edham.

"And the same is true in reverse." Jolin nodded toward the jungle. "In the Di-system some of those plants might flourish, others might contrive to exist by changing form to suit slightly different conditions—but many might wither and die for lack of one titanium atom in each ten thousand molecules of soil—or for lack of something else equally dispersed."

"I have been told all this," Edham reminded. "I do not fear the death of metabolic imbalance. By all accounts it comes insidiously, without pain." Cold-eyed, he studied the world beneath.

"But I do dislike the notion of involuntary change. Admittedly one survives when gradually altered by Nature to fit the new framework but one cannot be sure of the manner of one's change or the picture it presents in the end. There are so many possibilities, some of them repulsive.

"Yes." Jolin admitted it solemnly. "It is that I would find the most repugnant—alteration out of recognition. It is death which is not death. It is severance from one's own kind plus the torment of being something strange and new amid older unchanged life-forms that hate the strange and new. It is utter loneliness." He shuddered without shame. "I could not bear it."

"I could," said Edham, "if absolutely necessary." He paused, added in the same flat voice. "For a while."

Rafel changed the subject by appearing at the blister. "That is a fair sample down below. Most of the planet is the same. It spawns ferociously." He cupped his chin in his hand, regarded the tangle of life for awhile, then said, "We cannot sit down in any old place. We'll search the world and make a landing in the most attractive spot."

Edham said, "Or the least unattractive."

He did not smile when Rafel looked at him as if striving to discern what lay behind the mask. He was accustomed to the long penetrating gaze of those large eyes. As always it was an attempted estimating—and none can weigh the soul. So he met Rafel's questing orbs with a tantalizing blankness that provided inward amusement for himself but did not irritate the other.

"Perhaps you are right," conceded Rafel. He shrugged and went away.

Presently the venturis lengthened their blasts to a multitude of fire-spears. The jungle leaves swayed and cowered while unseen forms beneath them sent up a cacophony of noise.

The ship soared a mile higher, moved forward. The clouds stabbed it with hot forks.

2.

Sphere of Wrath

*P*ARALLELING THE EQUATOR ON A ROUTE WHERE THE sub-tropics merged into the temperate zone, the Disian vessel traveled at sedate pace. There was no need for great speed, no urgency. Accurate observation of the land was the prime purpose; it was not possible to find sanctuary at high velocity. So the ship roamed on, circumnavigating the world four times while its crew watched and waited for a haven of gentleness in this domain of savagery.

It was a sphere of wrath, hot, violent and seething with the sperm of a million things, great and small. Its clouds hung black and belly-bloated. Its trees climbed upon the bodies of their forbears as they fought hugely toward the blanketed sun.

Its animal forms were drinkers of blood, eaters of meat, feeders upon all other kinds, upon their own kind and upon their own young. They battled and copulated with an appalling frenzy, howling in labor, screaming in death and giving up their offal.

There was a horrid pseudo-life even beneath the earth. In certain places the surface crawled and rolled and heaved while great fissures opened and steam burst forth. A river bent down into a hole and was spewed out boiling.

Topless mountains volleyed meteor-streams that curved through the clouds and fired the jungle. The quivering surface emitted tremendous groans and the river hissed deafeningly and the mountains cannonaded again and again and again.

The atmosphere was heavy, thick, moist and somehow enervating and invigorating at one and the same time. It was invisibly striated with smells—the odors of wood-rot, wet leaves, sulphur, steam, crushed funguses, burning bark, cooling lava, and decay.

To search all this for a resting place was to seek a lesser hell and that they found on the fourth time around. There was a raised valley between rounded hills with slow-moving yellow rivers flowing at either side. The valley was broad and large— the hills silent, without inward fires. No steam arose from vents in the solidly founded ground.

The trees, shrubs, vines and creepers were all present together with the hot-blooded things that hunted beneath them. The same smells came up, the same noises. But purely by contrast with other parts of the world the valley seemed a little more sheltered, a little more stable, a little less racked with the strains of competing life.

Lowering his vessel, Captain Rafel took it along the valley with assault-beams blazing at full intensity. Every living thing beneath promptly resolved itself to an ash so fine that much hung suspended while some slowly settled.

The trees and the tangles beneath the trees and the monsters who lurked in the tangles all became ash. From one end of the valley to the other, all ash. From hill-base to hill-base, nothing but thin unsoiled stalks of ash quavering like new-born ghosts. The very ground was sterilized to a depth of twenty feet.

They ripped a cloud and rain came down and laid the reluctant dust. Over a smaller central area of the valley they beam-baked the mud so formed and converted it to the hard cake of an emergency landing place. On this the ship sat, touching soil lightly, letting its weight be felt gradually and forming an earthly cup in which to rest.

The crew emerged, six hundred strong. They knew exactly what to do and needed no orders. It was a familiar task— they had planted a Granor many times before.

Dragging out their machines, the wall-builders began to cut huge stone blocks from the hills, to move them along and around the valley, to mount them one upon another and fuse them together. Heavily armed, the guard squads patrolled beyond them near the burned rim of the jungle and kept hostile shapes at bay. Well inside the walls the prefab-erectors busied themselves assembling the sections of a small, compact house.

The biological party divided itself, extracted from the ship's cargo space a load of Disian seeds, tubers, cuttings, shoots and baby plants. These they unwrapped with loving care and proceeded to set in the alien earth according to a scheme conceived long in the past and executed time and time again in places spread across half creation's span.

Rafel hung around, watching. The wall arose and a raucous antagonism beyond the wall was quieted with a distant blast and the momentary shine of a beam. The house swung together, every addition making it more like a house. A quadruple row of tiny green growths already stretched from his feet to the base of the eastward wall. More plants, larger and darker, were being set beyond them.

"This performance, I presume, has the boredom of repetition," suggested Edham, joining him.

"Not at all. I look at today—but I see tomorrow." He glanced at the other, his eyes bright, luminous. "What do *you* see?"

Edham thought a moment, said, "I am given to vizualize a few lines from that ancient saga called *The Granor of Theta Ten.* Doubtless they are familiar to you." He carried on and recited them, speaking with a peculiar lack of emotion that somehow lent point to the words.

> *"They labor'd without rest or cease*
> *To make the land more fair,*
> *And builded him a place of peace*
> *Five thousand cubits square."*

"The verse is appropriate," said Rafel. "It cannot be otherwise since the technique has remained the same."

"But not the tomorrows?"

"Not the tomorrows," Rafel admitted with some reluctance. "Nature will not have us everywhere."

"Nor have us exactly as we are."

"Sometimes." Rafel felt that he was being pushed where he had no desire to go. "And sometimes not." He counterpushed with a proposal. "Come with me and explore beyond the walls."

"It is a useful idea," said Edham, betraying no hint of humor. "One should know one's neighbors."

Getting two pairs of scout-wings from the ship they struggled into the harness, each tightening the other's buckles. The wings swept white and gleaming from their shoulders as they switched on the tiny propulsors and soared. There was a certain trickiness in using this personal mode of flight, each user's pleasure being proportionate to his own dexterity.

Crossing the northward wall, already man-height and still growing, they floated wide-winged above the jungle's trees. Their closer approach made visible many things formerly hidden though others lurked lower and remained unseen. There were great worms in some tree-tops, sinuous, sliding, many-colored creatures that writhed up the trunks and lay along the branches and stared with beady unblinking eyes. There were other entities, barrel-bodied, beetle-browed, that swung from limb to limb and yelled at the winged forms above.

"A-a-ah! *A-a-ah!*"

And from faraway came the answering call of their fellows, red-eyed and toothy, "A-a-ah!"

At one point where a rocky outcrop made a space of barrenness in the warring vegetation, there slumbered an eater too gigantic to be eaten. It was a slate-gray monstrosity, stupidly evil of face, massive of body, with a high serration running along its back. Its balloonlike belly shrank and filled as it breathed and its tail curved away through tree-gap after tree-gap. With tiny eyes closed it snored in a manner that shook the shrubs before its nose.

Rafel had swooped daringly close to get a better look at the slumberer and as he curved upward on wide-set wings, coming low over a tree, a many-hued worm stabbed half its length at him from where it lay concealed in the foliage.

So much swifter was his own reaction that he had time only to glimpse the soft elastic mouth and darting tongue before his beam sliced the thing in three. The parts fell near to the slate-gray sleeper and continued to jerk around with raw ends. The sleeper opened one eye, stared with dull disinterest at the squirming pieces, grunted deep down and closed the eye again.

"That," remarked Rafel, unruffled, is "another item for my collection of cosmic incongruities—ambition in a worm."

Edham said, "Sometimes I wonder whether anyone else

has us similarly rated."

"When we meet them—if ever we meet them—we shall not try to get them down our gullets," promised Rafel.

"What else shall we do?"

"We will allow *them* to swallow *us*." Rafel gave him a sly smile. "We have never found any difficulty in permitting the unavoidable."

"Neither shall I." He did not smile back. "In a way I shall have complete control of this world—I shall sit upon it and permit everything." Edham deftly tilted against a side-current, swung straight. "Let us view this river."

The westward waterway over which they skimmed was the broader of the two at either side of the valley. Slow-moving and sullen, its depths were yellow and full of life. Small shapes occasionally leaped from its undersurface to escape larger pursuers and now and again the big ones jumped amid a shower of drops to avoid the monstrous. Logs floated downstream past other half-submerged things that strove to look like logs.

A black hook-beaked flyer fell from the clouds, coming silently on broad leathery surfaces, and plunged at Rafel while he was studying a log that had reptilian eyes. Edham sliced its head off in mid-air. The body shot straight to the water but did not touch it.

Great jaws came out of the river and caught it at the last moment, then sank from sight. A few lazy bubbles arose. The log which had drawn Rafel's attention split at one end and yawned, exposing many teeth.

"Here life is a phase—death an incident," Edham commented. "What a world!"

"To face alone," added Rafel.

Edham laughed without showing it.

3.

Sanctuary

THE ENCAMPMENT WAS COMPLETE IN EVERY DETAIL ON
the fortieth day. Its walls stood a hundred cubits high
by ten cubits thick, solid, jointless, four-square, without a break except for one armorplate door in the
center of the side that faced south. The living house was
finished and equipped.

The instrument shed stood near it, the tool shed adjoined
it and the transparent house for incubating plants was right
behind. Apart from that occupied by the space-ship, the rest
of the area within the walls was a parade-ground for Disian
plants in companies and battalions.

Rafel had a schematic diagram spread across the table
inside the house and his long slender forefinger shifted from
point to point as he spoke.

"As you know your main task will be to keep check on
all this. Every plant-section must be covered not less than
once in five days. Every stage of growth must be carefully
noted. Any departure from the norm must be recorded in the
fullest possible detail. Any failure to develop must likewise
be entered.

"Take special note of comparative rates of progress for
they are important. If the hard-fruited trees do well while the
soft-fruiting bushes do not, we want to know in what way
they differ, item by item, for such information is invaluable."

"I have had all this at the training college," Edham remarked. "We may never know why some Di-plants flourish
in alien conditions while others do not, but it is sufficient to
learn which can survive."

"Exactly," agreed Rafel. "Where enough of them cling
to existence, so can we. It is essential to know in advance how

many can live and of what kinds. That is real knowledge." He mused a little while over the graph. "I find it galling that we are reduced to animal status by one dismal fact—that any world can resist our settlement by resisting our digestive juices."

"Kalteniel has the problem solved. His characters are never guilty of any animal function. Would that I were one of them."

"That brings me to the most emphatic point." Rafel's great eyes looked straight and steadily into his. "This also is something you've had before, had it until you're sick of it, but before I go it must be said again. That is the strictest rule of Granor-planting—the Granor must not be left without being told again. Until such time as we return you will subsist solely upon foods of Di-origin."

"I know, I know."

"The stores we leave will last far beyond your fifth harvest—if there *are* any harvests. You are free to eke out your preserved supplies with fresh stuff grown within these walls—if any does grow." His voice grew sharp, authoritative. "But of the foods native to this world you must not eat!"

His long schooling at the College of Granors made itself felt as Edham squared his shoulders and obediently echoed, "Of native fruits I must not eat."

"Remember that—always remember," Rafel emphasized. "The food natural to this earth may be quite innocuous. Possibly you might wax fat upon it, more so than upon Di-foods. If so we are lucky indeed. But the time for testing the matter is not yet.

"Be satisfied that already you are breathing alien air of unknown potentialities, that you are continually subjected to the rays of an alien sun with hidden powers, that you remain within alien gravitational and magnetic fields—and the total long-term effects of all these are pure guesswork until such time as you have eliminated the guesses.

"So do not be venturesome or impatient. Remember that enough is enough and rest content with the hazards already imposed upon you."

"Do you suspect me of excessive zeal?" asked Edham.

"I have no suspicions—but I do have memories."

"Of what?"

"Of many things." He hesitated, went on, "My mind holds vivid pictures I would give much to forget. For example I see the Granor of the unnamed world near Arka. He suffered unanticipated disaster to his stores, became hungry and thirsty long before our return. And when we came back—"

"Go on," urged Edham.

"I remember his lonely distorted shape crawling into the dark as our ship lifted and cut him off forever from his kind. What he had was terrible, incurable and contagious. So he crept humbly into the dark and waited for the deeper darkness of the end. His name is upon the obelisk."

"Where mine will never be," capped Edham. "I shall live and grow fat out of sheer spite."

Rafel said severely, "There is nothing funny about it. There is nothing funny."

"I am not jesting. I am trying only to reassure you."

At that moment Jolin came along to bid farewell and Rafel said to him, "*He* is attempting to comfort *me.*"

"It would be more logical if I were the subject of his solicitude," returned Jolin morbidly. "The weight upon his spirit is equalled by the weight upon my mind."

"Did you choose that unnamed world near Arka?" Edham asked him.

"No, thank the broad heavens! That one was not my mistake."

"Neither will this one be."

"Now he's comforting *you.*" Rafel spread his hands to indicate helplessness. "What can one do with a person who insists on giving what he is supposed to receive?"

Gazing at the sky Edham suggested, "Leave him to his fearsome task of lazing around and permitting the unavoidable."

Jolin swallowed, said uneasily, "It's not going to be quite that." Then he changed his mind, hurriedly finished. "Farewell!" He shook hands and went, his features worried.

"He's somewhat sensitive for a planetary surveyor," opined Edham, gazing after him.

"He has seen too much," Rafel corrected. "As I have done." He too shook hands, returned to the ship, paused in its open lock to wag a warning finger and utter a final, "Remember!"

The lock closed. Edham backed well away from the venturis. Presently the tubes spouted fire and dust flew around and a great wave of warmth went through the walled area. Voices beyond the walls set up a chorus of hoots and screams.

Slowly the vessel rose, teetering and repeatedly correcting its plane until it had gained stabilizing speed. The lone watcher stood there while it was reduced to a tiny shining circle entering a cloud. It vanished into a black belly. He sighed and sat upon a handy rock.

"I am the Granor of the Green World, a seed of Di planted to discover just what happens to me. I am the lowliest tool of a super-agronomy, the test-piece, the fleshly nurseling among a million vegetable ones. If I live here my kind will live here. If I change my kind will change. If I die my kind will die. For better or for worse I am the Granor of the Green World."

Beyond the walls, "A-a-ah! *A-a-ah!*"

Of course the first night was the worst. The felon caged for life can hear and sometimes see evidence of the workaday world outside. The ship-wrecked survivor upon a deserted island can scan the horizon hopefully, week by week, tempor by tempor. But one with an entire planet to himself knows an isolation that cannot be more complete. The Granor is alone, utterly alone.

He lay on his air-cushioned bunk within the prefabricated house while the world's gloom thickened toward midnight and sleep refused to come. His mind insisted upon busying itself with calculations of tempors and velocities which would enable it to place the approximate position of the departing vessel.

His eyes kept opening to stare at the pearls of condensation shining on the ceiling. He could have cleared these away at one turn of a handy switch but he had not noticed them because he was looking at an imaginary space-ship. All the time his ears were straining to catch outside noises, of which there were plenty.

There had been a peculiar hush when the hidden sun went down and twilight came and coldness flowed in. The daytime noises had subsided—the night howlers had been slow to appear. Now, as the earth turned farther around from the warmth, the hairy things that shouted, "A-a-ah!" were silent and other creatures with different voices built up their own characteristic din.

For almost a quarter tempor two of them—huge and invisible—fought with shrill screams and much flapping of batwings right over his roof. In the end one landed upon the roof, gasped and bubbled awhile, made many scratching scrabbling sounds before it took off and vanished into the dark. It left an acrid smell as of strange blood.

Eastward, just outside the wall, a pair of unknown shapes of unknown tonnage battled tremendously, emitting piercing whistles at intervals and causing the faintest of tremors in the ground. Edham pressed a hand on the floor to sense the quivers, slight but discernible.

To cap the rest the wind built itself up to a loud moan that sounded as if the world itself were registering its agony. Distant trees thrashed and great limbs broke loose and tattered objects flew through the air.

The moan went up a hundred cycles where the airstream hit the wall, dropped lower as it sped across the planted area. Clouds rushed close-packed across the sky, seeming to be held in space while the earth rotated independently.

As the tempors crept nearer to morning Edham dozed without really sleeping. He had fragmentary dreams of the great city of Dise upon the planet also called Dise beneath the sun name Di. At no time had he scorned the city, yet he had failed to enjoy it as others had enjoyed it.

Now he wanted it. They had warned him at the college that it is natural to desire lost things when it is too late. He must conquer the yearning—but he wanted the city.

Dawn found him heavy-eyed and restless. The hurricane had gone, the heatmeter's hand already had begun to move along its scale and the same bellowers were back with their sounds. Taking the top package from the nearest pile in his ground-level stockroom he opened it, ate a four-course breakfast.

The torn wrappings lay across his knees while he ate and he could see the lettering—*Sunup Meal* 1. The sight did not please him despite his long training. This irritation was no more than evidence of an incongruity which for centuries had bedeviled the worthy tutors at the College of Granors, namely, that trainees are selected as natural pioneers—and men who are natural pioneers do not take kindly to regimentation.

Thus he scowled at the lettering because he knew that when the correct tempor chimed he would open *Noon Meal* 1 and later *Sundown Meal* 1 and tomorrow *Sunup Meal* 2.

He was being fed prepared fodder at prescribed times exactly like an exhibit in the zoo.

Finishing, he got mild satisfaction out of burning the wrappings with their offending inscription. He went out to inspect the Di-nursery, hoping for work. Already there was a little for him to do. Limbs and pieces of bark and strips of frond and thousands of leaves ripped from outer trees lay scattered all over the place.

Patiently he gathered this rubbish into the bare circle where the ship had squatted and beamed it to ash. That filled in his morning and after the noon meal he spent a couple of tempors tending plants that had suffered slight damage overnight.

A short time before sunset he got out his wings, had an awkward job with the harness, which was not easy to fit singlehanded. The tiny propulsor drove him to the top of the wall, where he strolled along its broad flat crest with pinions folded and gleaming.

The toothy ones in the jungle snarled and gibbered in anger at the unearthly sight.

At a point near the corner where the wall right-angled northward a local objector waddled out of its hiding place, came right to the base of the impassable rampart and stood directly below him. Staring upward with red eyes that burned beneath projecting brows, it drummed resoundingly upon its chest, made deep grunting sounds and drooled saliva.

Its attitude was challenging, an unmistakable invitation to come down and settle once for all the question of who was the superior life-form. Edham answered it by pausing in his walk, giving glare for glare and laughing inside of himself until the creature foamed with fury.

At the height of its rage he calmly spread his wings, glided within the walls and out of its sight.

4.

Lonely Vigil

*T*HERE WAS LITTLE SLEEP THAT NIGHT EITHER. HE MADE a fitting end to an imperfect day by consuming *Sundown Meal 1*, recited his brief notes into his autorecorder, had a short time with a pictorialized story taken from his small library, then composed himself upon his bunk.

Soon the rain came. It sounded as if someone high above were throwing away an unwanted ocean. He had never heard anything like it. The skies thundered and the ground thundered and the jungle bent over. There was alarm in his mind comparable to the noise in his ears for he had visions of tender sucklings being bombarded out of existence.

Kalteniel would have countered this menace by shielding the whole area under a force-screen. A Granor has no such means available since he must rely upon what exists in reality rather than in the imagination.

Disian science had produced effective power-beams, which could perform work or be concentrated destructively, but there was no known way in which to spread a beam without loss of power to the point of impotence. In grim fact there was nothing to discipline the torrent but the pumps.

His restlessness soon turned to action. Getting a transparent waterproof sheath from a nearby hook he pulled it over himself like an upended sack, went out with his powerful handlight shining through the protecting material. The rain battered at him furiously and ran over the sheath in such a heavy stream that it blurred his vision.

Despite this he made his way to the instrument shed wherein were his power-plant and the pumps which were connected with the area's irrigation system. The squat heavy atomic engine needed no starting for it was built to run continuously until due for replacement in several years' time. He put the six pumps into operation one by one, letting the engine take up the load in stages.

Very soon their joint output meter registered eight aquabulks per millitempor, an accurate indication of the great quantity pouring from the clouds. He remained in the shed for part of the night, nursing the pumps, watching the meters and listening to the downpour.

When eventually outside sounds were replaced by an amazing calm and the output meter showed a drop, he stopped the pumps, returned to the house, voiced a complaint into his autorecorder before laying down on his bunk.

"I can switch from the house everything switchable excepting the pumps. This world being what it is, remote control of those would be a convenience."

That was telling them. At some future time on some similar planet a Granor would be able to cope with a flood at the touch of a hand. They might even arrange it for *him* the trip after next—if he were still living at that time. If he were still . . . Slumber stepped in and drove the speculation from his mind.

Three weeks of backbreaking toil were needed to make good the damage. He finished with sore fingers and a crick in the spine. Had all the growths suffered he could not have coped in time to save them. But the bulbs and tubers had squatted undisturbed while the baby trees had survived the overnight ordeal.

Only the smallest, most delicate surface plants had been washed out and the major part of these he had been able to restore. Perhaps ten percent were beyond rescue. At least there had been no further disaster while the job was in hand.

With the midday task complete, he bathed, gave his aching back some radiant heat treatment, consumed *Noon Meal 22*, dictated his notes to the autorecorder.

"Sectors ten to eighteen have been reset. The loss numbers about one in ten. All other sectors remain rooted. The six end rows in sector nine are turning from green to yellow and their leaves show first signs of shriveling.

"The whole of the trees in twenty-four to forty are advancing at above normal rate, appear healthy and vigorous and seem likely to grow much larger than their usual size. There is nothing to report about remaining sectors."

Gazing absently at the mouthpiece into which he had spoken, he thought awhile, added, "I have examined myself in the mirror and see nothing unusual except that I look physically tired. To date my sleep has been inadequate. My weight has gone down by one twentieth. Doubtless these things will correct themselves in due course."

The listening machine got no more than that, the bare facts. At the college his brevity often had been deplored. They liked garrulous Granors who filled in the picture with a wealth of detail. It did not matter that the babblers were compounding with an unnatural situation by talking to themselves, using spool after spool of recording tape to hear their own voices.

According to the tutors, much information of great value had been sorted out from such seemingly inconsequential chatter. Edham did not feel that he had yet got to the self-conversational stage or that he would ever get to it. So far as he was concerned, when the time came to pray for a voice it must be another's voice, different, new.

A full day of lounging in the library, watching selections from pictorialized books, served to refresh him and take away the aches. The Disian breed recovers swiftly, is resilient. That is to say, the fleshly Disians.

The vegetable ones varied for no known reason. Thus the yellowing plants in sector nine turned yellower and slowly released their frail hold on life while the burgeoning *bodhi* trees in twenty-four to forty continued to progress at rates almost detectable between successive sundowns.

He took samples of the dying ones, dissecting them, subjecting thin slivers of cross-section to microscopic inspection, analysing the roots and the dirt in which they had been buried.

Either the cause of the casualties was something too minute and elusive to identify with what he had available—or more probably it was beyond identification in the light of present-day knowledge. It might well be seated in improperly understood plant-psychology, the mysterious reasons why one growth made itself at home while another died rather than endure the strangeness.

What little he did discover went into the notes. Characteristically all hazard and speculation were left out. The bare facts as usual. On the day the last member of the six rows was definitely dead and all the growths in sector twelve began to show first signs of surrendering the battle, he recorded the matter impassively.

Two months later, after he had beamed to dust the faded remnants of sector twelve, he sickened himself. The temperature of his blood arose, he perspired profusely, felt weak and muddle-minded. His digestive system went haywire.

Frequent doses of the likeliest drugs had no effect. The disease put him on his back, too exhausted to weed the acres or carry out inspections, make notes or do anything else than let it run its course—to recovery or the end.

Between spells of delirium he listened for outer disaster, wondering whether—if necessity proved dire enough—he could lift and thumb his attack-beam or crawl to the pumps. Experimentally he made two attempts to begin the crawl, failed both times.

He was many five-day reports overdue when eventually the illness relaxed its hold. The rain had come almost every night and sometimes by day but never in a menacing torrent. The plants still stood undisturbed. He was alive though thin and weak. There was much for which to be thankful.

The autorecorder got a curt uncomplaining description of his sickness, its symptoms, its progress. He did not bother to emphasize that he was breathing alien air, drinking distilled alien water but eating Disian food, that therefore the food was not to blame.

Let the machine's future listeners draw their own conclusions—that was their job. His was to be the subject of the operation and tell how it felt, stage by stage, even though the knife sank deep. The Granor is a seed of his race. It is helpful to plant a seed that can talk, even though laconically.

In the third year, when the *bodhi* trees fruited tremendously and became smothered with their typical golden balls of succulence, the *ahbodhi* trees produced a lesser load of distorted discolored objects that were repulsively sour to the taste.

The two kinds were related, different varieties of the same

species, yet one had spawned and the other miscarried. One had mastered circumstances, the other been mastered by them— almost like people.

Edham got a thought out of that, a dark suspicion. He did not record it because it was not yet a self-evident fact. But the notion kept circling tentatively in his mind, without hardening. It gained strength nearer the year's end when ten allied breeds of bushes produced crops as eatable as any on their home territory—but at different dates, in different sizes, shapes and colors.

All tasted the same. All gave the same responses to his perhaps inadequate analysis. All provided a welcome freshness for his digestive juices and nourished him to the same extent. Yet all were different.

"If I live my kind can live. If I live my kind will settle here, build new cities, a new world. They will have natural increase—but will that increase be natural? Will their children be the same?"

No answer—no way of telling. It was entirely his own mystery, as unsatisfactory and frustrating as Jolin's sad puzzle. So he held it in restraint without putting it aside, and gladly ate of such of the crop as was eatable. He had consumed *Sunup Meal* 1100 already and was more than eager for a change of diet.

"I am now going out of count with the packaged food," he recorded, "by reason of using part of the crop. There are yet no signs of anything seeding apart from the usual influx of local weeds. The crop has to be protected not only from these but also from periodic attacks of flying things, occurring always during daylight tempors, never at night.

"So far I have killed about four hundred raiders and lost little. There has been nothing to show why night-time flyers are not similarly attracted. I have examined myself and appear the same except that my color remains heightened."

Propagation eventually followed the same course as the fruiting, delays where there had been delays, intervals matching intervals, differences where there had been differences. Something in the rays of the concealed sun or the soil or the rain or the air was creating new varieties and thrusting a subtle wedge between existing ones to force them further apart.

Nevertheless he noted every item, patiently set the seed, drove off the winged monsters whose bellies yearned for the grains as much as for the fruits. Aware by training that what he had eaten of this his first crop, though of Di-origin, was alien grown, he watched himself more frequently for secondary effects. There were none visible and when one did come it caught him unknowing, unsuspicious.

He was winged for one of his boredom-breaking strolls around the wall and a pleasant exchange of insults with his neighbors when a black thing came down from the sky, intent on plunder. Many a seed was being coddled by the ash of such a visitor but this time he did not wait for it to land before dissolving it in smoke.

A sudden unfamiliar feeling swept irresistibly over him. His veins swelled, his eyes blazed, he spread his wings and bulleted upward to meet it. The creature died halfway down from a cloud and as he beamed it he heard a yell of triumph in his own voice.

Sitting on top of the wall, pinions folded, the midjoints pointing high above his shoulders, legs dangling down on the jungle side, he pondered the phenomenon. It was unwonted bellicosity. That any Disian can display belligerence was not in itself surprising. No kind can settle a thousand worlds without taking the offensive whenever the occasion demanded it. The point was that he had displayed uncontrolled animosity at the drop of a meal wrapper without real need to do so. It was lack of self-discipline. It was unreason.

The subject stewed in his mind a full tempor, during which he gave grave consideration to the possible state of his liver, his gall bladder, his kidneys or, alternatively, the subtler effect upon his mentality of three years of isolation.

Before he had finished his speculations the chest-drummer or its twin brother shambled out of the jungle shadows, stood directly below him, glared up red-eyed and roared its hate. On other days when this had happened he'd contented himself with an answering mock-glare guaranteed to make the creature put over an interesting exhibition of animal frenzy. This time his own eyes blazed. He bent forward—and spat upon it.

5.

The Sound of a Voice

FOR A CONSIDERABLE TIME AFTERWARDS HE WAS broody, introspective, frequently consulted the mirror. There was no physical change that he could pin down as more than imaginary. The hair on his head seemed thicker, more wiry, harder to subdue. His eyes held a constant hint of aggressiveness—or so he fancied. He could not be sure.

Sheer self-discipline kept him away from the walls while he concentrated upon the plants, his progress reports and the potentially alterable phenomenon of his own body. On four occasions he bit his lips as he beamed a flying raider, coolly, carefully, with determined disregard of that part of him which screamed for closer battle.

Nothing of this went into the autorecorder, not a jot, not a hint. All the transformations he could perceive were duly noted but not those only half-seen or dimly suspected.

With the end of winter and the coming of spring the rising tide of his blood swamped his restraint. Day after day, tempor after tempor, he had paced his enclosure from one end to the other, to and fro, to and fro, like a caged animal. The skies retained their everlasting gray but the fresher air was cool and warm by turns. Putting on his wings he soared to the wall, strolled along its crest.

A slate-colored colossus, resembling that monstrous sleeper of long ago, was standing close to the base on the southern side and rubbing its back against the stone to scrape off unseeable parasites. The process created loud rasping sounds and sent up an odor of pungent hide.

Standing directly above it and looking down into the smell, Edham felt his mouth open of its own accord and he bawled an ugly name at it. The monster ceased its scratching, looked stupidly around in every direction but upward. He called it again. It discovered him, focused eyes incongruously small in so tremendous a head.

Releasing an angry snort of such power that Edham felt the wind of it many cubits above, the thing reared itself against the wall, tried to claw him down, found him out of reach by more than a man-length. It gave another snort of imbecilic disappointment, fell back to ground with a rousing thud. Its stench was strong, acrid.

For the first time since his almost forgotten trip with Rafel the winged Edham left the enclosure. With no thought of rules and regulations and temporarily forgetful of past training he spread his pinions and dived off the wall—outward. His bold swoop carried him straight across the other's serrated back, his feet touching it in passing. It twisted with twenty-ton clumsiness, clawed at him and missed. Behemoth swiping a wasp.

Edham landed lightly in thick grass. His opponent snuffled eagerly and charged. He soared again at the very last instant, his eyes afire. The thing tossed its head as its own momentum carried it beneath him, touched a foot. He beamed away the tip of its tail as it passed. The jungle was full of spectators, howling and hooting at the pair of them. The tree-tops quivered and gave forth noises.

Coming down into the grass once more he whirled around in readiness for another charge. His lungs were big, his breath came fast and some strange appetite within him was satiating itself upon he knew not what.

The slate gray nightmare had lumbered around in a small circle, snuffing all the while. Finding him, it fixed tiny eyes upon him, expanded its nostrils to keep his scent and launched itself forward. The ponderous beat of its oncoming feet resounded far through the ground and vibrated up the trees to where the hidden audience stank and gibbered.

With wings folded Edham waited for the creature to be almost upon him. He remained stock still until he could see the wetness upon a huge misshapen tooth. Then he sprang aside. Too much tonnage carried the other on, unable to swerve. He rayed away another section of its tail.

By now the peculiar hunger within him had gone. He opened wings to soar, found himself anchored. A weirdly patterned worm in the undergrowth had coiled itself around one ankle. It had beady unblinking eyes that watched him fixedly as coil after coil came slithering through the grass.

The slate-gray monster came back thunderously, cheered on by the crowd. Edham chopped the worm at random, arose sluggishly with the severed portion still clinging as if unconscious of its loss. The slate-gray monster was almost upon him.

For an awful moment he thought he was not going to make it. Power poured through the propulsor and his wings swept wide while the beady-eyed thing clung raw-ended and tried to summon its missing length.

Dragging it with him he went up, frantically shaking his leg. It dropped off barely in time to save him and sudden release of the burden caused him to shoot skyward almost from under the twenty-tonner's nose.

This close escape eased the peculiar gnawing inside him. Gaining the wall he sat on its top, drew long relieved breaths and perspired. There were queer disconnected thoughts running through his mind, the inconsequential notions of an uneasy sleep.

"Life is beautiful because of death, like light in the darkness. To battle is to live and to live is to be not-dead. I must fight or be dead. I must live. A Granor must live."

He looked down upon his recent opponent, now snorting around defeatedly and echoed in bemused manner, "A Granor? What is a Granor?"

Then he stood up and yelled at the jungle, "I am Man! Look, I am Man!"

The ship's return was like the occurrence of a major miracle. True, after most of six years it should have been expected or at least hoped for. But six years can be six tempors or as many centuries, according to the circumstances. By the time it came back it was to Edham little more than the figment of a half-forgotten dream.

He stiffened with incredulity when the clouds were blown apart and the vessel appeared. A multitude of emotions electrified his being while he watched the shining thing come down.

A conflicting mixture of surly resentment and ecstatic anticipation took hold of him as though somehow he had become two individuals in one body, each reacting in its own way. The vision of the ship had precipitated a sort of spiritual schizophrenia.

Rafel was first out. His big luminous eyes alive with pleasure he seized Edham's hand, winced at the power of its grasp.

"Here we are, not merely up to time, but early." His hands went to either side of the other's shoulders, patting them, estimating their width. "My, but you look splendid! You're bigger, broader, heavier and it's all muscle. This place must suit you. Jolin will be overjoyed."

"Jolin," murmured Edham, looking around.

"He's not with us this trip," Rafel went on. "No point in him judging the same planet twice. He has gone with Razudiel to look over a new system beyond Neo-Dise."

"So?" said Edham, staring at the ship.

"Well, aren't you pleased to see us?" Rafel regarded him more carefully. "You never did say much but now you seem almost speechless." His smile followed quickly, full of sympathy. "I guess you're a little overwhelmed by company and the sound of a voice."

"The sound of a voice," repeated Edham, speaking as if from far away.

Taking his arm, Rafel led him toward the ship. "The first part of your task—the stage of silence—is ended. The worst is over. The next will be shorter and sweeter—if the medicos pass you."

"If," said Edham.

"There seems little likelihood that they won't," encouraged Rafel. "I have never seen a Granor looking in such excellent trim."

"I am not fattening myself for the kill," Edham assured. "And what is more I am laughing." He nodded toward the wall. "As I have laughed at them, loud, long and often." He paused, licked his lips, added with strange satisfaction, "They do not like my laughing."

Sobering, Rafel became thoughtful as he took Edham into the ship, handed him over to the medicos.

There were six of these examiners, tall, coldly professional, white-coated. Stripping him they went over him cell by cell, made him breathe down a tube so that the contents of his lungs bubbled into an inverted bottle, took blood samples from various parts of him, took hair and nail clippings, even a skin section.

They rayed him, studied his insides upon a fluorescent screen from four different angles, discussed his spleen in incomprehensible jargon. They photographed the lining of his stomach with a button camera at the end of a flexible tube, used a powerful light beam and a magnaglass to examine his tongue, throat and epiglottis. They asked a hundred questions.

"You have a seed molar. Did the first one expel itself in normal manner or did you have to extract it?"

"When did you first observe the appearance of body-hair?"

"Did you make a note of it in your autorecorder?" ·

"Did it appear simultaneously in all places where now evident, or did it start in one place and spread from there?"

He asked, "Does hair matter?"

"Most certainly."

"Why?"

They became evasive. "Hair upon the body is not a normal feature of our kind—and every change matters."

"So I *have* changed?"

The chief examiner said, "Look, everyone alters from birth to death."

"As *I* have?"

"This is a routine investigation and not a debate," reminded the examiner. "Leave it to us to decide which physical phenomena are significant and which are not."

Edham said, "Don't bellow at me."

"I am not bellowing. I spoke in perfectly ordinary tones." He gestured to an assistant. "Have a look at his ears."

They went over the ears, presently put down upon a form the words, *Aural sense preternaturally sharpened*.

A bit later, "How did you acquire those scars on the calf-muscle of your right leg?"

He stared down at the leg, twisting himself to see the marks, "Fighting a wild thing. It clawed me."

They were tempted to ask why he had not beamed it before it got that near but refrained. Such questions were for the psychoanalysts.

In due time the latter had their turn and put it to him, "Is your hand-projector still energized and efficient?"

"Yes."

"Why didn't you use it?"

"I please myself. I am an individual."

"We have not the slightest desire to challenge your rights as such," soothed the other. "We are merely interested in your reasons for doing whatever you saw fit to do. We cannot and would not force you to give an explanation."

"You'd have a hot time trying," assured Edham, involuntarily tightening his fist.

The expert was very observant. Calmly he regarded the fist, estimated the degree of muscular contraction, the amount of mental tension behind it. Edham forced the hand to open, the fingers to relax. The other was not deceived.

"Have you been beyond the walls?"

"Yes."

"Have you actually landed outside the walls?"

"Yes."

"Often?"

"Yes."

"Knowing that it was contrary to instructions?"

"Yes."

"And dangerous?"

Edham said nothing.

The expert wrote down a couple of little squiggles meaning, *Co-operative with reluctance—but truthful,* before he went off on another tack.

"Members of the crew are checking over the state of the plantation and condition of the ramparts. Beyond the wall they have found a bloodthirsty looking creature, thick-furred, with striped markings. It is dead. It appears to have expired recently, in mid-spring, claws extended, mouth open."

He stared at Edham, who remained silent. He placed an object on his desk. "It was pierced by four of those."

The object was a long slender arrow.

"It is well-made," commented the expert. "Skillfully constructed with a needle-sharp metal head. The bow from which it came must have been powerful."

"It was," Edham acknowledged indifferently.

"Did you shoot this creature from the wall-top or were you in the outside grass?"

"The grass."

"A bow, a bow and arrows," commented the other, poking the pointed and feathered shaft away from him. "He uses a primitive type of weapon in lieu of a modern beam-projector." His gaze lifted, he surveyed Edham curiously. "It would be nice to learn the logic on which such a preference is based."

Edham said, "The targets are just as primitive. They struggle with what they've got, what they can make themselves."

"I see." The leading questioner glanced at his silently listening fellows, returned his attention to Edham. "You cannot manufacture a projector which needs all the craft of an experienced armorer—but you can make a bow. You derive satisfaction from that?"

"Yes."

"Why?"

Both his fists hardened and whitened as Edham leaned forward and snapped, "I am Man!"

"That will be all," said the other.

6.

The Redhead

*E*DHAM NEVER SAW THE REPORTS. WRITTEN CONCLU-
sions invariably are withheld from the Granor. His
only clue lay in the length of the deliberations and the
frequent summoning of Rafel, who looked a mite
more solemn at each successive visit. It was evident that there
was some difference of opinion, some profound uncertainty
which made the question of triumph or failure highly debatable.

Eventually he would know their decision from what they
did with him. If he had changed in manner not to their liking
but had nothing contagious, they would put a black mark against
the planet and take him home.

If he were afflicted with something unwanted, incurable
and uncontrollable, they would abandon him along with his ac-
cursed world and add his name to those upon the obelisk. But
if failure were not yet certain and success a possibility, no matter how remote, they would push him into the second stage of
his task.

It was four days before he knew. In that time the crew
had attended to all repairs, overhauled the engine and pumps,
installed a remote control for the latter, supplied fresh spools
for his autorecorder, recharged his beam, supplied new wings
and propulsion, landed a huge load of packaged meals, all
duly numbered. They did not touch the plants. The living
would go on living—the dead stay dead.

There were eight females with the crew. Moving around
together in a lithe colorful bunch, they explored the house, the
instrument shed, the plantation. In single file they trotted along
the wall-top, chattering like birds, laughing in lilting tones and
exclaiming from time to time over the few exotic flowers visible
in the jungle.

All were young, strong, well-shaped. All studied Edham with clear frank eyes at every opportunity, weighing him up, estimating him. For his part he tried to avoid them. Their presence was closely linked with his fate. He was acutely conscious of the fact and embarrassed by the uncertainty of his position.

In the late afternoon of the fourth day Rafel came to him. "The conference is over. I am more than glad to hear the end of it. Yours has been a difficult case."

"I know I am hairy."

Rafel did not smile. He went on, "They say you have changed and in all probability will continue to do so. The purely physical features of it are innocuous. They are nothing to worry about, nothing to fear. Indeed, some of them are advantageous."

"Come to the worst," Edham suggested impatiently.

"It is the psychological shift that has them bothered. They detect an abnormal combativeness which, in theory, could grow until it becomes completely irrational."

"This life of mine is abnormal. What do they expect?" The dullness of a routine worker in Dise?"

"All your troubles and trials have been taken into account," said Rafel. "After considering everything—even the impetuosity of the pioneer, even boredom—they find more bellicosity than can be explained, more than is natural or necessary. It is the little extra you have absorbed from this bellicose world. You may continue to absorb it. At saturation point—if you live to reach it—where will you be?"

"Sitting around and *not* permitting everything," Edham answered. "And laughing."

Letting it pass Rafel continued, "Anyway, the second stage of this planet-probing task is shorter, less trying. You should come to no great harm if we carry on awhile. Besides, we would deserve to lose a world if we let go of it at the first setback." He looked straight at Edham. "Do you want to be taken home while the going is still good?"

Edham said in level tones, "To return voluntarily would be to return in disgrace, to be pointed out as the Granor who came back screaming. Do you think I would enjoy that? How would you like a bust on the nose?"

"There you go again!" said Rafel shrugging good-humoredly. "Well, the die is cast. It is for you to go through the second stage."

"With whom?"

"Of the eight Companions who have seen you and looked over this place, six have volunteered."

"Two don't like me, eh?"

"Not necessarily," denied Rafel. "For some reason which is beyond my mere male mind there are always two who want to see the next place. No matter how many Companions I take out, invariably I return with two—eagerly awaiting yet another world."

"Feminine curiosity," ventured Edham.

"The six have taken first pick as is the right of their sex. It is now your turn."

"Which six?"

Rafel nodded toward somewhere behind the other's back. "They are over there. The pair of transgalactic tourists are in the ship."

Without looking around Edham said, "If the tall, slender one with the flaming hair is among them—

"The redhead. So be it. You have chosen your Companion as she has chosen you." Rafel eyed the sky. "I will perform the ceremony of association this evening if you are agreeable. We will depart at the fourth tempor of tomorrow."

With the morning they were summoned to the vessel, the Granor and his Companion.

Rafel began with, "We are ready to boost. Is there anything you desire, anything you wish to ask before we go?"

"No," replied Edham.

"Are you satisfied with each other?" He smiled as he read the answer in their faces. "We shall return in about three and a half years. I hope then to find evidence in favor of systematic settlement.

"If so, a time may come when more Disians share your world, building it to greatness." His gaze shifted from one face to the other. "You will have much honor."

"Darn the honor," said Edham. "Give me the fun."

Trying to frown his disapproval, Rafel found it far from easy. He switched the subject. "Any alterations in yourselves will be the results of or adjustment to local conditions. Comparatively speaking it will be slow, insidious. It cannot have the swiftness and extremism of radical mutation." He stopped, rubbed his forehead while he sought around for further words.

"Meaning our children?" Edham prompted.

Rafel seized upon it gratefully. "We could learn more of real significance from your children than we can ever learn from you. Apart from other yet undetected peculiarities this planet has a deal of radioactivity. What does it mean to our kind? What might it do?" He spread helpless hands. "We don't know."

"All in good time," offered Edham.

"Your children are very much to be desired—by us," Rafel went on. "Nevertheless I advise you not to have any unless desired by you."

The redhead put it tartly, "The Ancient College of Granors' Companions is not a consortium for the stupid and—"

Hurriedly, Rafel countered her. "I am reminding you that Dise imposes no duty upon you in this particular respect. You are completely free to please yourselves."

"That goes for me, too," she said, blandly shoving him off balance.

Recovering he stood up, made his voice serious. "Except in one respect—you will eat nothing native to this world. It is strictly forbidden. When the time comes to try subsisting on local products, you will be informed."

"Boxed-up meals." She sighed regretfully. "Enriched, concentrated, reduced, fastened down and caged. I took a tedious course on them—*How to Make Packaged Food Interesting.* Oh, well." She patted her flaming hair, tucked a curl behind her ear. "There are other interests."

Eyeing her somewhat askance Rafel avoided the subject, held out his hand.

The two stood side by side watching the ship go up. It shrank as before, was swallowed up by a cloud, was gone.

"And that is that," remarked Edham, sensing the loss and yet glad of it.

"What now, Flabby?" she inquired.

"I think that for a start—" His voice petered out, his eyes suddenly burned at her. "What was that you called me?"

She repeated it with annoying gusto, a smile on her oval face, and she turned slightly sidewise. A growl sounded low in his chest. He pounced at her, hands out, fingers wide. She was away like the wind, hair streaming.

It was a full and arduous tempor before he cornered her by the southern wall. The laughter of their struggle brought answering howls and screams from the other side of the ramparts.

More imaginative treatment of meals plus the comfort of her presence transformed the area into a haven of peace and satisfaction—for a time. Edham lazed around, ignored the jungle, enjoyed his new-found domesticity.

The girl had a seemingly endless capacity for keeping him amused, occupying his attention, diverting his energies from former paths. When his spell of idleness wore off she found him numerous tasks and when she came to the end of those she invented new ones. He performed them all with the casual uncomplaining air of one who has known the weight of time on his hands.

Now and again she tantalized him, apparently on sheer impulse born of some feminine quirk. Invariably he failed to notice that such occasions were carefully chosen.

Thus, for example, there was that moment he stood at the west end, close by the wall, looking longingly at the top and sensing once more the urge to go out and do battle and shout with triumph until exhausted. His eyes were shining, his chest was out, brown-skinned with hairs upon it.

She came silently behind him, noting every detail, and said, "See here, Rugbust, I—" Then she turned and fled for her life, long slender legs moving with the grace of a ballet-dancer's.

Three jumps behind her he collided with the door of the instrument shed as she slammed it against him. He could hear her squealing with excitement. Scrambling onto the roof, his muscles bulged as he began to tear up a sheet and make a gap big enough to drop through. She came out and immediately he realized that he'd been fooled. Her wings had been hidden within. She emerged on white pinions, soared gracefully, waggled pink toes just beyond leaping distance from his head.

Perforce he had to go back to the house, don his own

wings. It was near nightfall before he got her at tremendous height in the base of a cloud. By then he was tired and hungry, precisely as she had calculated.

None of this went into the autorecorder. The blithe waste of propulsor-power was part of the mating game and there were no dutiful confessions for the ears of others.

They did not have a real difference until a hundred days later when he came in for the noon meal and found flowers upon the table. He glowered at the blooms, then at her.

"Where did you get these?"

"In the jungle." The reply was made with disturbing matter-of-factness as she placed a steaming dish upon the table and seated herself.

"So you have been outside the walls without my knowledge while my attention was diverted elsewhere?"

"Of course."

"There are dangerous creatures in the jungle."

"I know it."

He was chewing his bottom lip and glowering at her now. "You could be torn to pieces."

"So could you." Her eyes came up, faintly accusing and at the same time expressing the resignation of one who has tried in vain to control a mischievous child.

"I know how to look after myself."

"So do I."

"Hah!" he exclaimed. *"Hah!"*

She snapped at him. "All right, Fungus-front, go out and see for yourself. It's just over the south wall."

Giving her a look he went out, investigated, came back and said, "You killed it while you had both feet on the ground. You beamed it face to face."

"That's me," she admitted. "Man to man!"

"It wasn't a man. Neither are you."

Putting shapely elbows on the table she rested her chin in one hand and made her voice sugar-sweet. "What I like about you is your swift grasp of things."

"Then how about this?" he retorted, making a quick grab across the table, fingers crooked for a coil of thick red hair.

The snatch missed solely because the table jumped. The floor jumped with it. The house performed a brief jig. A dull cavernous rumbling sounded from east to west. The stony ramparts quivered along their full length. The rumble ended in a faraway crack.

"What was that?" she asked, sitting erect, wide-eyed, startled.

"A quake." He leaned back, stared at his grabbing hand while he cooled off. "They come once in awhile. Elsewhere they're more frequent and much more violent. Elsewhere they're really something!"

She thought it over for awhile, said suddenly, "Do you believe in precognition?"

"It is a subject that has been argued for a thousand years and will be for another thousand. I have no opinion about it." He studied her curiously. "Why do you ask?"

"To take unnecessary risks is against the rules. Yet despite that, despite your training, despite my attempts to divert you, the jungle calls you—until you obey." Her long fingers toyed with each other nervously.

"So last evening, when you thought yourself unobserved, you went outside with your bow. And this morning I went outside for flowers—the flowers you have never brought me."

He flinched at that and began, "I would gladly bring them if you did not criticize the getting and—"

"You misunderstand me. I am not criticizing you. Not any more." The hands folded. "You see I feel as you do— *I* yearn to go outside."

"*You* do?"

"The desire grows, encouraged by your bad example." Her gaze upon him was thoughtful, speculative. "Do you suppose that something may be impelling us to get accustomed to the jungle—while there is time?"

It made him vaguely uneasy.

"Instinct is a peculiar thing," she went on. "It comes to animals and birds as a mixture of precognition and ancestral memory and helps them survive." The steadiness of her gaze unsettled him as she finished, "Why do *you* crave the green hell?"

"I get restless."

"Why?"

"Kind of have the fidgets sometimes."

"Why?"

"Oh, heck!" he said, giving it up.

"Take me with you next time you go out," she pleaded. "Two together are safer than one—and I get such a wonderful feeling of freedom beyond the walls."

It was his turn to come back with, "Why?"

"Because I know that this world will take us only on its own terms. Not on ours but on its own. We must be ready."

"My luck," he commented, making a mock-frown at the ceiling. "Just my luck. I need a Companion who is pink and soft and warm and understanding. I pick one and what do I get? A seer! A long-legged second-sighter! A prophet of disaster! A red witch!"

"Think of the remarkable children we could have," she jibed. "With your hair and my magical powers. Furry demons."

"Be quiet," he ordered. His shoulders hunched to rid themselves of a cold little shiver. There are jokes—and there are jokes.

7.

Rejected

ISASTER CAME IN THE MIDSUMMER OF EDHAM'S eighth year and his Companion's second. There was no warning, no preliminary sounding of some deep note of doom. Indeed at first there was nothing to show that an experiment was being ended in order that a new one might begin. All that happened was that the sun shone.

It was the first time they had seen the sun from this planet's surface. Up to date there had been only the great blanket of cloud overhead, darkening or glowing and pouring heat by day, deepening the nights and hiding the stars. Always the fierce primary had been concealed.

Now the clouds broke widely, revealing a bronze-blue sky in which the sun burned with awful vim and sent down stinging rays. Edham studied it through a dark glass, saw a great spot upon its tormented surface. The visual radioscope in his instrument shed picked up a mass of flickering shadows and swiftly changing checkered patterns indicative of violent disturbances across all bands.

By day and by night the heat was terrific. At first it did not bother the red-haired Companion. She came from Ultra-Dise, a planet far hotter than Dise itself, and thus was well fitted to endure the blaze. But as the sun burned on, week upon week, she began to wilt along with the barely surviving plants, along with the wilting jungle.

In the seventh week the last tortured Disian plant gave up its eight-year-old battle and lay in the hot dust. Smoke from fires in the dehydrated jungle drifted over the walled area, brought with it a stench of burning flesh and hide. A small quake came, followed by another and another while still the orb flamed in the sky and the shrinking rivers steamed.

With the death of the last *bodhi* tree the Companion's uncomplaining endurance ended. She posed taut but tired in the hot shadow of the instrument shed, looked across the barren area shimmering with heat-waves.

"There is that deep cave we found in the mountainside far across the river. It is cool, comfortable and has water at its back. I think it might have been better had we moved there when first we discovered it."

"A Granor does not desert his post for the sake of comfort." He wiped his forehead with the back of a hairy hand, kept his eyes away from the blazing thing in the sky.

"I know, I know. I am with you while there is duty to be done." She surveyed the dust of their hopes. "There is now no post to desert—nothing but four walls. The alien sun has eaten everything. Are we going to let it consume us too?"

"We should hang on and wait for Rafel," he said.

"What—for at least another year and a half? Of what use to Rafel are whitened bones?"

"We have enough food."

"One cannot live on food alone. One must have water and sleep. One *must* have sleep." She eyed him slantwise. "How much have you slept?"

"Little. It is too hot. We must suffer until the clouds come back."

"Not me," she declared flatly. "What is left to merit the suffering? Nothing! Tonight I shall slumber peacefully in the cool of the cave even if I sleep alone, even if it is my last sleep on this world." With that she went for her wings.

He remained, pondering gloomily. After awhile he put on his wings and followed her—as she had known he would.

They were asleep in the cave ten nights afterward when the great quake that shook their mountain range flattened the distant plantation's south wall, blocked the west river, created a great, shallow stinking lake which lapped close to the remaining ramparts. Thirsty monsters, half-crazed by heat, made the lake their drinking place, the broken area their stamping-ground.

Throughout the following week Edham battled more savage life-forms than he had tackled in any one year. Under the merciless sun he swooped down wide-winged, beamed them away from the house, rescued packages of food and took them to the cave. He made trips by night, expecting less opposition, but they were there in even greater numbers, red-toothed and eager for him.

Thus the food stocks were laboriously reduced in loads pitifully small. The cost approximated one killing per package plus the risk of his own violent ending. The area swarmed with ferocious forms as did every place within easy reach of water. The world screamed for water and, having got it, wanted flesh.

On something over his one hundredth trip he returned to the cave so borne down by his burden that he barely escaped the brown scalded tops of trees from which menacing worms had long vanished. At that point his propulsor expired. Too-frequent usage and heavy overloading had dried up the power source. The wings were useless.

Food is more important than flight. Using his Companion's equipment he continued the trips, transported to the cave more than half the stock of the distant house before the second propulsor failed. They were landbound. They were at one with the animals, the things that crept through the shadows and could never reach the sky.

It seemed a major blow to Edham since the remaining stores now were ten days' march away with every step disputed. To his Companion it was a secret relief. Now she had him close by and did not have to scan the skies at every flight, praying for his safe return.

Both beam projectors continued to function long after clouds had reappeared to hide the sun and right through the raging winter. One petered out with the spring—the other eighty days later. They turned to bows, fought the reviving jungle, consumed its fruits, ate of its flesh, grew heavy yet more agile.

They quaffed the undistilled water which seeped from the rock at the back of the cave and they did not fall ill, they did not die. Neither the water nor the food nor the past torment of that violent sun made them diseased or misshapen.

No change was apparent to them except that the longer they knew the jungle the more it seemed like home—for they did not realize that they had developed a swift, abiding fury equal to its own.

Eternal hope kept them from being completely absorbed by this world. No matter how powerfully surged the passions it induced within them they held fast to respective memories of Dise and Ultra-Dise and to the dream of being found on Rafel's return.

Yet, strangely, along with the desire to be discovered lurked another frequently-repressed wish that neither mentioned to the other and that they denied even to themselves—the hope that discovery would not mean removal. This world had not yet taken them body and soul but it was establishing by insidious means a claim that grew stronger tempor by tempor, day by day.

"I have found golden grain to the east, Bristle-body. I don't know how or why the animals have missed it. Big, beautiful heads of grain."

"Probably it isn't fit to eat."

"I tried it on myself a week ago."

"You—" His deeply tanned face went taut. "You might have died."

"So might you this morning when you fought that beast which we did not need for meat."

"It was interested in the cave. I permit nothing near the cave." He bunched a fist. "I am Man!"

"Then you can make me a stone grinder," she said. "If I had a grinder I could make flour and bread and cakes."

"*Cakes!*" he spat. "In this place."

"You'll see," she promised, not the least bit disturbed by his attitude. "Fruit cakes and meat patties. Real food!"

"Forbidden food."

"What else is there?"

"The packages I took such pains to get."

"They will not last. Eventually we shall have to subsist only on what this world has to offer and chance what it does to us. We might as well start now. I'm not afraid."

"Not afraid but impetuous."

She studied his heavily muscular body, clad in the colorful skin of some animal he had slaughtered, shifted her gaze to the powerful bow grasped in his right hand and said, "Listen to who's talking."

"I will make a grinder and you can have your cakes," he agreed, conscious of unspoken accusations. "And may the stars preserve us!"

"From what? From this world's fruits? We have been eating them already and flesh as well. Can *more* fruit do any worse?"

'If their dangerous properties are accumulative we can step over the margin between enough and too much. Besides you and I might gorge ourselves to the limit of our capacity without ill effect upon ourselves but—but—"

"Our children?"

"Yes."

She took a step toward him. "Do you wish for children?"

"Do you?" he countered.

"Of course."

"No matter what they may be like—or *not* like?"

"They would still be ours," she pointed out.

"Unrecognizably perhaps."

"I would always know my own—and I am not afraid."

"But as I have already said you are impetuous," he gave back more gently. "Wouldn't it be better first to wait for the vessel and learn our fate?"

"Perhaps," she admitted relaxing.

She watched him as he tightened his bow, watched him stride down the path from the cave and enter between the trees. Something far back in the trees screamed its anger at his coming while she still watched.

"A-a-ah!"

The great vessel from Dise—it was like some misty figment of a bygone dream. A phantom of the past, hoped for yet feared.

A thing of dreams it seemed when at last it did come down. Deep in their cave at dead of night they heard a whine come through the sky and resolve itself to the thunderous roar of hot venturis.

They ran to the cave's mouth, saw a ring of crimson spears floating over the distant plantation. The spears shortened, went out. Thunder ceased. For a moment they gazed at each other like people who have seen the impossible come to pass.

Edham got the tiny signal generator which he had rescued from the house, drew out its telescopic antenna, cranked the handle bemusedly. Somewhere over there, far away in the dark, loops were swinging to get his bearing. But his thoughts were not of that. They were of the threatening upheaval to his way of life.

Winged members of the crew arrived and took them high above the trees, back to the ship. There was huge excitement and much congratulating before they were passed along to the examiners.

The poking and prying was much longer, more tedious than before and almost unbearably irritating—but the decision came more quickly.

Rafel summoned them before him. "The plantation has ceased to exist through no fault of yours. All Di-growths have long gone, this world having proved too much for them." His tones were solemn, regretful. "In the circumstances we must reject this planet. It is unsuitable for settlement." Then he added, "But I can comfort Jolin by telling him that he was not entirely wrong."

Edham said, "How do you mean?"

"I said this planet *is* of no use to us. Someday it may be. We have tried it too early, many centuries too early."

"So it seems," commented Edham, dryly. "If we two can survive among the beasts, so can others."

Rafel shot back at him, "In what shape?"

There was no effective answer, no answer at all. Edham fidgeted with the sheer impotence of it, stared back at him, said nothing.

"I have the examiners' report here," Rafel went on, eyeing the written scroll. "I am not permitted to give it to you in detail but I can state the conclusions. They say you may stay here or return to Dise—at your own choice."

Silent up to that moment the redhead shrewdly noted his forced impassiveness, asked, "Suppose we elect to go back, what then?"

With great reluctance, Rafel told her, "There must be no issue of your association."

"So that's the snag. Always a Companion but never a

mother."

"I am sorry. Truly I am sorry. The basic law must be obeyed even when it thwarts the rights of individuals, and that law says Disians remain Disians now and forevermore. The law says un-Disians are non-Disians except when scientifically produced under proper control. Much as I would like to do so, for your sake it is beyond the power of a mere ship's commander to modify a basic law and—"

"I prefer to stay," she interrupted. Her air was too positive, too decided to permit argument.

Rafel's gaze moved inquiringly to Edham, who responded with, "Since you reject it this world is ours, entirely ours, every stick and stone of it ours! Who would surrender a world for the comfort of Dise?"

"You sadden me," said Rafel. He sighed resignedly. "So be it. I shall put a red mark against this planet to indicate that it is not condemned for all time, that it may be suitable in the future." With slight emphasis, looking at Edham, he repeated, "The distant future."

"I know what you mean," Edham assured. "And I do not care. A Granor does not care—can you believe that?"

"Most certainly. To be a Granor one must not care—much."

"Anyway I've a feeling about this," chipped in the Companion, blithely exercising her feminine precognition. "In the distant future to which you refer the next visit may be from *here*. What of the law of Dise then?"

"They will permit the unavoidable," remarked Edham, giving Rafel no time to reply.

Frowning a little Rafel shrugged it off. "We shall give you new wings, new beam projectors, anything else you may require. They will last awhile and be of some help. More than that I cannot do. When those things are exhausted there will be no further help and you will have to continue as best you can."

"We have managed without them. We can do so again."

"I know. I shall make a full report upon it. Your names will be honored in your respective colleges and you will be remembered."

"While we hasten to forget," remarked Edham.

It embarrassed Rafel. He covered up by saying, "May the eternal stars be with you," and went away.

In due time Edham watched the ship go up and noted with only a hint of surprise that the finality of its departure created no emotion within him. There were queer insubstantial tentacles holding him to the dirt of this restless world, alienating him from that other world of his youth. His psychic shape had changed invisibly.

It was geohypnosis, the cunning fascination of a sphere.

The ship went through the clouds. In silence they used their new wings to transport equipment to the cave. The task was easier this time for the great vessel's blasting arrival and fiery departure had driven every hostile form from the vicinity.

Three-walled, open-ended and dead beneath the twilight sky, the area that once had been a place of hope held them musing a little while on their final trip. In the days when it flourished and was thought of as a sometime-city the woman had blessed it with its future name. To please her he had carved it upon the wall now broken by one belly-heave of a world not yet ready for names or walls.

He was gazing set-faced at the shattered name when she asked, "What is the matter?"

"I am laughing."

She grasped his hand. "Come—come with me."

So together they fled from Para-Dise and set forth into the land and begat many children, all of their own shape but none truly of their kind.

The first was a murderer.

The second, his victim.

The fifth had a yellow skin and tilted eyes.

Only the tenth had red hair.

The twelfth was born black.

But the seed of this seed subdued and mastered the stormy world which some call Terra.

The Witness

No COURT IN HISTORY HAD DRAWN SO MUCH WORLD
attention. Six television cameras swivelled slowly
as they followed red and black-robed legal lights
parading solemnly to their seats. Ten microphones sent the creaking of shoes and rustling of papers over
national networks in both hemispheres. Two hundred reporters
and special correspondents filled a gallery reserved for them
alone. Forty representatives of cultural organizations stared
acoss the court at twice their number of governmental and diplomatic officials sitting blank-faced and impassive.

Tradition had gone by the board; procedure resembled
nothing familiar to the average lawyer, for this was a special
occasion devised to suit a special case. Technique had been
adapted to cope with a new and extraordinary culprit, while the
dignity of justice was upheld by means of stagy trimmings.

There were five judges and no jury, but a billion citizens
were in their homes watching and listening, determined to en-
sure fair play. Ideas of what constituted fair play were as
varied as the unseen audience, and most of them unreasoning,
purely emotional. A minority of spectators hoped for life, many
lusted for death, while the waverers compromised in favor of
arbitrary expulsion, each according to how he had been in-
fluenced by the vast flood of colorful and bigoted propaganda
preceding this event.

The judges took their places with the casual unconcern of
those too old and deeply sunk in wisdom to notice the lime-
light. A hush fell, broken only by the ticking of the large clock
over their rostrum. It was the hour of ten in the morning of
May 17, 1977. The microphones sent the ticking around the
world. The cameras showed the judges, the clock, and finally

settled on the center of all this attention: the creature in the defendant's box.

Six months ago this latter object had been the sensation of the century, the focal point of a few wild hopes and many wilder fears. Since then it had appeared so often on video screens, magazine and newspaper pages, that the public sense of amazement had departed, while the hopes and fears remained. It had slowly degenerated to a cartoon character contemptuously dubbed "Spike," depicted as halfway between a hopelessly malformed imbecile and the crafty emissary of a craftier other-world enemy. Familiarity had bred contempt, but not enough of it to kill the fears.

Its name was Maeth and it came from some planet in the region of Procyon. Three feet high, bright green, with feet that were mere pads, and stubby limbs fitted with suckers and cilia, it was covered in spiky protrusions and looked somewhat like an educated cactus. Except for its eyes, great golden eyes that looked upon men in naive expectation of mercy, because it had never done anyone any harm. A toad, a wistful toad, with jewels in its head.

Pompously, a black gowned official announced, "This special court, held by international agreement, and convened within the area of jurisdiction of the Federal Government of the United States of America, is now in session! Silence!"

The middle judge glanced at his fellows, adjusted his spectacles, peered gravely at the toad, or cactus, or whatever it might be. "Maeth of Procyon, we are given to understand that you can neither hear nor speak, but can comprehend us telepathically and respond visually."

Cameras focused as Maeth turned to the blackboard immediately behind him and chalked one word. "Yes."

"You are accused," the judge went on, "generally of illegal entry into this world known as Earth and specifically into the United States of America. Do you plead guilty or not guilty?"

"How else can one enter?" inquired Maeth, in bold white letters.

The judge frowned. "Kindly answer my question."

"Not guilty."

"You have been provided with defending counsel—have you any objection to him?"

"Blessed be the peacemaker."

Few relished that crack. It smacked of the Devil quoting Scripture.

Making a sign, the judge leaned back, polished his glasses. Adjusting the robes on his shoulders, the prosecuting attorney came to his feet. He was tall, hatchet-faced, sharp-eyed.

"First witness!"

A thin, reedy man came out the well of the court, took his chair, sat uncomfortably, with fidgeting hands.

"Name?"

"Samuel Nall."

"You farm outside Danville?"

"Yes, sir. I—."

"Do not call me 'sir'. Just reply to my questions. It was upon your farm that this creature made its landing?"

"Your Honors, I object!" Mr. Defender stood up, a fat, florid man, but deceptively nimble-witted. "My client is a person, not a creature. It should therefore be referred to as the defendant."

"Objection overruled," snapped the middle judge. "Proceed, Mr. Prosecutor."

"It was upon your farm that this *creature* landed?"

"Yes," said Samuel Nall, staring pridefully at the cameras. "It come down all of a sudden and—."

"Confine yourself to the question. The arrival was accompanied by much destruction?"

"Yes."

"How much?"

"Two barns and a lot of crops. I'm down three thousand dollars."

"Did this *creature* show any remorse?"

"None." Nall scowled across the court. "Acted like it couldn't care less."

Mr. Prosecutor seated himself, throwing a mock smile at the fat man. "Your witness."

Standing up, the latter eyed Nall benevolently and inquired, "Were these barns of yours octagonal towers with walls having movable louvres and with barometrically-controlled roofs?"

Nall waggled his eyebrows and uttered a faint, "Huh?"

"Never mind. Dismiss that query and answer me this one: were your crops composed of foozles and bi-colored merkins?"

In desperation, Nall said, "It was ripe barley."

"Dear me! Barley—how strange! Don't you know what foozles and merkins are? Wouldn't you recognize them if you saw them?"

"I reckon not," admitted Farmer Nall, with much reluctance.

"Permit me to observe that you seem singularly lacking in perceptive faculties," remarked Mr. Defender, tartly. "Indeed, I am really sorry for you. Can you detect sorrow in my face?"

"I dunno," said Nall, feeling that his throne before the cameras was becoming somehow like a bed of nails.

"In other words, you cannot recognize remorse when you see it?"

"Objection!" roared Mr. Prosecutor, coming up crimson. "The witness cannot reasonably be expected—." He stopped as his opponent sat down. Recovering swiftly, he growled, "Next witness!"

Number two was big, beefy, clad in blue, and had all the assurance of one long familiar with courts and the tedious processes of the law.

"Name?"

"Joseph Higginson."

"You are an officer of Danville police?"

"Correct."

"You were summoned by the first witness?"

"I was."

Mr. Prosecutor wore the smile of one in complete command of circumstances as he went on, "Discovering what had occurred, you tried to apprehend the cause of it, did you not?"

"I sure did." Officer Higginson turned his head, threw a scowl at the golden eyes pleading in the box.

"And what happened?"

"It paralyzed me with a look."

The judge on the left interjected, "You appear to have recovered. How extensive was this paralysis, and how long did it last?"

"It was complete, Your Honor, but it wore off after a couple of hours."

"By which time," said Mr. Prosecutor, taking over again, "this outlandish object had made good its escape?"

Lugubriously, "Yes."

"It therefore obstructed a police officer in the execution of his duty, assaulted a police officer, and resisted arrest?"

"It did," agreed Higginson, with emphasis.

"Your witness." Mr. Prosecutor seated himself, well satisfied.

Mr. Defender arose, hooked thumbs in vest-holes, and inquired with disarming amiability, "You can recognize another police official when you see him?"

"Naturally."

"Very well. There is one at present seated in the public section. Kindly point him out for the benefit of this court."

Higginson looked carefully over the small audience which represented in person the vaster audience beyond. Cameras swung in imitation of his search. Judges, reporters, officials, all looked the same way.

"He must be in plain clothes," declared Higginson, giving up.

The middle judge interposed mildly, "This court can hardly accept witness's inability to recognize a plain clothes officer as evidence."

"No, Your Honor," agreed Mr. Defender. His plump features registered frustration and disappointment which gladdened the heart of his watching opponent. Then, satisfied that the other had reached the heights, he plunged him to the depths by brightening and adding, "But the said official is in full uniform."

Mr. Prosecutor changed faces like swapping masks. Higginson got a crick in the neck as he took in the audience again.

"Olive-drab with red trimmings," Mr. Defender went on. "He is a Provost Marshal of the Corps of Military Police."

"You didn't tell me that," Higginson pointed out. He was openly aggrieved.

"Did you tell the defendant that you were a police officer?"

The witness reddened, opened his mouth, closed it, gazed appealingly at the prosecuting attorney.

"Answer the question!" insisted a judge.

"No, I did not tell it."

"Why not?"

Mopping his forhead, Higginson said in hoarse tones, "Didn't think it was necessary. It was obvious, wasn't it?"

"It is for me to put the questions; for you to provide the answers. Do you agree that the Provost Marshal is obvious?"

"Objection!" Mr. Prosecutor waved for attention. "Opinions are not evidence."

"Sustained!" responded the middle judge. He eyed defending attorney over his glasses. "This court takes cognizance of the fact that there was no need for witness to offer vocally any information available to defendant telepathically. Proceed with your examination."

Mr. Defender returned his attention to Higginson and asked "Precisely what were you doing at the moment you were paralyzed?"

"Aiming my gun."

"And about to fire?"

"Yes."

"At the defendant?"

"Yes."

"Is it your habit to fire first and ask questions afterward?"

"The witness's habits are not relevant," put in the middle judge. He looked at Higginson. "You may ignore that question."

Officer Higginson grinned his satisfaction and duly ignored it.

"From what range were you about to fire?" pursued defending attorney.

"Fifty or sixty yards."

"So far? You are an excellent marksman?"

Higginson nodded, without pride, and warily. The plump man, he had decided, was a distinct pain in the neck.

"About what time do you hope to get home for supper?"

Caught on one foot by this sudden shift of attack, the witness gaped and said, "Maybe midnight."

"Your wife will be happy to know that. Were it not for the radio and video, you could not have told her vocally, could you?"

"I can't bawl from here to Dansville," assured Higginson, slightly sarcastic.

"Of course not. Such a distance is completely beyond range of the unaided human voice." Mr. Defender rubbed his chin, mused awhile, suddenly demanded, "Can you bawl *telepathically* for fifty to sixty yards?"

No reply.

"Or is your mental limit in keeping with what the defendant assures me to be the normal limit of twenty-five to thirty yards?"

Higginson screwed up his eyes and said nothing.

"Don't you know?"

"No."

"A pity!" commented Mr. Defender, shaking his head sadly and taking a seat.

The third witness was a swarthy, olive-skinned character who stared sullenly at his boots while the prosecuting attorney got to work.

"Name?"

"Dominic Lolordo." He gave it in an undertone, as if reluctant to have it coupled with his image on the video.

"You operate a sea-food restaurant?"

"Yes."

"Do you recognize the creature in that box?"

His eyes slid sidewise. "Yes."

"In what circumstances did you last see it?"

"In my joint, after hours."

"It had forced an entrance, had it not, shortly before dawn, and it awakened you while plundering the place?"

"That's correct."

"You did not try to catch it?"

Lolordo made a face. "Catch that? *Look* at it!"

"Appearance alone would not deter you if you were being robbed," Mr. Prosecutor suggested meaningly. "Surely there was something else?"

"It had walked in through the window," said Lolordo, his voice rising considerably. "Right through the window, leaving a hole its own shape. It went out the same way, making another hole. No broken glass around, no splinters, nothing. What can you do with a green nightmare that walks through glass as if it wasn't there?"

"Seeing this demonstration of supernormal powers, you

ran for assistance?"

"You bet!"

"But it came too late? This unscrupulous plunderer had gone?"

"Yes."

The questioner handed over with a gesture, and defending attorney began.

"You assert that you were plundered? Of what?"

"Stuff."

"That is not an answer."

"Ain't it?" Lolordo yawned with exaggerated disinterest.

The middle judge bent forward, frowning heavily. "Does the witness desire to be committed for contempt?"

"Lobsters and oysters," said Lolordo, hurriedly and with bad grace.

"In other words, a square meal?" inquired Mr. Defender.

"If that's what you want to call it."

"Was it being consumed as if the defendant were ravenously hungry?"

"I didn't stick around to see. I took one look and went on my way—fast."

"So that if defendant picked up enough of your thoughts to realize that a felonious act had been committed, there was no opportunity to apologize or make restitution?"

No reply.

"And, in any case, your departing thoughts were violently hostile?"

"I wasn't hot-footing for a bouquet," assured Lolordo.

Mr. Defender said to the judges, "This witness is impertinent. I have no further use for him."

The judges conferred, and the middle one decided coldly, "The witness will be detained within the precincts of this court until the case has been decided."

Lolordo stamped away from his seat, glowering right and left.

"Fourth witness!"

The chair was taken by a middle-aged, dapper man who resembled the movie notion of a bank president or an eminent surgeon. He could have been cast equally well for either part.

"Name?"

"Winthrop Allain."

"You are a resident professor of zoology, are you not?" inquired the prosecuting attorney.

"That is correct."

"You recognize the creature in the box?"

"I ought to. I have been in close communication with it for many weeks."

Mr. Prosecutor made an impatient gesture. "In what circumstances did you first encounter it?"

An answer to that one seemed unnecessary. The whole world knew the circumstances, had been told them time and time again with many fanciful frills.

Nevertheless, Allain responded, "It appeared in the zoo some two hours after closing time. How it got there I don't know."

"It was snooping around, seeing all there was to see, making mental note of everything?"

Hesitantly, "Well—."

"Was it or was it not looking over the place?"

"It certainly saw a good bit of the zoo before the keepers discovered it, but—."

"Please do not embellish your answers, Professor Allain," said Mr. Prosecutor, firmly. "Let us continue: owing to the great furore created by this strange object's arrival and subsequent exploits, your keepers had no difficulty in recognizing it?"

"None at all. They reported to me at once."

"What did you do then?"

"I attended to the matter myself. I found it a warm and comfortable apartment in the unused section of the Reptile House."

The entire court along with the cameras peered respectfully at the expert who could treat such an occasion with such nonchalance.

"How did you achieve that without suffering paralysis, disintegration or some other unnatural fate?" Mr. Prosecutor's voice had a touch of acid. "Did you graciously extend a cordial invitation?"

The witness, dryly, "Precisely!"

"There is a time and place for humor, Professor," reproved Mr. Prosecutor, with some severity. "However, the court understands that you classified this nightmarish entity as a reptile and managed to put it in its proper place."

"Nonsense! The Reptile House was immediately available, convenient and acceptable. The defendant is unclassifiable."

Dismissing that with a contemptuous gesture, the prosecuting attorney went on, "You are not prepared to tell this court by what means you overcame this creature's menacing powers and succeeded in trapping it?"

"I did not trap it. I knew it was sentient and treated it as such."

"If we can rely upon the evidence of other witnesses," said Mr. Prosecutor, tartly, "you were fortunate to have any choice about the matter. Why did this caricature permit you to make the contact it denied to others?"

"Because it recognized my mind as of a type accustomed to dealing with non-human forms. With considerable logic it assumed that contact with me would be far easier than with any others."

"With considerable logic," echoed prosecuting attorney, turning toward the judges. "I ask Your Honors to make especial note of that remark, bearing in mind that the witness has a distinguished status." He returned his attention to Allain. "By that, you mean it is intelligent?"

"Indubitably!"

"You have had many weeks in which to study the mind of this unwanted invader. Just how intelligent would you say it is?"

"As much so as we are, though in a different way."

"Do you consider this sample to be fairly representative of its race?"

"I have no reason to suppose otherwise."

"Which race, therefore, equals us in brain-power?"

"Very probably." Professor Allain rubbed his chin and mused a moment. "Yes, insofar as one can relate things which are not the same, I'd say they are our intellectual equals."

"Perhaps our superiors, not only in brains, but also in numbers?" persisted Mr. Prosecutor.

"I don't know. I doubt it."

"The possibility cannot be ruled out?"

"Such data as is available is far from sufficient and therefore I—."

"Do not evade my question. There is a possibility, no matter how remote, that the life-form represented by this monster now standing before us is the direst menace humanity has ever been called upon to face?"

"Anything can be construed as a menace if you insist, but—."

"*A menace,* yes or no?"

The middle judge interjected profoundly, "Witness cannot be required to provide a positive answer to a hypothetical question.".

Not fazed in the least, Mr. Prosecutor bowed. "Very well, Your Honor, I will put it differently." He resumed with Allain. "In your expert estimation, is the intelligence quotient of this life-form high enough to enable it to conquer, subdue and enslave humanity if it so desired?"

"I do not know."

"That is your only answer?"

"I'm afraid so."

"It is quite satisfactory," commented Mr. Prosecutor, throwing a significant look through the cameras at the unseen but billion-strong jury, "inasmuch as it admits the possibility of peril, extreme peril."

"I did not say that," protested Allain.

"Neither have you said the contrary," retorted the other. He seated himself, confident and pleased. "Your witness."

Mr. Defender began heavily, "Professor Allain, have your various hand-outs concerning the defendant been reported factually?"

"Without exception, they have been grossly distorted," said Allain, grimly. He cast a cold look at the big group of reporters who grinned back arrogantly.

"Defendant has repeatedly been described as a spy who must receive drastic treatment lest worse befall. Does your data support that theory?"

"No."

"What status do you assign to the defendant?"

"A refugee," said Allain.

"It is impossible for the defendant's motives to be hostile?"

"Nothing is impossible," said Professor Allain, honest though the heavens fall. "The smartest of us can be fooled. But I don't think I am fooled. That is my opinion, for what it is worth."

Mr. Defender sighed, "As I have been reminded, opinions are not evidence." He sat down murmuring. "Most unfortunate! Most unfortunate!"

"Fifth witness!"

"Tenth witness!"

"Sixteenth witness!"

That one, number sixteen, ended the prosecution's roster. Four or five times as many witnesses could have been produced, but these were the pick of the bunch. They had something cogent to offer, something calculated to help the public to decide once and for all—at least with its prejudices if not with its brains—whether gallivanting life-forms were to be tolerated or given the bum's rush, or worse. The question at issue was the ephemeral one of public safety, and it was for the public to say whether or not they were going to take any risks. With this in mind, the evidence of the sixteen made a formidable indictment against the queer, golden-eyed thing on trial for its liberty or even its life.

Conscious that he was leading on points, Mr. Prosecutor came erect, gazed authoritatively at the defendant.

"Just why did you come to this world?"

"To escape my own."

"Do you expect us to believe that?"

"I expect nothing," chalked Maeth laboriously. "I merely hope."

"You hope for what?"

"For kindness."

It disconcerted the questioner. Left with no room for a telling retort, he was silent a moment while he sought another angle.

"Then your own world did not please you? What was wrong with it?"

"Everything," responded Maeth.

"Meaning you were a misfit?"

"Yes."

"Nevertheless you view *this* world as a suitable dumping-ground for misfits?"

No reply.

"I suggest that your plea is nonsense, your whole story a sheer fabrication. I suggest that your motives in coming here are deeper and darker than you dare admit. I will go further and put it to you that you do not come even from the region of Procyon, but from somewhere a good deal nearer, such as Mars."

Still no reply.

"Are you aware that austronautical engineers have subjected your damaged ship to long and careful examination and made a report on it?"

Maeth stood there, pathetically patient, eyes looking into the distance as if in search of peace, and said nothing.

"Are you aware that they have reported that while your vessel is far in advance of anything yet developed by us, and while it is undoubtedly capable of traveling far outside this solar system, it is not able to reach Alpha Centauri, much less Procyon?"

"That is true," wrote Maeth on the board.

"Yet you maintain that you came from the region of Procyon?"

"Yes."

The prosecuting attorney spread despairing hands. "You have heard defendant, Your Honors. His ship cannot reach here from Procyon. All the same, it came from Procyon. This creature cannot manage to be consistent, either because it is dimwitted or, more probably, an ineffectual liar. I therefore see little purpose in continuing my—."

"I rode on a rock," scrawled Maeth.

"There!" Mr. Prosecutor pointed sardonically at the blackboard. "Defendant rode on a rock. That is the escape from a self-created impasse—a rock, no less!" He frowned at the box. "You must have ridden a long, long way."

"I did."

"So you sat your ship on this rock and saved fuel by letting it carry you many millions of miles? Have you any idea of the mathematical odds against finding a wandering asteroid in any section of space?"

"They are very large," admitted Maeth.

"Yet you discovered the very asteroid to bring you all the way here? Most astonishing spacemanship, is it not?"

"It did not bring me all the way. It brought me most of the way."

"All right," agreed Mr. Prosecutor, with airy contempt. "Ninety-nine millions instead of one hundred millions or whatever the distance is supposed to be. It is still amazing."

"Moreover," continued Maeth, writing steadily, "I did not select one to bring me here, as you imply. I thankfully used the only visible rock to take me anywhere. I had no specific destination. I fled into the void at random, putting my trust in the fates."

"So some other rock might have borne you some place else, might it not?"

"Or no place at all," Maeth put morbidly. "The fates were kind."

"Don't be too sure of that." Mr. Prosecutor hooked thumbs in vest pockets and studied the other with sinister expression. "If your real purposes, your real motives are in fact those which have been attributed to you by our ever-alert news-services, it is to be expected that you would have a cover-up story replete with plausibility. You have given this court such a story but have offered no concrete evidence in proof. We are left with nothing but your unsupported word—and the word of an ill-formed alien, an unknown quantity, at that!" He paused, ended, "Can you not submit to this court something more material than a series of bald assertations?"

"I have no way of combating disbelief," wrote Maeth, slowly and tiredly, "except with trust."

Mr. Prosecutor countered that one by striking hard and ruthlessly. "How many others of your kind are now upon this world, following their dastardly designs while you distract attention by posing in the full glare of publicity?"

The court, the hidden audience, had not thought of that. Half a dozen reporters quietly kicked themselves for not having conceived it first and played it up for all it was worth. It had been assumed from the beginning that the alien in their hands was the only one on the planet. Yet there might well be more, a dozen, a hundred, hiding in the less frequented places, skulking in the shadows, biding their time. People stared at each other and fidgeted uneasily.

"I came alone," Maeth put on the board.

"I accept that statement. It may be the only truthful one you have made. Experts report that your vessel is a single-seater scout, so obviously you came in it alone. But how many other vessels came about the same time?"

"None."

"It would be a comfort to think so," remarked Mr. Prosecutor, thereby discomforting his listeners. "Doubtless, your world has many other ships, much larger and more powerful than yours?"

"Many," admitted Maeth. "But they can go no farther or faster. They can only bear greater loads."

"How did you come by your own ship?"

"I stole it."

"Indeed?" The prosecuting attorney raised his eyebrows, gave a little laugh. "A self-confessed thief!" He assumed an air of broadminded understanding. "It is expected, of course, that one would suffer less by confessing to theft rather than espionage." He let that sink in before attempting another hard blow. "Would you care to tell us how many other bold and adventurous males are ready or making ready to follow your path to conquest?"

Defending attorney stood up and said, "I advise my client not to answer."

His opponent waved him down, turned to the judges. "Your Honor, I am ready to state my case."

They consulted the clock, talked in undertones between themselves, then said, "Proceed."

The speech for the prosecution was able, devastating and long. It reviewed the evidence, drew dark conclusions, implied many things from which the hidden audience could draw other and still darker conclusions. This is not to say that Mr. Prosecutor had any real hatred of or fear of the stranger at the gate; it was merely that he was doing his specialized job with ability that was considerable.

"This case, with its own new and peculiar routine," he reminded, "will go down in legal annals. As from today it will constitute a precedent by which we shall determine our attitude toward future visitors from space. And the final arbiters of that attitude will be *you*, the members of the general public, who will reap the reward of outside alliances or"—he paused, hardened his voice—"suffer the sorrows of other-world enmities. Allow me to emphasize that the rewards can be small, pitifully small—while the sorrows can be immense!"

Clearing his throat, he had a sip of water, started to get into his stride. "In trying to decide what should be done for the best we have no basis for forming conclusions other than that provided by the fantastic example who will be the subject of your verdict."

Turning, he stared at Maeth while he went on. "This creature has not been put on oath because we know of no oath binding upon it. Its ethics—if any—are its own, having little in common with ours. All we do know is that its far-fetched and highly imaginative story places such a strain upon human credulity that any one of us might be forgiven for deeming it a shameless liar."

Maeth's large eyes closed in pain, but Mr. Prosecutor went determinedly on. "While the question of its truthfulness or lack of same may remain a matter for speculation, we do have some evidence based upon fact. We know, for instance, that it has no respect for property or the law, which forms of respect are the very foundation-stones of the civilization we have builded through the centuries and intend to preserve against all comers."

He overdid it there. Maeth was too small, too wide-eyed and alone to fit the part of a ruthless destroyer of civilizations. Nevertheless, the picture would serve to sway opinions. Some thousands, probably millions, would argue that when in doubt it is best to play safe.

"A thief. More than that: a self-admitted thief who steals not only from us but also from his own," declared the prosecuting attorney, quite unconscious of switching his pronoun from neuter to male. "A destroyer, and an intelligent one, possibly the forerunner of a host of destroyers. I say that advisedly, for where one can go an army can follow." Dismissing the question of whence said army was going to get its flock of trans-cosmic asteroids, he added, "A dozen armies!"

His voice rising and falling, hardening and softening, he played expertly upon the emotions of his listeners as a master would play on a giant organ, appealing to world patriotism, pandering to parochialism, justifying prejudices, enlarging fears— fear of self, fear of others, fear of the strange in shape, fear of tomorrow, fear of the unknown. Solemnity, ridicule, sonorousness, sarcasm, all were weapons in his vocal armory.

"He," Mr. Prosecutor said, pointing at Maeth and still using the male pronoun, "he pleads for admission as a citizen of this world. Do we take him with all his faults and follies, with all his supernormal powers and eccentric aptitudes, with all his hidden motives that may become clear only when it is too late? Or, if indeed he be as pure and innocent as he would have us believe, would it not be better to inflict upon him a grave injustice rather than court infinitely greater injustices to a great number?"

Challengingly he stared around. "If we take him,. as a refugee, who will have him? Who will accept the society of a creature with which the average human has no joint understanding?" He gave a short, sharp laugh. "Oh, yes, there have been requests for the pleasure of his company. Incredible as it may seem, there are people who want him."

Holding up a letter for all to see, he continued, "This person offers him a home. Why? Well, the writer claims that he himself was a spiky thing in Procyon during his eighth incarnation." He tossed the letter on his desk. "The crackpots are always with us. Fortunately, the course of human history will be decided by calmly reasoning citizens and not by incurable nuts."

For a further half hour he carried on, a constant flow of words which concluded with, "In human affairs there is a swift end for the human spy, quick riddance for the suspected spy. I can conceive of no reason why any alien form deserves treatment more merciful than that which we accord to fellow humans. Here, we have before us one who at very least is an undesirable character, at most the first espionage agent of a formidable enemy. It is the prosecution's case that you have to consider *only* whether it is in the best interest of public safety that he be rewarded with death or with summary expulsion into the space from which he came. The weight of evidence rules out all other alternatives. You will not have failed to note that the witnesses who have appeared are overwhelmingly for the prosecution. Is it not remarkable that there is not one witness for the defense?" He waited to give it time to sink home, then drove it further by repeating, "Not one!"

Another sip of water, after which he seated himself, carefully smoothed the legs of his pants.

One thing seemed fairly clear: Maeth was a stinker.

Mr. Defender created a mild stir right at the start by rising and saying, "Your Honors, the defense does not intend to state its case."

The judges peered at him as if he were a sight ten times more strange than his own client. They pawed papers, talked together in whispers.

In due time the middle one inquired, "By that, do you mean that you surrender to verdict by public poll?"

"Eventually, of course, Your Honor, but not just yet. I wish to produce evidence for my side and will be content to let my case rest on that."

"Proceed," ordered the judge, frowning doubtfully.

Addressing Maeth, the defending attorney said, "On your home world all are like you, namely, telepathic and non-vocal?"

"Yes, everyone."

"They share a common neural band, or, to put it more simply, they think with a communal mind?"

"Yes."

"That is the essential feature in which your home world differs from this one of ours: that its people share a racial mind, thinking common thoughts?"

"Yes," chalked Maeth.

"Tell this court about your parents."

Maeth's eyes closed a moment, as if the mind behind them had gone far, far away.

"My parents were freaks of nature. They drifted from the common band until they had almost lost contact with the race-mind."

"That was something the race-mind could not tolerate?" asked Mr. Defender gently.

"No."

"So they were killed—*for having minds of their own?*"

A long pause and a slow, "Yes." The scrawl on the board was thin, shaky, barely decipherable.

"As you would have been had you not fled in sheer desperation?"

"Yes."

Mr. Defender eyed the judges. "I would like to put further questions to the fourth witness."

They signed agreement, and Professor Allain found his

way back to the chair.

"Professor, as an expert who has made a long, personal study of my client, will you tell this court whether defendant is old or young."

"Young," said Allain promptly.

"Very young?"

"Fairly young," Allain responded. "Not quite an adult."

"Thank you." Mr. Defender let his mild, guileless gaze roam over the court. There was nothing in his plump features to warn them of the coming wallop. In quieter tones, he asked, "Male or female?"

"Female," said Allain.

A reporter dropped a book. That was the only sound for most of a minute. Then came a deep indrawn hiss of breath, a rapid ticking as cameras traversed to focus on Maeth, a running murmur of surprise from one end of the court to the other.

Back of the gallery, the most pungent cartoonist of the day tore up his latest effort, a sketch of defendant strapped to a rocket hell-bent for the Moon. It was captioned, "Spike's Hike." What could one call it—him—*her*, now? Spikina? He raked his hair, sought a new tack, knowing that there was none. You just can't crucify a small and lonely female.

Mr. Prosecutor sat with firmed lips and the fatalistic air of one who has had eighty per cent of the ground snatched from under his feet. He knew his public. He could estimate their reaction to within ten thousand votes, plus or minus.

All stared at the golden eyes. They were still large, but somehow had become soft and luminous in a way not noticed before. You could see that now. Having been told, you could really *see* that they were feminine. And in some peculiar, inexplicable manner the outlines around them had become subdued, less outlandish, even vaguely and remotely human!

With effective technique, the defending attorney gave them plenty of time to stew their thoughts before carefully he struck again.

"Your Honors, there is one witness for my side."

Mr. Prosecutor rocked back, stared searchingly around the court. The judges polished their glasses, looked around also. One of them motioned to a court official who promptly bawled in stentorian tones.

"Defense witness!"

It shuttled around the great room in echoing murmurs. "Defense witness! There is a witness for the defense!"

A bald-headed little man came self-consciously from the public section, bearing a large envelope. Reaching the chair, he did not take it himself, but instead placed upon it a photograph blown up to four feet by three.

Court and cameras gave the picture no more than the briefest glance, for it was instantly recognizable. A lady holding a lamp.

Rising with a disapproving frown, the prosecuting attorney complained, "Your Honors, if my learned opponent is permitted to treat the Statue of Liberty as a witness he will thereby bring into ridicule the proceedings of this—."

A judge waved him down with the acid comment, "The bench is fully capable of asserting the dignity of this court." He shifted his attention to Mr. Defender, eyeing him over the tops of his glasses. "A witness may be defined as one able to assist the jury in arriving at a just conclusion."

"I am aware of that, Your Honor," assured Mr. Defender, not in the least disturbed.

"Very well." The judge leaned back, slightly baffled. "Let the court hear witness's statement."

Mr. Defender signed to the little man who immediately produced another large photograph and placed it over the first.

This was of the enormous plinth, with Liberty's bronze skirt-drapes barely visible at its top. There were words on the plinth, written bold and large. Some in the court gave the picture only another swift look, since they knew the words by heart, but others read them right through, once, twice, even three times.

Many had never seen the words before, including some who had passed near by them twice daily, for years. Cameras picked up the words, transmitted them pictorially to millions to whom they were new. An announcer recited them over the radio.

> *Send me your tired, your poor,*
> *Your huddled masses yearning to breathe free.*
> *The wretched refuse of your teeming shore,*
> *Send these, the homeless, tempest-tost to me—*
> *I lift my Lamp beside the Golden Door.*

In the deep, heart-searching silence that followed nobody noticed that Mr. Defender had bowed deeply to the judges and resumed his seat. The defense rested, having nothing more to add.

Midnight. A large stone cell with a metal grille, a bed, a table, two chairs and a radio in one corner. Maeth and the plump man sat there conversing, examining correspondence, watching the clock.

"The opposition picked a sloppy one with that crackpot's letter," remarked Mr. Defender. He could not refrain from expressing himself vocally though he knew full well that the other was hearing only the thoughts within his mind. He tapped a heavy forefinger on the bunch of missives at which they had been looking. "I could easily have countered him with this bunch written from a week ago to way back. But what was the use? They prove nothing except that all people don't think alike."

He sighed, stretched his arms wide and yawned, had his twentieth or thirtieth look at the clock, picked up another letter. "Listen to this one." He read it aloud.

"My son, aged thirteen, keeps pestering us to offer your client a home for at least a little while. I really don't know whether we are being wise in giving way to him, but we shall certainly suffer if we don't. We have a spare room here, and if your client is clean about the house and don't mind a bit of steam around on wash-days—."

His voice petered out as he had to yawn again. "They say it will be six in the morning before this public poll is complete. Bet you it's at least eight o'clock and maybe ten. They're always late with these things." He jerked around in vain effort to make himself more comfortable in his hard chair. "However, I'm staying with you until we've seen this through, one way or the other. And don't kid yourself I'm the only friend you've got." He pointed to the letters. "You've plenty there, and none of them certifiable."

Maeth ceased perusal of a note in uneven, spidery writing, reached for pencil and paper and scribbled, "Allain did not teach me enough words. What is a 'veteran'?" Having had it explained, she said, "I like this writer best. He has been hurt. If I am freed I will accept his invitation."

"Let me see." Taking the note, Mr. Defender read it, murmuring, "Um . . . um . . ." as he went along. He handed it back. "The choice is yours. You'll have something in common, anyway, since you'll both be coping with a cock-eyed world." Throwing a glance at the wall, he added, "That clock has gone into a crawl. It's going to take us a week to get to morning."

Somebody opened the grille with a jangle of keys, and Mr. Prosecutor came in. Grinning at his rival, he said, "Al, you sure make it tough for yourself in clink—you don't even use the comforts provided."

"Meaning what?"

"The radio."

Mr. Defender gave a disdainful sniff. "Darn the radio. Noise, noise, noise. We've been busy reading—in peace and quiet." Sudden suspicion flooded his ample features. "What have we missed on the radio, if anything?"

"The midnight news." Mr. Prosecutor leaned on the edge of the table, still grinning. "They have thrown up the poll."

"They can't do that!" The defending attorney stood up, flushed with anger. "It was by international agreement that this case was— "

"They can do it in certain circumstances," interrupted the other. "Which are that a torrent of votes overwhelmingly in favor of your client has already made further counting a waste of time." He turned to Maeth, finished, "Just between you and me, Funny-face, I was never more happy to lose a fight."

The man in the back room was nearing middle age, prematurely gray, and had long slender fingers that were sensitive tools. He was listening to the radio when the door-bell rang. There was no video in the room, only the radio softly playing a Polynesian melody. The bell jarred through the music, causing him to switch off and come upright. Very deliberately he moved around the room, through the door and into the passage.

Strange for anyone to call in the early evening. Not often that people came then. The mailman occasionally turned up in the morning and one or two tradesmen toward midday. Rarely did somebody appear later, all too rarely. He was not expecting a visitor, either.

He trod gently along the passage toward the front door, his feet silent on the thick carpet, his right hand brushing the wall.

There was something mighty queer about this summons because as he neared the door he conceived the weird notion that he knew in advance who was waiting outside. The picture crept into his mind, shadowy but discernible, as if insinuated by some means he could not define, as if hopefully projected by one of those beyond the door. It was a picture of a big, plump, confident man accompanied by something small, all green and golden.

Despite past trials and stern testings which had made him what he was today, his nerves were passably good and he was not subject to delusions, or had not yet developed a tendency to delusions. So he was puzzled, even a little upset by preconceptions without any basis. He had never known a big, heavy man such as his brain was picturing, not even in other more normal days. As for the second one . . .

Here and there, of course, are people with greatly sharpened senses, with odd aptitudes developed to an extreme. That was to be expected, for the fates were kind and provided compensations. Without them, it would be hard to get around. But he knew his own, and they included none like this.

His fingers, usually so precise, fumbled badly as they sought the door-latch, almost as if they had temporarily forgotten where it was placed. Then, finding it, they began to turn the lock, and at that point a thin piping voice came into his mind as clearly as a tinkling bell.

"Open please—*I am your eyes!*"

Last Blast

*T*HE BLOW WAS DELIVERED IN A MANNER FULL OF LOGIC and devoid of sentiment, that is to say, suddenly and without warning. It was a hundred or a thousand times more fearsome than the latest hell-bomb but took longer to demonstate the fact. Nobody opposed it or tried to strike back for the plain reason that nobody knew they'd been hit.

And when realization came, it was too late—as had been intended.

A rather appalling simplicity was the outstanding characteristic of the unknown enemy's technique. One long, silvery cigar came out of the sky, dropped seven bombs in planned positions and went away. It wasn't noticed. At minimum altitude of twenty miles and lowest velocity of four thousand eight hundred per hour, the thing remained too high and fast to be discovered by the naked eye. Neither did radar screens register its passing. They were not alerted because in orthodox thought there was nothing for which to watch. The world was at peace, without fear, and had been for more than half a century.

The bombs landed and burst without spectacular brilliance or tremendous noise or detectable concussion. They looked as formidable as so many bottles of stale beer tossed overboard by an irresponsible spacehand for they were nothing but small, brittle spheres containing a thin, slightly cloudy liquid. The spheres hit Earth and shattered. The liquid splashed around.

This spread of droplets was the beginning of the end, creating the certitude that humankind would pass out not with a bang but with a whimper. The greatest scoop in history for any journalism able to see the shape of things to come. But no newspaper mentioned it the next day. No radio network voiced one excited word about it. They didn't know. They didn't suspect. They had been killed—but needed time to die.

Humanity remained untroubled for at least a little while when every second counted and every split-second added long steps to the march of death. Some folk worried but it was about health, babies, taxes, stocks and shares; other folk, hopes of heavenly salvation; anything but poison from the skies.

The first to gripe was Barton Maguire, a farmer in Iowa. The last to react were the seven human beings on the Moon. Maguire's surly complaints served as the original warning. One of the Lunar seven made the final move.

Men on the Moon were no novelty. Twenty successive landings had boiled away a world's capacity for amazement. A feat is remarkable only the first time. Do it again and it reduces to pretty good. Twenty times becomes ordinary.

Only a ship on Venus or Mars would bring a repeat of those wild international celebrations of sixteen years ago. Such another whoopee had yet to come and by the looks of things there would be a long wait. Thirty million miles come to more than a hop, skip and jump.

Meanwhile men had to be content with a satellite as their sole cosmic plaything. The group on the Moon were there because the playing had begun. Their task was not complicated, not immensely difficult, but it was valuable as a source of essential data. They were extracting a sample of the new toy.

To this purpose they had considerable tonnage of equipment ferried over in four loads. Within an air-tight sanctuary, shaped like an inverted ice-cream cone, they worked upon a minor crater that had no name, tended a nuclear engine and serviced a drill that brought up a constant succession of cores each of which told a story. An expert could cast a sharp eye over these cylinders of extra-terrestrial plasma and declare that to the limit of the bore the Moon was made thus and so. Later, analysts would use them to list its riches in hydrocarbonates and metallic ores, if any.

Seven men consorting cheek by jowl under a dunce's cap and parted from the rest of humanity by a quarter million miles. There were moments when it irked; times when the engine moaned and the drill churned and the great rig trembled to its peak far beyond allotted hours—because men must battle the immediate task lest instead they battle each other.

Wilkin, government metallurgist, was the least sociable of the bunch. A gaunt, elderly individual with pale eyes fronted by steel-rimmed glasses, he had the dreary pessimism of the liverish and nursed the resentment of one handed a young man's job when near retirement. Somewhere back in the stuffy haunts of bureaucracy his tongue had stabbed a superior. The Moon was his sentence.

Liveliest of the lot was Yarbridge, thickset, tow-haired—the radio operator; a one-time ham who gloried in running a station where none had been run before. The small but powerful transmitter-receiver was his personal juju complete with call-name of *Yarboo*. He had an advantage over the rest—he had the comfort of his god and a thousand invisible friends behind the god. He had been conditioned to the company of voices in the dark. About the only thing he missed was the morning mail with its QSL cards.

The busiest and, therefore, the least touchy man was James Holland, tall, gangling, freckled. Though the youngest member of the party he was quiet, thoughtful, studious. He had to be. As the atomechanic he'd spent four years studying nuclear engines and reckoned he'd devote another forty to absorbing latest advances.

Some fast brainwork had been required to learn how to cope with the contraption he'd got here, for it was way ahead of anything he'd seen at the International Power Institute—one quarter the size, one eighth the mass, and it ran on thorium. It resembled a pair of Diesels coupled nose to nose with the hot-stuff cased between the fan-drives. Probably it would be out of date within a year. Holland tended to pore over books and blueprints in determination to keep up with the times.

The remaining quartet were curiously alike in many respects, big chested, hard-eyed, untidy, ruthlessly expert at various card games and lavishly supplied with adjectives. All four had made a career of sticking pins in Earth's heart for the big oil companies. They knew how to do it and did it well, vituperatively but efficiently.

The day the bombs dropped there were forty-six cores lying outside the Moon-dome. They reposed in a neat row, placed in order of extraction, each tagged at both ends with a plastic numeral by way of doubled check. The quantity of them indicated a bore-depth of nine hundred twenty feet. The nuclear engine moaned soft and low while the drill rotated and sank slowly, ever so slowly, toward the thousand mark.

An untouched case of whisky atop a small mountain of sealed food patiently bided this first celebration-point. At one thousand feet a bottle would be broached, some sort of petty celebration organized. There were twelve bottles in the case but that didn't mean a probing limit of twelve thousand feet. The drive would continue so long as the engine could' rotate the lengthening mass of steel tube, so long as a ship could bring more shafts, more cutting-heads, more whisky.

Ambling to the dome's center point, Yarbridge eyed a white ring where the turning shaft had been touched with chalk at a measured point. He kept quiet while a driller timed the ring's descent to ground level. The chalk circle disappeared and the other put his watch away.

"How's she going?" asked Yarbridge, not really caring.

"Cool and steady." The driller bit a ragged end from a thumbnail. "What's the latest from over there?"

"Gale warning in the Atlantic. Vesuvius is spewing sky-high and the Italians are evacuating the area around it. A Czech stratoliner has crashed. Seventy dead, no survivors. They were burned alive."

"Humph! Nothing ever happens." He put spit on a finger, used it to make a wet ring on the shaft. "Luck!"

"What's that for? Hoping to hit a gold reef?"

"Hoping we don't have to change a cutter too soon."

Yarbridge nodded. He could see what it meant. Real sweat. They'd have to haul up most of a thousand feet of stuff, detach it section by section to get at the worn head. Then fix a new cutter and reverse the whole process, linking up section by section as the toothy bit went down. It would have to be done again and again and again but nobody was yearning for it.

In short time he tired of studying the shaft and started what they had come to call the Sing Sing hitch, namely, a bored, aimless walk to and fro or around the rim of the circular space in which they were confined. Day and night some fidgety soul was performing this trek. When two did it simultaneously and passed each other for the tenth time, each generated mild thoughts of mayhem.

He wouldn't have been mooching but for the home planet's Asiatic face. The great hemispherical antenna atop the dome

did not trap much worth having when confronted by Chinese,
Malays and Dyaks. Caterwaulings from Shanghai, tin prices
from Singapore and a little boogie from Tokyo. The thousand
with the kit to beam him were concentrated around the corner
and temporarily silent. These were the siesta hours of his elec-
tronic god.

Finally he sat on a packing case near the engine, watched
Holland check over the linked generator that provided heat,
power and light. It struck him as faintly ironic that they could
and did use electric razors while millions on Earth lacked the
juice to run them.

"James," he said, "why am I like the Moon?"

Holland turned a freckled face toward him. "Don't you
know?"

"Perhaps," said Yarbridge, "it's because I'm bored." He
brooded a moment, asked, "Aren't you?"

"No."

"Why not?"

The other thought a while, said slowly, "Like you, I have
an interest. But mine doesn't wax and wane with exterior conditions. It remains constant."

"I guess you're right. Maybe I've become too dependent
upon a box of tricks. I should have learned to play poker."

"Fat lot of money you'd have coming at the end of this,"
opined Holland. "Those four would have stripped you."

"Or I might get their wads."

"I doubt it."

"Yes, and so do they judging by the number of times
they've wanted me to join them." He glanced around. "Where's
old Sourpuss? Hiding in a crate?"

Nodding toward the trap in the dome's wall, Holland informed, "Put on a headpiece and went out for another look at
the last core. He muttered something about that inch-wide stri-
ation of red dirt being ferrous oxide."

"What does that signify?"

"Nothing of importance. It isn't worth digging up. Too
thin and too deep."

"The truth is that he doesn't give a darn for that core or
any other," suggested Yarbridge. "He's escaping six faces that
give him the gripes. A two hours' supply of oxygen means
that temporarily he can get away from it all. Why doesn't he

join the Foreign Legion?"

"He's an old dog compelled to learn new tricks," said Holland solemnly. "As a young one in the same fix, I sympathize with him."

"They ought to let him go home," Yarbridge commented. "They ought to send us a guitar player in his place. Or, better still, half a dozen slinky brunettes from the chorus line. Rumor has it there are twenty more points selected for further test bores. If so, we'll be stuck here quite a spell."

"Suits me. I'm out of mischief, perfecting my education and making money fast." He gave a sly grin. "Being neither married nor brunette-starved, I can afford to wait."

Yarbridge stood up, stretched himself, made a face. "Oh, well, shortly the sunny side."

The other knew what he meant. They were swinging away from Earth's dark hemisphere and round to her illuminated face. That meant an additional diversion in circumstances where each one was precious, to be savored to the utmost. Some intelligent official back home had seen fit to include in their equipment a small telescope, only x200, with four-inch object lens. It had proved considerably a morale-booster. Men could and did stare through it for hours, drinking the scene with avid thirst, and telling each other thumping lies about the wealth of detail to be discerned in their own back yards.

They cleaned, polished and fondled the spyglass, treating it with loving care, for it made the faraway seem near. It provided illusionary comfort. Soon it would reverse that role and create realistic pain. It sharpened any eye in search of peace and beauty—but magnified turmoil and tragedy with equal impartiality.

A direct pointer to coming trouble was not immediately recognized as such either by the seven on the Moon or the teeming masses of Earth. Even specialized minds summoned to deal with it were motivated more by curiosity than alarm. It formed a minor item in a news bulletin picked up from KDTH at Dubuque, Iowa.

"Experts from the Department of Agriculture at Washington are flying to the farm of Barton Maguire, near Dubuque. In an interview Maguire said that a field has developed grass-rot."

It was forgotten before the succeeding item had been

voiced halfway through. KDTH began to fade. Yarbridge
searched around, picked up a lively performance of *"La Cum-
parsita"* from Rio de Janeiro, hummed in off-key accompani-
ment. Wilkin lay nearby on his oxygen-inflated mattress and
frowned through his spectacles. Two drillers off duty played
cards with deadly earnestness.

Two days later WCBM at Baltimore, made intermittent by
static, let go half a sentence. ". . . Eminent botanists and biolo-
gists rushed by the United Nations Food Commission to the
farm of Barton Maguire, in Iowa."

James Holland, having a turn at the telescope, removed his
attention, said to nobody in particular, "Who's this Maguire?
I'm sure I've heard his name before."

"There are millions of them," grunted a driller. He planted
a queen on his opponent's nine, confiscated both cards. "They
swarm out of the ground every St. Patrick's Day."

Letting it pass, Holland had another look at Earth. In full
sunlight it was a spectacle of which one could never tire, a
vision infinitely more satisfying than the other planets or the
host of stars. And it kept steady, without faltering behind a
shivering atmosphere. The chief snag was that if one stared
too intently and too long one began to imagine things. The
brain gained ascendancy over the eyes, forcing them to detect
a non-existent dot in mid-Atlantic and call it a liner. Or con-
vert a line to a road and conjure vehicles along it.

He was again at the 'scope next day when Yarbridge brought
in a voice that for some time had been dimly muttering, "Yarboo! Come in Yarboo!" It boosted to fair strength.
For a couple of minutes Yarbridge and the other slapped backs,
chewed technicalities, exchanged love to Margaret for love to
Jeannie, swapped a couple of corny insults. Then again Holland's attention was drawn away as the distant ham spoke more
seriously and in lower tones.

"Something fishy is going on. Lot of rumors flying
around. They say that troops have been rushed north with
flame throwers. A guy told me he'd been turned back by the
National Guard outside Dubuque. He thinks a flying saucer
has landed and the authorities are keeping it quiet. You can
take that as bunk. How many saucers have you found up
there?"

"None," said Yarbridge.

"It's bound to happen some day," ventured the other. "But I don't believe it's happened yet. This saucer stuff is a lot of scuttlebutt. All the same, there's a general feeling of suspicion that something is going on and we're not being told. See if you can raise a station farther north—maybe you'll be given a hair-raiser."

"You could do that yourself." Digging a small book out of a breast pocket, Yarbridge consulted it. "There are a dozen or more in and around Dubuque."

"Hah! You're telling me? Their cards are stuck on my wall. Try getting them!"

"You mean they're not operating?"

"Definitely not!" A pause, then, "That's why I say there's something peculiar afoot. If anything of national or international interest were taking place up there, they'd be bawling all over the bands. But they aren't. You know what *that* means!"

"Shut down and sealed by official order."

"That's how it looks—and I don't like it."

"Me neither." Yarbridge glanced at an Earth-chronometer ticking to one side of his rig. "Will you be around at eighteen hours G.M.T.?"

"Yes, if I'm not in the clink."

"All right. I'll let you know what I find."

He added a bit more, switched off, turned in his swivel seat and said to Holland, "I've known that boy for ten years. He's as excitable as a porcelain Buddha and doesn't tell tales for the fun of it. Furthermore, all the hams in Dubuque won't drop dead on the same day."

A hairy driller passing by caught the last remark, stopped and informed, "They might, if they were holding a weekly meeting and some nut let go a bomb. Years ago we lost a complete crew that way during a native revolt."

Ignoring it, Yarbridge went on, "Can you see anything extraordinary in Iowa?"

"What, with this glass?" Holland made a disparaging gesture. "We need one umpteen times the size."

"I suppose so." He switched on, resumed probing the ether. "If we can't use our eyes, we'll have to depend on our ears. I'll try bringing in Jerry, who lives at—"

He broke off as his slow-motion dial hit a peaky point and a Canadian voice came out the speaker: ". . . At Ottawa this morning. After a hurried meal the Russian delegation left by air for Iowa, having refused press interviews. Circles close to the United States Government say that an exchange of agricultural technologists has been arranged and that an American party flew to Omsk last night."

Holland got up from the 'scope, put hands on lean hips and said, "That's Iowa again."

"I know." Yarbridge sounded a little grim. "How about adding another heater or two? I feel cold."

"You'll be colder if major ructions take place across there," remarked Wilkin, morbidly gratified. "Fine fix we'll be in, cut off from the rest."

"Why should there be trouble?" asked Yarbridge with a touch of defiance. "We have outgrown world wars. There hasn't been so much as a diplomatic clash for half a century. Everyone is peaceful and happy these days."

"Are they?" Wilkin cocked a sardonic eyebrow.

"They darned well ought to be!"

"*Ought* and *is* are different words," Wilkin pointed out.

"You should know!" snapped Yarbridge.

"What do you mean by that?" His pale eyes narrowing behind his glasses, Wilkin sat up.

Hurriedly Holland chipped in. "If people had the patience to wait for the heaters, there'd be no need to warm up their tempers." He started off toward the switchboard, adding, "I can take a hint. I'll turn them on at once. No rest for the wicked."

It served to crack up the acrimonius byplay. It was a conversational gambit frequently adopted by a third party when two men showed signs of rubbing each other the wrong way. Strange conditions breed strange conventions, including that of drowning other people's differences in one's own sorrows.

Here, the problem of how to live together perforce had been solved, haphazardly but adequately. On Earth it was soon to prove unsolvable. The unknown enemy had complicated it beyond solution merely by shifting its crux from the brain to the belly.

Possession of power creates a peculiar hiatus in the reasoning part of the brain. There's one lesson that authority is mentally incapable of learning, namely, that truth will out. The more determinedly and persistently truth is thrust down the well, the bigger the bounce when finally she emerges.

By the end of a week authority still wore a pin on its lips but the Lunar seven had learned via Yarbridge and a hundred hams that Iowa was under martial law and its state lines held by troops against all but those holding official permits to cross. Also that the German and Brazilian armies had been partially mobilized with the consent of the United Nations. The Australian Government had voted itself powers unheard-of except in time of war. Planes and unspecified supplies were being rushed to south China for reasons not stated.

Two more days and the stubborn secrecy of the powers-that-be was burst wide open by the sheer necessity of world-wide publicity. This point marked the second step forward in the natural march of events foreseen by those who had provided the root cause.

Yarbridge could have picked up the official announcement from any professional radio station in any known language. By luck he got it from WBAX at Wilkes-Barre.

"A previously unknown phenomenon afflicting the holding of Farmer Barton Maguire, outside Dubuque, Iowa, has been found by experts to be caused by the presence of a filterable virus that is responsible for the ultra-rapid decomposition of chlorophyll. The same virus has also appeared in Brazil, Germany, mid-Russia, China, Pakistan and Rhodesia. Its origin is unknown."

"Well, that's a consolation," commented Yarbridge as the faraway announcer paused for breath. "I'd expected something worse."

"You couldn't!" contradicted Wilkin.

WBAX continued with: "This disease can be spread by contact and borne from one place to another by animals or birds. The government, therefore, prohibits all movements of livestock whether near an affected area or not. Dogs, cats and other domestic creatures must be kept under control. Any found wandering loose will be destroyed on sight without compensation to owners."

"They're becoming tough," observed a driller, thoughtfully. "It can't be for nothing—the public wouldn't stand for it." He pulled at an ear, finished, "I reckon it's serious."

"Shut up and listen," ordered Yarbridge.

"Under the Emergency Powers Act of 1988 the government takes authority to seize any property found to be contaminated and use thereon any measures that may be deemed necessary to destroy the virus. All citizens are required to report affected areas without delay to the nearest post office, police station or military camp. Failure to do so is punishable by a fine of one thousand U.N. dollars or one year's imprisonment."

"Hell's bells!" the driller ejaculated. "Sounds like they're scared."

"Sh-h-h!"

"The following description of symptoms has been issued for the benefit of the public," went on WBAX. "First occurs a bleaching of green leaves which turn gray and dry within forty-eight hours. They are then brittle and lifeless, will readily crumble between the fingers. The process spreads from point of origin in a rapidly increasing circle, destroying plant life over a progressively greater area. The inside of such an area is not dangerous since the virus remains active only at the rim where it can continue to feed on chlorophyll. The rim, therefore, is the danger point; pending arrival of expert assistance the rim should be thoroughly burned by any means at hand and then given similar treatment at any point where advance is found to continue. The Department of Agriculture assures listeners that there is no reason for undue apprehension and that every effort is being made to find a satisfactory method of combating this menace."

Wilken wiped his glasses and said, "That last lullaby tells two things. One, that they regard it as a genuine menace. Two, that they haven't found what they call a satisfactory method of dealing with it."

"They will," assured Yarbridge.

"Will they?" asked Wilkin.

"You like to think they won't, eh?" inquired the driller, glowering at him.

"I see things as they are and not as I'd prefer to see them," answered Wilkin, stiffly. "My dream world has long been dead."

"The real one is alive. It will go on living."

"The former is factual; the latter hypothetical."

The other let his fists dangle. "When a guy turns to ten-dollar words, I give up."

He went away, sadly shaking his head in the manner of one unable to cope with an idiot. Wilkin finished shining his glasses, carefully fitted them on his nose, eyed Holland as if inviting further comment.

Holland obliged with, "One thing they didn't tell us."

"What's that?"

"Rate of spread."

"Yes," agreed Wilkin. He fiddled his fingers, watched himself doing it. "They didn't tell us."

"Maybe they forgot," offered Yarbridge. "Or didn't think it especially important."

"It could be five inches a month," ventured Holland. "It could be twenty miles per day."

"Now don't start giving me the willies," Yarbridge protested.

"If you want a real headache," suggested Wilkin, "go to bed and think it over. Take away chlorophyll and see what's left."

"It means nothing to me. I don't eat the lousy stuff."

"You're lucky," said Wilkin in the same even tone. "You should survive as the last man."

Yarbridge scowled, said to Holland, "What is he talking about?"

"Something that may never happen."

"I might have guessed it." He sniffed his contempt.

"Or may," said Wilkin.

"There are the oceans," Holland told him, "full of fish."

"How nice!" said Wilkin. He lay down, closed his eyes.

Confused with having half his attention on the radio and only half on this erratic conversation, Yarbridge demanded, "Look here, what has fish got to do with it? Why bring them up?"

Wilkin did not bother to reply.

Holland said, "Oh forget it," and strolled toward his engine.

"This can't go on for another couple of years," informed Yarbridge, speaking to thin air. "Not when guys go off the beam after four months."

He reached for his microphone, called a person named Jerry without enthusiasm—and without result.

At the thousand-foot mark the barber shop quartet didn't

sound so hot and the whisky lacked zip. The celebration had all the joyous verve of a wake held around a frowning corpse. For one thing, they'd been delayed by need to replace a cutter. For another, there were those shenanigans next door, a quarter million miles away.

So they finished the bottle, listened while four cold sober drillers bellowed a bawdy song, put on one or two artificial grins, told one or two unfunny anecdotes. Then somehow they broke it up before properly begun, returned in silence to duty or to bed.

Men were quiet after that, speaking when necessary, tending to hang around the radio receiver or play with the 'scope. Faces became set. The nuclear engine gave out its low whine; the drill went round and round, was drawn up, forced down, rotated again. More cores were stacked outside without anyone knowing or caring whether they held dirt or diamonds. The task had been reduced to a job and the job to a mere function.

As the days drifted by the radio told that the British, Dutch and Belgian governments had brought in a complicated system of food rationing. The United States authorities took control of all cereals and fixed the retail price of bread. Canada followed suit. In the Argentine a million men slaved to build along the northern frontier something described as the Fire Curtain. The Ukrainian Republic made heated protest to the United Nations about what it called infringement of rights of sovereignty, but nothing was said about what had raised Ukrainian bile.

Obviously a thin, bedraggled veil of censorship continued to obscure the international scene. The dunkers of truth were still on the job. But Moonlisteners found significance in the occasional use of new words apparently coined on the spur of the moment and thrust into news bulletins.

"A gun battle took place in Milan early this morning when strong forces of Italian police surrounded a warehouse and trapped a band of chowjackers. Eighteen were killed, more than forty captured. The police lost six."

New York state troopers grabbed a bunch of beefleggers. The British sent to jail a smooth gentleman described as a burp-baron. Not to be outdone, the Germans raided a noisy plant in the Black Forest wherein large humans and large canines were cooperating in the production of dogburgers.

"Hear that?" exclaimed Yarbridge. "How do guys like those get away with it?"

"They didn't," someone pointed out.

"What I mean is where's the money in it?"

"At the right time, in the right place and in the right conditions there is money in dead rats," Wilkin opined.

"If I remember correctly," put in Holland, seriously, "they actually did eat rats during the seige of Paris."

"Go easy, will you?" Yarbridge thinned his lips. "My stomach can stand only so much."

"Be thankful that you're not in the part of Asia where they have two or three thousand to the square mile," advised Wilkin. "You would stand for something a good deal worse there. Or better, according to your gastronomic viewpoint."

"Such as what?"

"Stiffburgers."

"What?"

"Mock-pork—the dead feeding the living."

Yarbridge yellowed around the jawline. An off-duty driller—apparently asleep—opened a dark eye and stared at Wilkin. He maintained the gaze while he mulled things over, then rolled off his mattress, lumbered across and spoke in a deep rumble.

"I've had too much of you, you four-eyed runt!" He jerked a thumb skyward. "I've a wife and three kids over there. I've worry enough without you trying to be funny. Keep your noisy trap shut, see?"

"I wasn't trying to be funny," Wilkin denied. He wiped his glasses, peered at the big bulk without visible intimidation. "My only daughter is in Iowa."

"More shame to you then, acting the way you do. Hold your teeth together if you want to keep them."

Another driller came along, glanced from one to another, said, "Something wrong, Hank?"

"Nothing much, Joe. Only that I'm working myself up to break a certain gab's neck."

"What'll that buy you?"

"Satisfaction," informed Hank.

James Holland said soothingly, "Not all folk worry the same way. Some nurse it; some let it go bang; some hope for the best; some expect the worst."

"All right," conceded Hank. "Then he can switch fast from type four to type one."

"Thus shaping myself in your image," said Wilkin. Displaying unexpected nerve, he came to his feet, faced the other. "Why should I?"

"Because, Granpop, I've got this." His opponent showed a knobby fist half the size of a ham, "And I'm not particular about—"

Wilkin opened a hand, revealed a vest-pocket automatic three inches long. "I've got this—and I'm not finicky either." He waited a moment, his pale eyes level, then ended, "We've free speech here. You're not taking it away. Beat it, you hairy bum!"

The other studied him calculatingly up and down, then spat on the ground, turned and headed for the mid-section. Joe went with him. Wilkin reposed on his oxygen bag.

"You blundered there," Holland told him. "He's bothered about his family, as is natural. Some people are touchy when worried."

"So am I," said Wilkin.

"You look it," scoffed Yarbridge. "In my opinion—"

He shut up as Holland nudged him. The latter continued, "Anyway, this is no place to wave a gun around."

"It will be!" Wilkin promised.

The third inevitable step began when the Indian delegate to the United Nations Assembly made a long, impassioned speech that might have been cribbed from the late nineteen thirties. It was upon the same subject: the haves and the have-nots. It ended the same way—with an implied threat. It produced the same reaction: open pacification and secret preparation.

Dr. Francisca, chairman of the assembly, dexterously employed a procedural quibble to avoid a vote on the plain issue of who should give what to whom. He had a wary eye on the have-nots, present in full strength and ready to vote as one man. The danger of a complete split was avoided for twenty-four hours. At the end of that time India withdrew from the United Nations. China followed. So did every other nation whose crops could not keep pace with its needs.

Joe saw the first flash on Earth's dark side. The little

telescope wasn't popular when Earth resembled a great black ball against a blinding Sun, but occasionally it was used as the terminator approached. He was staring through it in the angled blaze of false twilight when he spotted a flash on Earth's sickle of darkness. Then another and another.

Quietly he left the 'scope, shook Yarbridge awake and whispered, "I've just seen lights over there."

"What of it? Why spoil my sleep?"

"Nobody's seen them before."

"Maybe they weren't looking. There isn't a constant watch as you know quite well."

"I've got a queer feeling about them. They were mighty big flashes."

Yarbridge emitted an imitation snore.

Nearby, Holland stirred, awoke, propped himself on an elbow, asked, "What's the matter now?"

"I don't know," said Joe. "I can't be sure, I want this tramp to check up on the radio."

"Well, what makes you think something may be wrong?"

"I've just seen three great flares on Earth's dark strip."

"Meteors," suggested Holland.

"Do you think so?"

"Could be." He eyed the other. "What else?"

"Atom bombs," said Joe.

"Nuts! They aren't *that* crazy."

"How can we tell?" Joe asked. "We know only what we hear. And that isn't enough."

"You're morbid."

"Maybe I am," said Joe, doggedly, "but I saw what I saw. Aren't you interested?"

"No."

The other frowned. "Why not?"

"Because I've swallowed a pill that you've yet to take. You'll have to gulp it down sooner or later and whether you like it or not."

"Meaning—?"

"There's nothing we can do. Positively nothing!"

Musing it with much reluctance, Joe finally admitted, "Yes, that's it. Until the ship comes we're trapped. We've got to sit here and watch. We've got to eat our fingers down to the knuckles and—"

Raising an irritated face from where he was lying, Wilkin harshed, "Then go gnaw them some place else. I need sleep even if you don't."

"Earth's dying," said Joe, taking no notice. "The drills are still and the derricks are down and the fields are aflame—and none of you care. Technicians! Bigbrains! And none of you care!"

"Get some shuteye, Joe," advised Holland. "A few sparks in a glass don't signify the crack of doom."

"All right." Resignedly he turned to leave, added with strange positiveness, "But we'll have that sleepy-eyed lunk at his bawl-box before breakfast—and we'll see who's right and who's wrong."

Yarbridge responded with another snore, a real one this time.

Reclining full length, James Holland stared at the stars visible through the transparency of the dome's conical cap. A blue one kept winking at him alongside the circular rim of the overhead antenna. After a while he closed his eyes but found it impossible to sleep. His brain droned drearily, "There's nothing we can do, nothing we can do."

In the small hours he ceased to court slumber, rolled off his mattress, crept silently past the others' feet and had a long look through the telescope.

There was a babble of insistent voices right across the ether, singsong ones, guttural ones, determined ones, hysterical ones. Ignoring the play of languages none could understand, Yarbridge felt around with his dials, picked up a station that did not identify itself with any call-sign or locale but was rapidly transmitting a series of figures in plain English.

It went on, "The first group of numbers will report for service by six o'clock this evening, the second group tomorrow, the third the day after. Unless he is totally blind or is certified under the Mental Deficiency Act, the failure of any citizen to report will result in the issue of a warrant for his arrest. This is the Federal Broadcasting Service radiating simultaneously from all stations."

"By hokey!" said Yarbridge. "Sounds like they've taken over the whole shebang from coast to—"

He broke off as the faraway voice continued, "Indian and Chinese forces crossed their borders in great strength at noon yesterday and are attempting to seize the Burmese rice-bowl and such wheat-growing areas of central Russia as the virus has not yet reached. A report that Germany is about to invade the Black Earth region of the Ukraine has been energetically denied in Berlin. The Italians indignantly repudiate a French accusation that they are preparing to attack the uncontaminated agricultural area of southeast France. In view of the serious international situation the President has declared a state of emergency and assumed all the powers to which he is entitled thereunder. His midnight speech emphasized that the time has come to honor our—"

The announcer ceased in mid-sentence. They waited a minute for him to resume but he didn't. Even the sizzle of background noise had gone.

Yarbridge turned a strained face over one shoulder, remarked to the small audience, "That's war—without saying so."

"I could have told you several hours ago," said Joe.

"I'd have bet on it a couple of weeks ago," capped Wilkin.

"How long is it since that virus stuff was first mentioned?" a driller inquired.

Consulting his logbook, Yarbridge informed, "Forty-seven days."

"And how long before this ship is due?"

"Thirty-two."

"Think it'll come?"

It was a shocking question.

Yarbridge passed a hand through tousled hair and growled, "Why not?"

"The ship isn't one of those thinking machines they have in stories," the other pointed out. "Men order it to be sent and other men bring it."

"Well?"

"Suppose they become too busy?"

"That's hardly—"

"Or the ship gets busted wide open?"

"There are two ships," Yarbridge reminded.

"So what? There's a war on. They're parked side by side, like stiffs in a morgue. Whatever wallops one will wallop both."

"The walloping won't be easy," put in Holland. "They've

got formidable defenses over there."

"What, after fifty years of peace? They never had enough even when they were having wars."

Joe chipped in with, "How about asking the spaceport to confirm date of arrival?"

Glooming at his instruments, Yarbridge said nothing.

"What's come over you?" persisted Joe. Suspicion grew into his beefy features. "You're here to maintain contact, aren't you? How about raising the spaceport?"

"I can try," said Yarbridge.

"Try? What d'you mean, try?" Joe glanced around at the listeners, added, "How long since you last spoke to the spaceport?"

"Nine days."

"Haven't you called since then?"

"Dozens of times. No reply."

"No reply," echoed Joe. He swallowed hard, stared at his feet, manifestly could think of nothing more to say.

Wilkin studied him with pale, calculating eyes.

"And you didn't tell us," broke in another driller, with unconcealed ire. "These fancy mechanics knew we're cut off but didn't tell us. We're too dim to understand. We're only oil boys, see?"

Holland said, "Now don't start dividing us into rival trade unions just because four of you happen to share the same skill. We're all in this together. The spaceport has something better to do than chat and hold our hands days after day. We've gone many a full week without speaking to it."

"Not when it's being called," retorted the other.

"Radio apparatus isn't infallible," said Yarbridge, not very convincingly. "They may have a technical hitch."

"I always thought you guys were too clever to have hitches."

"I wish to heaven we were!" said Holland, fervently. He rubbed a freckled chin, glanced toward the engine steadily droning on the farther side.

The others followed his gaze and went silent. They knew what he meant. The engine and its coupled generator provided light and they could dispense with that if necessary. Also power for the drill, the radio, the cooker and other items they could do without in a pinch. Also warmth via the numerous heaters placed equidistantly around the perimeter. They couldn't live through the Lunar nights without warmth. And finally oxygen by electrolysis of Moon-water eighty feet down. They couldn't survive without oxygen.

Frankly alarmed, one asked, "How much jollop have you got for that contraption?"

"You mean thorium oxide?"

"Yes."

"Sufficient for a couple of years."

"Then all you have to do is keep her going?"

"That's all," agreed Holland, straight-faced.

The other looked him up and down as if seeking an invisible joke at his own expense. Then he moved away to tend the drill.

Yarbridge used his mike. "Yarboo calling Booster One. Come in Booster One. Come in Booster One!"

He wasted his breath.

As the days rolled by they developed a tendency to ignore the radio most times or treat it with open skepticism when the temptation to listen became too much. The thousand friends behind Yarbridge's god had shrunk to little more than a dozen, the technical qualifications of the missing ones having drawn them into the detection and communications services of the armed forces.

The few survivors told little, though they could have said much. But they did not dare. Vertical beam antenna were now prohibited and their calls were monitored. They spoke briefly and pointlessly, with the extreme wariness of those peculiarly susceptible to the capital charge of disseminating information that might be useful to an enemy.

Yarbridge said wearily to Holland one day, "This is grim. Doesn't matter whether I get George in Memphis or Jules in Toulouse, he can't tell me so much as whether it's raining because somebody across the battle line might need that datum."

"If there *are* any battle lines," said Holland. He pawed his freckles, went on, "What beats me is that in all that gabble nobody mentions who's fighting whom."

"Everyone is fighting everyone," opined Wilkin, coming up behind him. "What else do you expect?"

"And when they do see fit to tell anything you get less than half of it," Yarbridge continued. "Listen to this."

He turned the volume control, brought up a British voice that had been murmuring almost indistinguishably: ". . . And several more robot planes were shot down over London last night. The rest of the country—"

Switching off, he said, "There's a sample. He doesn't say how many. He doesn't say who sent them. He doesn't say what happened to the bomb loads when the planes dropped or what damage was caused."

"Of course he doesn't say," put in Wilkin. "In fact it's a wonder he says anything at all. But it won't be for much longer."

"Why?"

"The lights are going down across the world. Would *you* squat there and count them out loud for the benefit of an unimportant gang upon the Moon?"

"Who says we're unimportant?" inquired Hank, joining them and displaying aggressiveness.

"I do," Wilkin informed. "Who cares for someone looking out the top window when there's a free-for-all in the street?"

"It can't last," decided the other, not caring to argue the point. "They haven't got the stuff. Half a century back they'd have been using supersonic missiles and all kinds of other gadgets. These days they haven't got 'em. Armaments have hit an all-time low."

"Who told you that?" inquired Wilkin.

"Everybody knows it."

"Do they?" He put on a lopsided smile. "Pity we can't ask them today."

Hank scowled, edged nearer the radio and rasped at Yarbridge, "Unimportant or not, we're entitled to know what's happened to our wives and kids. Why doesn't the spaceport—"

It was a gag, for as he got alongside Wilkin he swung a huge fist into the metallurgist's face and grunted with the force of the blow. Wilkin crashed one way while his glasses flew the other. The thing was done with such suddenness that Hank was astride the victim and frisking his pockets before the others had time to interfere. Breathing heavily, he came erect holding the little automatic.

"I never did like sneery guys with guns." His eyes challenged them as beside him Wilkin sat up and held hands to features. He moved over to Yarbridge. "All right, Porky, get busy and raise the spaceport."

"How?"

"He asks me how!" His big hand gave the other's shoulder a shove. "You know how. Let's see you do it—and fast!"

Yarbridge obliged, then said, "There you are. I can call until my tonsils drop out. Now let us see you do better."

"How can I tell that you're calling them in the right place?" He pointed to the dials. "Or, for that matter, that you're correctly tuned to get anybody on that set?"

"How do I know when a cutter is due to be swapped?" asked Yarbridge.

"Don't be funny with me!" A pulse was beating heavily in his forehead. "If the drill goes bust while I stand here a month, I'm going to—"

"You're going to do nothing we don't like," interjected Holland. "And you'd better give me that gun."

"You crazy?"

"Not yet."

"Me, neither," assured Hank. "So you can go take a walk."

"Thanks," said Holland. "I will." Shoving hands deep in pockets he ambled away, his lips pursed in a silent whistle.

Thirty seconds later the engine stopped. The drill ceased its weary grinding. The lights went out and there was no illumination save through the transparent peak of the otherwise opaque dome. The U-tubes set in the wall no longer fizzed and bubbled. No oxygen trickled into the interior and no hydrogen poured outside.

Hank crossed the circular area with a bull-like rush, gestured with the automatic. "Start her up."

"Sorry."

"I said start her up!"

"Do it yourself."

He examined the engine from end to end, seeking visible evidence of how to do it. Once or twice he toyed momentarily with a lever, stud or switch but thought better of it. He had all the layman's near-superstitious fear of hot-stuff.

"It's your job, not mine." He flourished the weapon again. "Go to it."

"I'm on strike," Holland informed. "My union has called

me out."

"If you don't do as you're told, Spotty-pan, I'll put a slug through your bean."

"Well," hazarded Holland, thoughtfully, "that might be one way to get her operating. But I doubt it."

The other drillers had clustered around by now and one demanded, "What's the big idea, cutting the engine?"

"He's trying to show us who's boss," Hank growled. "And I won't have it. No kid's going to push me around."

"There's nothing for it but to make him see sense," put in Joe. He rolled up his sleeves, revealed brawny arms.

"That'll take you a couple of minutes," Holland pointed out.

"So what?"

"You won't have that long."

Joe took a hurried step backward. "No? Why won't we?"

Glancing significantly at the engine which could be trusted to remain quiescent for a million years, Holland advised, "Wait and see."

"Give him the gun, Hank," said Joe, nervously.

"Go on, give it him," urged the rest as panic mounted.

"I think he's a liar," declared Hank, mulish. "I think he's taking us for a ride. He wouldn't lounge there easylike if something were about to happen."

"I'm hoping it won't." Holland ostentatiously consulted his wrist watch. "Because I'm betting that your nerves will crack before mine." Extracting a handkerchief, he mopped his forehead, had another look at the watch.

It was an effective gesture. The driller alongside Hank decided that more waiting would be unendurable. He made a snatch at the gun, got it, strove to twist it out of the other's grip. Stubborn to the last, Hank hung on. The remaining pair suddenly made up their minds and joined the fray, ignoring Hank's grunts and curses. The disputed weapon emitted a thin, hard crack and planted a slug in the dirt between stamping feet. It came loose. One of them tossed it toward the onlooker who was still doing his best to maintain a phony expression of strained anxiety.

"Start her up! For Pete's sake start her up!"

The struggle ceased by mutual consent and all four tried

to urge him with their eyes. He did things including several that weren't necessary and some they couldn't see. The engine moaned. He let in the generator clutch. The lights came on. The U-tubes bubbled and gassed.

"You big, awkward hophead!" one of them rumbled at Hank. "Why can't you leave well alone? Think we haven't got troubles enough?"

They went back to the drill. Hank stared a while at his own hands, opening and closing the fingers, favored Holland with a look of dark suspicion, then lumbered after the others.

Holland made for his sleeping space, picked up his helmet, checked the pressure in its little oxygen cylinder. He fitted the headpiece while Wilkin sat grimly nursing a split lip and Yarbridge watched in silence. Exiting via the double trap, he trudged through fine gray Lunar dust, past the stack of cores and at a suitable spot fired the gun until it was empty. Then he hurled it into the distance.

Returning, he removed the helmet, carefully placed it on its rack, lay down and studied the overhead circle of transparency. Wilkin still offered no remark.

After a while, Yarbridge said, "You were lucky to get away with that. I don't know that I'd have had the nerve to try it."

"Comes easier when you've done it once or twice before," Holland informed. "A few years ago I was compelled to learn that one needn't always be completely without means of defense. In the last resort there's often one thing that can be used and effectively."

"Such as what?"

"The other's fellow's ignorance."

"Suppose he isn't ignorant?"

"Then it's your hard luck." He smiled to himself, went on, "But everybody is ignorant by one standard if not by another. I'd be a prize sucker for a radio gag if you could think up a good one."

"I guessed so," agreed Yarbridge who had never given a thought to this aspect of his own ability.

He made up for lost time by commencing forthwith to examine the possibilities. As weeks and months rolled on and the situation worsened a crafty scheme or two might prove useful. Indeed, technical knowledge plus sharp wits might decide between life and death.

The ship did not come, neither on the appointed day nor a fortnight later. They required the extra two weeks to incubate to point of vocal expression the opinion that it would never arrive.

Other data supported this dread thought. The telescope had enough power to reveal numerous and sinister markings on Earth's land surface though not with clarity sufficient to determine their true nature. The instrument had to be used with imagination that might be over- or under-exercised according to the individual.

And night after night, day after day, brilliant flashes had been observed on the mother-globe, waxing and waning until finally they ceased.

Only seven stations could be heard across the full widths of the long, medium, short and ultra-short bands. They were unintelligible, radiating high-speed but very weak signals in code. A week later there were four. Ten days afterward there was one. Then that, too, went off the air. The ether was silent. Earth rolled along her appointed course, a black ball on the night side, a shining picture on the day side, and gave forth no single voice.

At that point they took stock of food supplies. Originally enough packaged meals and emergency rations had been dumped to last seven men for twenty months and nearly a third of that time had now passed. If they reduced consumption to the minimum and rigorously prevented all waste, the seven might live another sixteen months.

That much being known, the arithmetic of the situation became obvious to each man, though he kept it strictly to himself, coddling it within the secret recesses of his own mind. If one died, so much the better for the rest; they'd make out another eighteen or nineteen months. If two went under, the survivors would gain a further spell of life. Three deaths would permit the remaining four to eat until the engine stopped —and beyond that, if they could.

The environment was beginning to force a distorted picture into each mind, making it see that the others were not men with mouths, but mouths with men around them.

But this hidden reaction betrayed its presence in indirect ways. The hairy-chested quartet stopped the drill to cut down power consumption and—as they theorized—help eke out the precious reserve of hot-stuff. Holland noted the deed, deduced its purpose and did not bother to tell them that disintegration was held at a uniform rate regardless of power used. It could not be speeded up without danger nor slowed without ceasing to provide exploitable energy. Their action was futile.

One day Joe caught him away from the rest, sidled up, said, "I've been thinking."

"It's a healthy occupation," Holland approved.

"What if this gadget packs in?"

"Then it's my responsibility to get it going again."

"Yes, I know." He glanced around to make sure none were within hearing. "We're stuck here quite a spell. If anything happens to you, we're sunk."

"That's what I like about it," said Holland.

"I don't," declared Joe with some emphasis. "If you fall sick at the wrong time, it'll mean the end."

"Very true. So on no account must I become ill." He eyed the other shrewdly. "It might help if we reserved some whisky for an emergency. The way it's evaporating out of sealed bottles there won't be any left pretty soon."

"It isn't me—it's the others," said Joe.

"It would be!" indorsed Holland.

Joe blinked and went on, "Anyway, what I want to say is this: that it's your duty to teach someone else to handle this groan-machine. One isn't enough. We need another who knows how."

"Such as yourself?"

"I could learn."

"I don't doubt it," said Holland.

"Well, why shouldn't you show somebody?"

"I may come to regret it—if one can have regrets in one's sleep."

"What d'you mean by that?"

"If your thinking has been taken far enough, you know darned well what I mean."

"Smart, aren't you?" spat Joe, momentarily vicious.

"The circumstances compel me to be," assured Holland blandly. Crossing fingers, he held them under Joe's nose. "This is me. Don't you forget it!"

Yarbridge came across as Joe stamped away. "He looks

sour. You been rubbing him the wrong way?"

"He's just applied for the post of assistant atomechanic.
I turned him down."

"Did you tell him you've been instructing me?"

"No." He pondered briefly, explained, "Three of us have
completely different qualifications whereas the other four are
and always have been birds of a feather. Each of those four
knows what the others are doing and why they're doing it, at
any given moment. They understand each other in a way they
can't understand us. Our methods and functions defeat them.
No matter how irrational it may be, people often tend to dislike
what they're unable to understand."

"All the same, if there's a split in this group it's of their
own making," Yarbridge observed.

"Yes, but we mustn't blame them for it. The division is
in some ways as natural as the sunrise. So, if I'd told him
I'd picked you instead of a driller as standby mechanic, it
might aggravate matters."

Yarbridge gestured toward the food stack. "I fear they'll
be more than aggravated by the time we've eaten most of the
way down that. Sooner or later somebody's going to make us
put on a local version of what's happened on Earth."

"While there's life there's hope," said Holland.

"Of what? A miracle?"

"A ship."

"That *would* be a miracle," declared Yarbridge, flatly.

He was wrong. In due time a ship came, deliberately and
without benefit of supernatural forces.

It was ten months since those in the dome had first heard
mention of the virus and by now they'd almost forgotten its
existence. Events that followed had overshadowed the cause,
like a prolonged riot in which none can recall who or what
started it.

The food stack now stood at less than half its original
height. The drill remained sunk to the best part of two thousand feet, its drive-gears motionless, its shaft red-brown with
a fine layer of rust. The engine droned and shuddered, the
lights still burned, the numerous heaters gave protection against
night's exterior low of—150° C. Moon-water still surrendered
its oxygen and maintained the breath of life. The radio remained serviceable but had not been in operation for weeks.

Four oxygen-inflated beds were lined together on the perimeter, three more at the opposite side. This sleeping arrangement was symbolic of psychological antagonisms that no man wished to boost to a crisis yet no man was able to cure. Civilized conditioning persisted enough to hold the issue in precarious suspense at least for a little while longer, though each man knew deep in his soul that a time might come when one would starve to death while another sat and watched unmoved.

They were loafing around, four at one side and three at the other, each indulging the vacuous occupation of deciding what he could do with most if only it were there. Conscious of his age, physique, and the shape of things to come, Wilkin yearned for his lost gun. Hank ached for his wife and kids but refused to show it or mention it. Yarbridge's need was no more than a familiar voice seeking him out and calling him in. Holland's choice, vividly and tantalizingly depicted in his mind, was a two-gallon can of pineapple juice, cold or warm.

And the ship came.

It screamed overhead and howled into the distance and turned in a wide sweep and came back with a rising roar. The sounds cut off. The dome trembled slightly as great tonnage sat itself outside.

Hank stood up with little beads of moisture on his forehead. He had the expression of a sleepwalker. The others came to their feet seeking visible confirmation that all ears had heard the same.

"The ship!" said Yarbridge on a note of incredulity. "It can't be anything else but the ship!"

"Didn't make that sort of noise last time," observed Wilkin, unwilling to jump to conclusions. He felt vaguely around his pockets as if looking for something without knowing what. "Maybe it's a different one."

"Sounded different to me," confirmed Joe. "Bigger and faster."

"I'll take a look." Holland picked up his helmet.

A loud knocking sounded on the double-trap before he had time to fit the headpiece. He dumped it, went to the trap with six pairs of eyes watching, manipulated the locks.

The three who entered were not human.

Gray uniformed, gray-blue skinned and hairless, they came into the dome with the casual, unsurprised air of neigh-

bors wanting to borrow the mower. They had two arms and
two legs apparently formed of cords and cartilage rather than
muscle and bone, for they bent in a curve from end to end
instead of at a mid-joint. The six fingers of each hand were
similarly bendable and jointless.

Apart from these noteworthy features of strange coloring
and rubber skeletons they approximated to human appearance.
Their mouths looked natural, their eyes were of human type,
their ears normal enough though somewhat large. All three
stood a couple of inches above Holland, the tallest of his group.
All three were bald and hatless.

Wilkin was the first to break the silence. He peered over
the tops of his glasses as if to insure that they were not causing
an optical illusion, and said, "Who are *you?*"

"That doesn't matter," responded the foremost of the
trio. "Does it?"

"Where did you learn to speak English?" put in Holland,
having expected communication by means of signs and gestures. He felt behind to check that he wasn't flat on his mattress and deep in a ridiculous dream. His hand prodded Yarbridge's paunch.

"On your own world of course. Where else could we
learn it?"

"Can you take us back there?" inquired Hank, single-
mindedly dismissing everything in favor of one aim.

"We have come for that purpose." The alien glanced
around, noting everything but not curious. "We intend to
leave with the minimum of delay. Do whatever is necessary
before you depart and do it quickly."

It wasn't a request. It wasn't an order. It was a plain
statement of plain fact, devoid of either politeness or authority.
Somehow it created a cold impression that the speaker was not
in the habit of asking or telling, but rather of presenting a
realistic case and awaiting the inevitable result. An inhuman,
unemotional mind concerned only with facts.

They packed in a hurry, their minds filled with a thousand questions postponed by the glorious vision of escape. It
did not occur to any of them to view the newcomers as enemies
or treat them with hostility. They had no data to go upon.
So far as they were concerned the Martians—or whoever they
were—had turned up at long last and at the most opportune

time.

Each bearing a pack of personal belongings, they donned helmets, followed the three from the dome. Holland, the last out, switched off the nuclear engine, fastened the double-trap. Filing aboard a vessel several times the size of those with which they were familiar, they were conducted to a large cabin and left to themselves. The ship boosted immediately afterward, plunged toward Earth.

Nobody talked much. Shock of alien contact plus inward speculation of what was awaiting at the other end kept them fairly silent until the landing. The trip had taken fourteen hours, less than half the time they'd required on the outward journey nearly a year ago.

An alien not identifiable as one of those already seen appeared at the cabin, said, "We are grounded and you may leave. Follow me." Conducting them to the long ramp leading from the air lock, he pointed outward. "You will find food and accommodation in that camp. We'll summon you when required."

Descending the ramp they set feet on bare brown earth, paused to survey their surroundings. Straight ahead stood a large collection of hutments typical of an army training center. To the left were the outskirts of a medium-sized town. Mountains loomed in the far background and a small river flowed on the right.

"Where's this?" Yarbridge glanced around, noted that no alien had stayed with them. "Anyone recognize the place?"

"We can find out." Hoisting his pack, Holland started forward. "We've got tongues in our heads."

Hank moved up alongside him, recent differences forgotten. "What did that guy mean about calling us when wanted? Does he think we're going to squat in this dump until somebody whistles to us like dogs?"

Holland shrugged, offered no comment.

"If so, he's got another think coming," Hank went on. "I'm more than grateful for the hitch from up there but that doesn't mean I've got to wait for the official thank-you ceremony. I'm going home and fast! What's the use of making for this camp?"

"Before you know which way to go and how to get there, you've got to find out where you are."

"You may be a thousand miles from home," Yarbridge contributed. "With all the world to pick from you can't expect those aliens to dump you in your own back yard."

"I don't care if it's a million miles. I'll make it if I have to crawl it. I've a wife and kids."

"I had a daughter," said Wilkin, dull-toned. "And I doubt whether I'll ever see her again."

"Shut up, Misery!" growled Hank.

Passing through the main gates they went to the first hut. It contained forty Chinese, men and women, who eyed them with blank indifference. They tried the second. That held a weird mixture of races including a half-naked brown man with a bone through his nose.

"Anyone know English?" called Holland.

A trembling oldster came from the back. He had a long, untended beard and hot but rheumy eyes.

"I do, my son."

"What goes here?"

"What goes?" He had a moment of muddled mystification before his lined features cleared. "Ah, my son, you seek enlightenment?"

"That is the idea," agreed Holland. "More or less."

"You are inspired," informed the other, grasping him by the arm. "For you have come to the right place and the right person. I have been privileged to save the world. I saved it upon my knees, a sinner crying at the gates of heaven. I prayed while the city fell and children screamed and the unrepentant died." The grip tightened, the eyes grew hotter. "Until finally my voice was heard and help came from the skies. Listen, my son, if you, too, will have the grace—"

"Sorry, dad, some other time." Holland pulled gently away.

They transferred attention to the third hut, leaving the oldster querulously mumbling in his beard. Outside the door of this adjoining place a big brawny man stood watching their approach.

He rasped as they reached him, "Another bunch, eh? Where did they find you?"

"On the Moon," Holland told him.

"So?" He studied them from beneath bushy brows, then offered, "Some folks don't know when they're well off. Why didn't you stay there?"

"Would you?"

"Hah! You bet your shirt I would!" He spat on the ground. "Unless I could find a way to drop it on this alien mob that has darned near wiped out humanity."

Hank pushed forward, his beefy features working. "It doesn't look wiped out to me."

"It wouldn't," agreed the other, giving him a calculating up and down. "We're all here in this camp and in that town. All sixty thousand of us. There aren't any more except a scattered few being found and dragged in like you."

"There aren't any more?" Hank had difficulty in understanding it. "You mean—?"

"The world is empty save for this collection of racial remnants." He waved a hand to indicate the local area. "This is us—Homer Saps."

"You sure you know what you're talking about?" asked Yarbridge.

"I ought to, mister. I've been here most of a month." He gave them another shrewdly estimating look-over, went on, "My name's Deacon. I'm an Australian, not that that means anything these days. If you fellows are wanting some place to bunk, you'd better come in here. We've room for ten and we'd rather have you than a gang of half-wild, half-witted Dyaks or Hottentots."

They followed him inside. Spring beds were lined against both walls, each with a cupboard and arms-rack. A tattered and faded military notice in English flapped behind the door. Some thirty men, mostly white, observed their entrance apathetically. One of them had the broad, flat features and monkish haircut of an Eskimo.

Slinging his pack onto a vacant bed, Holland inquired, "Just where are we?"

"Outside a place called Kaystown in Alberta. It jumped up in two or three years after someone struck oil. Nearest dump of any size was Lethbridge."

"*Was?*"

"Half of it's flat and the rest is empty."

He sat on the springs, stared at the wall, subconsciously noted that the windows needed washing. After a while, he asked, "How do you know these aliens caused it all?"

"They told me so."

"They openly boasted of it?"

"No, I can't say they bragged," admitted Deacon with a mite of reluctance. He looked as though he'd have enjoyed another forceful spit had he been outside. "They're neither conscience-stricken or triumphant. They mentioned it as an accomplished fact, like saying that two and two make four."

"I wonder," mused Holland.

"You wonder what?"

"Whether they're opportunists. Whether they're kidding. Maybe they're cashing in on a ready-made situation. Maybe they're grabbing the discredit in order to establish psychological mastery."

"You think they mightn't have done it?" Deacon's features hardened.

"It's possible."

"Won't pay you to talk that way around here."

"Why not?"

"You've had it easy on the Moon, little as you may know it. You've not tasted what most folk down here have experienced. And they're touchy, see? They don't like these aliens and they won't be amiable toward anyone who does like them." He leaned forward. "There's hatred all around, long, fierce, all-consuming. If you sniff, you can smell it. If you look, you can see it."

"Then why don't they do something about it? Sixty thousand against one ship—heck, they could swamp it!"

"The idea has been stewed until it's boiled to rags," Deacon informed. "For one thing, they have weapons and we haven't. For another, what they've done before they can do again."

"What are you getting at?"

"They dropped a virus. It ate green stuff at faster than walking pace. It killed the grass and everything that lives on grass directly or indirectly. But it left the seeds lying below ground. So now they're coming up; the grass is returning. All that those rubber-legged caricatures need do is sling out another dose of poison. That would wipe out the new crop and the only seeds still down would be the ones that refused to germinate. It would mean finish!"

One of the listeners put in, "Besides, what's the use of

jumping the ship unless we can catch them all together? We can't. They've a flock of little boats constantly roaming the world."

"And there are plenty more aliens wherever they've come from," contributed another.

"Do you know where they came from?" Holland asked Deacon.

"Nowhere around this neck of the cosmos. Some faraway star that hasn't a number, much less a name. That's what they say."

"Hm-m-m!" He pondered it for quite a time, then remarked, "So they're a long, long way from home. I'd like to know more about them."

"You'll know plenty before you're through," Deacon promised. "For myself, I'd like to see them at the seventh layer of the seventh hell!"

The summons came late next morning. One alien appeared armed with no more than blank indifference to the looks with which he was greeted. He went from hut to hut until he found the seven.

"Come with me."

Hank bristled forthwith. "Who does he think he—?"

He closed his trap as Holland jogged him with a sharp elbow. "Let's not become noisy just yet."

The alien stood watching them with blue, humanlike eyes. His strangely colored and impassive face gave no indication of whether he had heard the brief exchange.

Holland went out with Yarbridge close behind. The others hestitated, then followed. They walked to the ship without further remark, trailed their guide to a cabin in the nose occupied by four more of his kind.

Without preamble the biggest of the four picked on Joe and asked, "What is your profession?"

"Boring engineer," informed Joe. "A driller, like these," He indicated the other three.

"Driller of what?"

Joe explained it more fully.

"So four of you do the same thing." The other thought it over, turned to the guide, said, "They should interest Klaeth, he being a geologist. Take them to him."

Yarbridge's turn came next. Admitting that he was a

radio operator he was rewarded by being sent to interview an alien named Ygath. Then Wilkin was questioned.

"Ah!" exclaimed the alien. "A metallurgist, no less. That is gratifying. Mordan has been hoping to find one such as you."

Wilkin was conducted elsewhere. He followed his guide gloomily, his pale eyes dull behind his glasses. That left Holland as the last for treatment.

"And you?"

"Atomechanic."

"That tells us nothing. Just what do you *do?*"

"I tend and service atomic-powered engines."

"What do you mean by atomic-powered?"

Holland's back hairs gave a twitch but he permitted no surprise to show in his features. "It is power derived from the controlled decomposition of certain unstable elements or compounds."

"Metals?"

"Certain rare metals or their oxides."

"You had better stay here," declared the other. "I shall deal with you myself." He switched to a sibilant language as he addressed one of his companions who went away, returned in short time with a wad of papers.

"These are the documents you require, Drhan," he said, handing them over.

Scanning them rapidly, Drhan nodded approval, pointed to a tubular chair, told Holland, "You will sit there." When he was seated Drhan studied him a while, frankly trying to estimate his intelligence and capabilities. Finally he informed, "It was as well that we picked you and your friends off that dead satellite. You are all technicians and we are badly in need of technicians."

"Why?"

"Because we have acquired a world replete with things we do not understand."

"Indeed?" Holland cast a significant glance at the huge and complicated instrument board beneath the bow observation port. "Yet you're miles ahead of us there."

"You think so?"

"That's how it looks."

"It would," agreed Drhan. "But appearances can be de-

ceptive. We are backward in many branches of science. A
ship such as this is something we might not have developed of
our own accord for centuries to come. Fortunately, others did
the job for us. We have gained a big advance by proxy."
Without bothering to explain in greater detail he indulged another unconcealed summing up of his listener. "Now these
others teach us how to build ships and run them. In return we
permit them to eat."

"You permit them?" Holland sat up, feeling cold.

"Yes." The gray-blue face remained blank. "Though
backward in some respects we are advanced in others. Like
everyone else, we have developed weapons characteristic of the
subjects in which we excel. Ours are effective, as you have
seen for yourself. We do not destroy people. We are content
to destroy food and leave people to obliterate themselves in
the battle for the remaining crumbs. We persuade the opposition to slaughter itself."

"That must save you an awful lot of bother and heart-
ache," remarked Holland.

If the other perceived the sarcasm he did not show it, for
he added with the air of one stating an obvious and incontrovertible fact, "Take away food and you take away life. No
more is necessary, no more need be done."

"Why deprive us of ours? What have we done to you?"

The question did not accord with Drhan's alien logic because he had to mull it quite a time before he said, "You have
done nothing to us. Why should you? How could you? We
want your world because we need it. We have taken it because it would not have been given had we asked for it. We
struck effectively and without warning because that is the best
guarantee of success. Surely you can see the sense of that?"

"I can," admitted Holland, grimly.

Drhan went on, "Far, far in the past we stood urgently
in need of another world reasonably similar to our own but
could do nothing about it until we acquired ships. Then for
four hundred of your years we searched the cosmos around
us before we found one and seized it. In due time we had to
have another. It took us twice as long to discover. Now we
must have a third. There aren't many that fit our specification;
they're rather rare. It has required almost two thousand years
to find this one of yours."

"Two thousand? Do you live *that* long?"

"Of course not. Those two thousand years cover many expeditions sent out generation after generation."

"Do your people know that you've found this world?"

"Not yet. Not until some of us return to tell them. We have no means of sending signals so far. The ship will have to go back with precise details of location." His eyes gazed shrewdly into Holland's and for the first time his face showed the faintest glimmer of a smile. "From the viewpoint of your kind that is something worth knowing, as doubtless you have decided. It means that if you can permanently disable this vessel you will escape our attentions for another two thousand years. Doesn't it?"

"The idea is not without attraction," Holland admitted.

"Therefore I suggest that you discourage any hotheads from trying," advised Drhan. "There are few of you left. It would be a pity if there were none."

"Why leave any at all in the first place? You could have killed off the scattered survivors."

"And thus destroy the knowledge we must acquire?" He motioned toward the wad of papers lying on his desk. "Already we have done much exploring. And what have we found? That this world is full of ingenious machines some of which we understand, some of which we think we understand, and others of which we know nothing. But they are ours by right of conquest. They are a valuable part of our inheritance. We must learn to use them, know how to operate right down to basic principles. How are we to learn these things without waste of time?"

"How do you expect?"

"That those who know will teach us."

"Or what?"

"There is no 'or' about it," assured Drhan with all the positiveness of experience. "The will to resist weakens as the body shrivels and the belly becomes bloated with hunger. We know. We have seen it happen again and again."

"Unmoved?"

Once more his mind had to plow through unaccustomed labyrinths to catch the question and try to pin it down. And then he could not devise a satisfactory answer.

With mild complaint, he said, "I don't comprehend. The

issue is a simple one, namely, we or you. The result is perfectly proper and natural: the weak become subject to the strong."

"And the stupid to the clever?" suggested Holland.

"It is the same thing," declared Drhan. Picking up the papers, he sought through them, his fingers bending either way with equal facility. "Now, we have here several reports of certain great power machines devoid of visible fuel supplies. I presume that these are the atomic mechanisms of which you speak?"

"Probably."

"Then you will explain them to us."

Obediently Holland got on with the job of explaining.

Deacon made the springs squeak as he sat up and asked, "They try to pick your brains?"

"That was their purpose," conceded Yarbridge. "They know something of radio but haven't got as far as frequency modulation, let alone stereoscopic T.V. and suchlike stuff. They're just emerging from the spark-signal stage."

"How much did you tell them?"

"A fat lot. I can't hand out in one day what took me about three years to acquire."

"Don't tell 'em anything," Deacon ordered, making it sound authoritative. "Feed them a lot of useless guff instead. That's what I did. I was sitting with a ton of food in the loneliest part of Northern Territory when one of their little boats picked me up. I'd been prospecting in happy ignorance of what was happening elsewhere. I'd found a dollop of slaty flakes in a river bed and knew I'd struck osmiridium. Think I told them all that? Not on your life! I misled them up the garden path. You do the same if you want peace!"

"It's not so easy for us," put in Joe. "We can't kid them our drills bring up lots of little brass Buddhas."

"Say you go round poking for fresh water. Make it sound scientific and say you plant a drill wherever a hazel twig jerks around. That'll get them playing with bits of stick."

"You don't credit them with much intelligence, do you?" inquired Holland.

"Do you?" Deacon countered aggressively.

"Certainly."

"You would!" said Deacon, beginning to dislike Holland and not hesitating to show it. He glanced around the hut, found moral support in many faces. "I bet you think them a good deal sharper than what is left of your own kind?"

"Not necessarily."

"Backing out, eh?"

"Not at all. I say I don't think them dopey."

"Meaning you think we are dopey?"

"When you consider the present state of affairs there is much to be said for that theory," said Holland. "But I don't agree with it. Not just yet."

"Not here, you don't," observed Deacon, pointedly. "On that ship it may be different. Perhaps you change your mind to suit the company you keep. How much have you been telling them of what you know?"

"As much as can be told in a few hours."

"A Kahsam!" pronounced Deacon, gaining color.

Low murmurs sounded around the hut. Men fidgeted, rubbed their knuckles, eyed Holland with antagonism; all but the one who resembled an Eskimo and didn't know a word of English.

Holland began, "Not knowing what a Kahsam is supposed to be, I—"

"I'll tell you." Deacon stood up, walked heavily to the other's bedside. "First wise-boy they took on board was a bleary little goat named Kahsam, a professor of languages from some snoot college. He spent a fortnight teaching them English and was tickled to bits because they learned so fast. Overjoyed to help those who'd filled his college with corpses."

"Did he know that at the time?"

"Shut up and listen, will you? He did his stuff for two weeks and thought himself mighty cute. When they'd finished with him they dumped him in one of the most comfortable apartments in town, gave him a food priority certificate."

"That was nice," said Holland, lying back and surveying the other's angry features.

"First chance that came along we pulled him to pieces," informed Deacon, displaying savage satisfaction. "His playmates haven't missed him yet." Licking thick lips, he added with sinister meaning, "Since then we've got a name for any guy who willingly and persistently collaborates with the enemy.

He's a Kahsam. A traitor to his kind is a Kahsam. Sooner or later he goes the same way."

"I wouldn't care for that," admitted Holland, rubbing his freckles and grinning upward.

Irritated further by this airiness, Deacon went on, "I invited you and your bunch in here so as to keep other types out. That means I've a duty to warn you when you're sticking out your necks. You've an equal duty to take notice and not try us too far." He paused a moment, added, "Because what I've said isn't just talk!"

With that he returned to his bedspace, lay down and scowled at the roof. Other men studied him in silence, now and again frowned at the culprit. The Eskimo gazed steadily at nothing while Wilkin blinked at him through thick glasses and the four drillers proceeded to deal a worn and filthy pack of cards.

After a while Holland sighed introspectively, went out for a breath of night air and a look at the stars. A minute later Yarbridge joined him.

"That Deacon is a natural ringleader," whispered the radio operator.

"I know."

"He's a decent enough guy providing you don't offend his sense of what's right."

"True, brother, true."

"Then why try making an enemy of him?"

"I need enemies."

"Jumping jiminy!" said Yarbridge, low-voiced. "We're in enough of a mess without stirring up more."

"Worry not nor weep tears of dire despair," advised Holland, patting him on the back. "I am the Kahsam, not you."

"It's nothing to joke about," Yarbridge insisted, looking serious. "These survivors are jumpier than a flea in a hot oven and they can't be blamed for it. They've seen, heard and felt things that we avoided while on the Moon. They are pinned down here with too little to do and they can't escape because a man must eat while on the run."

"I am not lacking in imagination," Holland reminded.

"Then why don't you use some of it? If you insist on flaunting treachery in their faces, you're liable to beat it to the ship six yards ahead of a lynching party."

"You must have precognition," said Holland, patting him again. "Such a fate is my purpose, my desired aim."

Staring at him in the starlight, Yarbridge muttered, "I'll keep you out of trouble whether you like it or not."

"How?"

"First time you're not around I'll warn them that you're going off your nut."

The warning was effective for a time. He went to the ship every morning, returned to the hut each evening and was met with uneasy suspicion rather than open hostility. Their ready acceptance of Yarbridge's diagnosis was natural in the strange circumstances for not a day passed without some man running amuck in the nearby town or some woman creating an hysterical scene as overtaxed nerves finally snapped. It was understood by everyone that at any time a man or woman might prove unable to take it, be calm today, completely crazy tomorrow.

Thus the mental conditioning born of the situation impelled them to treat him much as one would a prospective lunatic and it was ten days before they found cause to revert to their original attitude. He entered the hut at dusk, sat on the end of his bed, spoke to Yarbridge.

"I won't be here tomorrow."

"How's that?"

"They're flying me south."

"Only you? Not the rest of us?"

"Only me. I'm going down in one of their little lifeboats. They want samples of hot-stuff to take back to their own world."

Erupting from his bed-space, Deacon loudly demanded, "Are you helping them get it?"

"Of course. It's buried deep in an abandoned plant covering six square miles. They don't even know what to look for— so how can they dig it out without help?"

"So much the better," said Deacon. "Left to themselves they'd never find it or recognize it when it was right in their rubbery mitts. But you have to open your dirty big trap!"

Somewhat mordantly, Wilkin chipped in, "We've got to look at things as they are rather than as we'd like them to be. I don't see how we can get by without playing ball even if we play no more than we can help."

"You wouldn't see," growled Deacon. "You're old and already half-dead behind those weak eyes." He put big fists on big hips. "Let me tell you something, mister: that virus can't live without food any more than we can. I got that straight from the rubber boys who invented the stuff. Twenty hours without chlorophyll kills it stone dead. Know what that means?"

Staring stonily forward, Wilkin did not reply.

"It means that this world has been virus-free for weeks, maybe some of it for months. If birds hadn't carted it around, it might have been free before then. The virus has eaten itself out of existence. Untouched seeds are coming up. North of the town are skeletal trees already forcing out new buds and leaves. There are acres of tiny shoots that will become badly thinned-out corn. When those lousy invaders beat it we shall be able to cope for keeps providing we can last out on canned stuff the first couple of months."

"They know we can cope," Wilkin answered dully. "Mordan said so."

"What else did he say?"

"They'd leave us in cold storage, be gone two and a half years and come back in great strength with many ships. By that time we should have far more food growing around than sixty thousand can eat—and if we want to keep it we'd better have the bands out and the flags flying for them."

"I'd as soon kiss a flock of crocodiles."

"What alternative do you suggest?" invited Holland.

"Not the one you've chosen," snapped Deacon, his complexion darkening. "I'll be a Kahsam for nobody."

"I'm with you there," declared Hank, standing up and scowling at Holland.

"Me, too," supported Joe. "Knuckling down can go too far. When a guy hands over atomic power for the asking, I reckon—"

Yarbridge shot to his feet and flapped pudgy hands. "Quit snapping and snarling. What do you bums know of atomics?"

"Not much," said Deacon. He jerked a heavy thumb in the general direction of the ship. "But it's more than those stinkers have any right to know. It's enough to tell me that atomic power is a gift too big for those we don't love."

"You said it!" endorsed a dozen voices emphatically.

"Furthermore," continued Deacon, encouraged without needing it, "you're a radio guy, not a nuclear specialist. So what do *you* know about it?"

"The stuff is dangerous to handle. It has to be moved with tongs half the length of a flagpole or, better still, by remote control. What will it do to that crowd if in their innocence they start playing with it like sand?"

Taken aback, Deacon eyed him uncertainly. "You think the radiations will burn them to crisps?"

"I don't know for sure." Yarbridge gestured toward Holland, who was reposing carelessly on his bed and listening with academic interest. "But he does! And on the Moon he made a remark I haven't forgotten. He said that when you're without any other means of resistance you can take advantage of your opponent's ignorance."

"So that's the idea!" Deacon stewed it a moment, said to Holland, "Why didn't you tell us instead of lolling around and watching us go on the boil?"

"Because it is not the idea," Holland informed. "They know that radiation is highly lethal and that the stuff must be handled with extreme care. I told them."

"You did?" Deacon seemed unable to believe his ears. Eventually he rasped, "There you are, men, a Kahsam!"

"He's kidding us," suggested Yarbridge, bewildered and reproachful.

"I told them," repeated Holland, irritatingly matter of fact. Putting feet on the floor he braced himself. "They took a steel safe out of one of the town's banks this morning and have lugged it on board as a suitable cupboard for samples."

"That's right," endorsed a gaunt, blue-jowled man at the other end of the hut. "I saw them carting it away and wondered—"

"They're not having it *all* their own way," asserted Deacon, veins swelling in his neck. "Without this dirty Kahsam they'll be stumped!"

So saying, he made a mad-bull rush for the traitor's bedspace. A dozen others jumped with him. Anticipating this, Holland had come to his feet, ready and prepared even while looking casual. Now he leaped the Eskimo, bed and all, shot through the door into outer darkness. He ran for the ship, moving in long, lithe strides that heavier men would find hard to overtake.

Behind him occurred the precise sort of delay for which he had hoped. Fury is impetuous, possessed of no time or inclination for thought; therefore the enraged dozen attempted the impossible by trying to get through the door in a solid bunch. They jammed together, cursing vividly, until Deacon, Hank and a couple of others tore themselves free by main force and raced after the fugitive. Forty or fifty from neighboring huts emerged and joined the chase on general principles.

It was most of a mile to the space vessel and Holland made it two hundred yards ahead of a skinny but whipcord-muscled pursuer who had shown a surprising turn of speed. A bright light bloomed above the ship's lowered ramp as an alien guard detected the oncoming rush of feet. Holland ran up the ramp and through the open lock unopposed by the guard. Two more guards appeared, motioned him farther inward before they joined the third at the lock.

The one who had switched the light bawled, "Hold it!" About to mount the ramp, the skinny runner paused, glanced behind in search of support, glowered up at the guard. The rest of the pack arrived, milled around and cursed while each waited for someone to bell the cat.

"Go away," ordered the guard.

Deacon planted a big boot on the ramp, told him, "We want that louse you've just taken aboard."

"What've you got against lice?" called a voice from the back. "He's a stinking Kahsam!"

"Go away," repeated the guard, not interested in reasons or causes.

For a moment it seemed as if Deacon were about to take the lead and thus precipitate the general rush, but he thought better of it when the guard produced a high-pressure hand-spray. His companions continued to fidget around murmuring oaths and threats.

His eyes gleaming as he scowled up toward the ship's light, Deacon said to the guard, "All right, you can keep the dirty scut and welcome! And we mean keep him—for good!"

"Go away," repeated the guard, impassively.

They went slowly and defiantly, balked of their prey and voicing their disappointment with lavish use of adjectives. Standing behind an observation port, Holland watched them depart, then spoke to Drhan and Ygath at his side.

"They're in an ugly mood. It is hard for people to be coldly realistic after many highly emotional experiences."

"I suppose so," commented Drhan. He scratched a large ear with a flexible finger. "It is well that you have kept telling us of rising danger to yourself and that we held the lock open as you requested."

"We could have foreseen it without being told," remarked Ygath, "had we known the importance of this atomic power."

"Naturally they don't like us taking the biggest thing they've got," agreed Drhan. "I might feel the same way myself if the Shadids grabbed our best biological weapons." He glanced at Holland, went on, "Therefore we're so much the more indebted to one mentally capable of looking facts in the face. And that in turn creates a minor problem."

"Meaning me?" Holland asked.

"Yes. We cannot take you with us. We dare not leave you here, especially since we want your services when we return."

Ygath suggested, "We can establish him with adequate food supplies either on the other side of this world or upon the satellite. He would be beyond the reach of petty vengeance and should be safe enough until we return. Then he'll have our protection."

"Don't let it bother you," said Holland. "You can dump me here."

"What, after that scene outside?"

"I know my own kind. You're departing in two days' time. By then they'll have simmered down."

"Are you certain?"

"I'm fairly sure. They aren't without logic. They will realize that what has been done can't be undone. A few may argue that perhaps it's all for the best. The others will be soothed by your going even though you're coming back. Probably they'll get busy trying to plot a hot reception for you."

"Which will be more than futile," Drhan assured.

"I know it," agreed Holland.

They eyed him, seeking a double meaning, found his features showing the confidence of one who knows himself to be on the winning side. It pleased him even though deep in their hearts each had a mite of sympathy for Deacon.

Nobody likes a traitor, not even those who use him.

Mid-morning two days later a repeated thrum of propulsors drew the attention of those in the camp and the nearest outskirts of the town. Assembling, they watched in sour silence while several lifeboats zoomed back to the mother-ship and were taken on board. The large vessel then belly-slid through sandy soil, flared and roared, made a bound, finished at an upward tilt on the side of a small hill four miles farther away. Its tubes ceased their bellowing.

"Must be making ready to beat it," remarked Hank.

"Can't be too soon for me," said Joe.

"Wonder what's happened to Holland," Yarbridge ventured. He shifted restlessly, expecting vituperative reproof for mentioning the name. "Somehow I don't think he'll go with them."

"They'll dump him some place else," suggested a burly, red-haired man. "The devil looks after his own."

"I'd like to find him where he's planted," topped another, lending it menace.

Several voices supported that. They continued to observe the vessel now made too small by distance for them to discern individual activity around it. Nobody had binoculars; in bygone weeks that now seemed aeons all such instruments had been confiscated for the use of armies now dead and gone.

After most of an hour somebody reported, "One of them is coming this way. Maybe he wants to shake hands all round. No hard feelings and all that. It was just in fun. Rubber Boy loves Homer Sap."

Shading his eyes with a hairy hand, Deacon stared lengthily. "It isn't one of them. It's the Kahsam, no less!"

"He wouldn't dare," said the redhead incredulously.

"He would and he is," Deacon asserted. Again he studied the distant figure tramping steadily toward them. "And I can guess why."

"Why?" invited the other.

"Bet you he's bringing a message from his lords and masters telling us what they'll do to us if we touch one hair of his precious head."

"I'll take my chance on that," declared the redhead. He examined a clenched fist. It was big and rawboned.

"Lay off him, Lindsay," Deacon ordered. He cast a warning frown at all within hearing. "That goes for the rest of you, too. If the rubber boys are taking it skyward, we can well afford to wait until they're out of sight." His authoritative gaze went over each surly face. "Then we'll have him all to our little selves and what the eye doesn't see the heart won't grieve over!"

"Yes, that makes sense," Lindsay admitted with reluctance. Shoving hands in pockets, he controlled his emotions.

Following this cue, the others forced themselves to cool down. Presently Holland arrived at rapid pace, stopped a few yards from the mob and immediately in front of Deacon.

"They're waiting for the last lifeboat," he informed. "When they've got it aboard they're going home."

Nobody made remark. They stood together, hard-eyed, content to bide their time.

Licking his lips, Holland went on, "All right, if that's the way you feel." He moved forward. "Me, I'm not going to stand when I can sit."

"You'll neither stand nor sit pretty soon," screamed a nerve-strained voice at the back.

"Shut up!" roared Deacon, glaring over the heads of the front ranks. He threw a meaningful glance toward the alien ship, pretended to consult the watch he didn't possess.

They got it. Opening a path to permit Holland to pass, they closed in behind him, escorted him to the hut. Fifty crowded him. Three or four hundred massed outside the door. One man held a needle-sharp fishing spear made from a prong of a garden fork. Another carried a length of nylon cord scorched at both ends.

Squatting on the end of his bed, Holland wearily rubbed his freckles, favored Yarbridge with a tired grin and said, "I suppose all these gloomy looking gumps resent me shoveling hot-stuff aboard by the ton?"

"Well, haven't you?" inquired Yarbridge, hopefully.

"I gave them enough."

"One ounce is too much!" harshed Deacon, chipping in.

"What can you do with a mere ounce?" Holland asked.

"Close your gab!" advised Lindsay, scowling at him.

"Or use it to say prayers," suggested another.

A man outside called through the door, "The lifeboat's just come back. It won't be long now!"

Everyone stared the same way: at Holland.

He said to nobody in particular, "Naturally they wanted the whole works, blueprints, formulae, extraction techniques, samples of thorium, radium, uranium, plutonium, neptunium, the entire shebang. They wanted sufficient to enable them to set up in business way back home. I couldn't give it all—the stuff wasn't there."

"But you gave all you could?" invited Deacon.

"Yes, Beefy, I did. I gave them precisely enough. They will stash it in the safe and—"

A light of near-blinding brilliance flashed through the west-side windows. Beyond the door a man howled like a hungry wolf. Then the ground shuddered. The hut gave four violent jerks, a sidewall cracked and let more light pour in. There was no sound other than that of witnesses outside.

The bunch at the door ran west with one accord. Several in the hut chased after them. Deacon stood up, his heavy features mystified.

"In the name of glory, what was *that?*"

"I told you," said Holland. "I gave them enough."

Making up his mind, Deacon rushed out, looked westward. The others pressed behind, gazed at an immense gout of vapor rising more than four miles away. It was monstrous, frightening despite its familiarity. Nothing could be seen of the alien ship.

Swiveling on one heel, Deacon said in stifled tones, "That was your sweet trick."

"I needed hate here to establish trust and confidence there," explained Holland. "I got it—and it worked."

Turning his back upon him, Deacon bent down with elbows resting on knees. "You know what to do."

Holland surveyed the proferred rear end. "Great as the temptation may be, I resist it. Not because I forgive you. I think we can arrange a wallop more effective."

Coming up quickly, Deacon eyed him suspiciously. "Such as what?"

"According to statistics they had on that ship," Holland continued, ignoring the question, "humanity clung to a basic convention even in its death throes, namely, women and children first. Result: we survivors number more females than males."

"That's right," a voice endorsed. "About five to three."

"If we double our number every thirty years, we'll be a formidable swarm before one thousand, let alone two thousand. And we aren't starting from the trees and caves. We're starting with salvable parts of civilization and we still have the know-how." He jerked an indicative thumb toward the town. "Ten to one that somewhere in there are a couple of nuclear physicists and umpteen other experts who've been making like bricklayers while nosy aliens were around." He paused thoughtfully, finished, "And between the lot of us we must have learned some useful things about that ship. The next one just won't get this far. It will regret the attempt."

"So did that one!" bawled a voice.

It was like the snapping of a tense cord and brought a roar of triumphant cheers.

When the noise had died down, Holland said, "Large families will help. So when we get around to lawmaking"—he studied Deacon, walked round him a couple of times looking him up and down as if inspecting a prime hunk of beef—"we'll have to make bachelordom illegal."

Deacon flushed and let out an agonized yelp of, "Hey, you can't do that to me!"

"We can," assured Holland amid surrounding laughter. "And what's more, we shall!"

He was wrong there. Ten days before such a law was passed a buxom widow put the bee on Deacon.

Homo Saps

MAJESTICALLY THE LONG CARAVAN EMERGED FROM the thick belt of blue-green Martian *doltha* weed and paraded into the Saloma Desert. Forty-four camels stalked along with the swaying gait and high-faluting expressions of their kind. All were loaded. Beneath the burdens their deliberate, unhurried feet dug deeply into the long waves of fine, pinkish sand.

The forty-fifth animal, which was in the lead, was not a camel. It was daintier, more shapely, had a beige-colored coat and only one hump. A racing dromedary. But its expression was fully as supercilious as that worn by the others.

Sugden had the dromedary, Mitchell was on the following camel, and Ali Fa'oum formed the rearguard of one. The forty-two burdened beasts in between had modest loads and immodest odors. Ali, at the back, got the benefit of the last. It didn't matter. He was used to it. He'd miss it if it wasn't there.

Twisting in his seat, Sugden tilted his head toward the sinking sun, and said, "They'll put on the brakes pretty soon, I guess."

Mitchell nodded lugubriously. He'd sworn camels across Arabia, cursed them through the Northern Territory of Australia, and had oathed them three times around Mars. His patience was no better than on the day he'd started. Within his bosom burned a theory that if there had never been camels there would have been no such thing as Oriental fatalism.

Abruptly the dromedary stopped, went down fore legs first, back legs next and settled with a sickening heave. It didn't bother to look behind. There wasn't any need, anyway. The rest of the cavalcade followed suit, front legs first, hind legs next, the same heave. A box with loose fastenings parted from its indifferent bearer and flopped into the sand.

Ali, now compelled to dismount, did so. He found the fodder, distributed it along the resting line. Ignoring the white men, the animals ate slowly and with maddening deliberation, their disinterested eyes studying the far horizon. Ali started grooming them as they ate. He'd groomed them in Port Tewfik thirty years ago. He was still doing it. They still let him get on with it, their expressions lordly.

Lighting a cigarette, Sugden gave it a savage suck, and said, "And they talk about mules!"

Slowly the dromedary turned its head, gave him a contemptuous look. Then it resumed its contemplation of distance. It chewed monotonously and methodically its bottom lip pursed in silent scorn.

"Same distance, same time," voiced Mitchell sourly. Thumping the heel of his jackboot he killed a Martian twelve-legged sand spider. "Never more, never less. They clock on and clock off and they work no overtime."

"They've got us where they want us." Sugden blew a twin funnel of smoke from itching nostrils, stared distastefully at what had been the spider. "They're the only things that can cover these deserts apart from the Martians themselves. If we had tractors, we'd use tractors if there was any gasoline on this planet."

"Some day, when I'm bloated with riches," Mitchell pursued, "I'm going to be eccentric. I'm going to get them to build me a superhyperultra rocketship. One that'll carry some real tonnage."

"Then what?" inquired Sugden.

"Then start from where I left off here—only with elephants."

"Ha-ha!" laughed Sugden, with artificial violence.

The dromedary turned its head again. It made a squelching sound with its slowly moving mouth. The noise was repeated all the way along the line until the mount of Ali emitted the final salivary smack. Ali proceeded with his grooming.

Mitchell snorted and said, complainingly, "You'd think the whole darned lot had loose dental plates." He started to open up the thermic meal pack. "And they stink."

"And I don't like their faces," added Sugden.

"Me neither. Give me a cigarette, will you?" Mitchell lit it, let it hang from his bottom lip. "To think the Martians kowtow to them and treat us like dirt. Funny the way they've acted like that since the first camel was imported."

"Yeah, I'd like to get to the root of it sometime."

"Try talking to a Martian. Might as well talk to a gate-post, and—*yeouw*, this thermic's red-hot!" Mitchell coddled his fingers. "Sixty years and never a word out of thém. They ought to be able to talk, but won't." He heaved the meal pack onto its telescopic legs, slid out its trays. "Hi, Ali, come and give us a hand."

"No, sah. Finish these first. One hour."

"See?" Removing his solar topee, Mitchell flung it on the sand. "The stinkers first, us last."

The igloo-shaped lumps of Jenkinsville showed on the horizon at sunset next day. Nobody knew the Martian name of the place, but its first discoverer had been one Hiram Jenkins, originally of Key West, Florida. So from then on it was Jenkinsville. The place was precisely fourteen miles away. Nevertheless, the dromedary squatted and the rest did likewise.

Sugden dismounted with the usual scowl, raked out the usual battered cigarette, heard Mitchell air the usual curse. It couldn't have been a curse of much potency since the curve on the grief chart remained constant, with never a dip.

The same box fell into the sand again, making the same dismal thump. Phlegmatically, Ali got on with the feeding and grooming rigmarole. In superior silence the forty-five animals rested and masticated and gazed at nearby Jenkinsville much as Sugden had gazed at the squashed spider.

"I've a persistent notion," said Sugden, his sand-chafed eyes on the energetic Mr. Fa'oum, "that he sneaks up at mid-night and worships them. First time I catch him I'll prove he can't salaam without presenting his rumps for suitable retalia-tion."

"Humph!" Mitchell wrestled with the meal pack, burned his fingers as he'd done a thousand times before, let out his thousandth *yeouw!* "Hi, Ali!"

"One hour," said Ali, firmly.

"I'm clinging to life," announced Mitchell, speaking to the general outlines of Jenkinsville, "so's I can outlive the lot.

One by one, as they die on me, I'm going to skin 'em. I'll make foot mats of their stinking pelts. I'll get married, wipe my feet coming in and going out and every time the cuckoo clock puts the bean on me."

The sixth camel from the front rumbled its insides. Slowly the rumble moved from stomach to gullet, ended in an emphatic burp. Taking its blank eyes off Jenkinsville, the dromedary looked backward with open approval. Mitchell enjoyed a furious kick at the thermic, denting its side.

"Now, now!" said Sugden.

Mitchell gave him a look of sudden death, twitched a tray from the thermic. He did it wholeheartedly. The tray shot clean out of the container, tilted against his ineffectual grasp, poured a mess of hot beans in tomato sauce over his jackboots. Ali paused and watched as he brought a bundle of night coats to the complacent camels. Sugden stared at Mitchell. So did Ali. Also the camels.

Looking first at Sugden, then at his boots, Mitchell said, "Notice that?"

"Yes, I've noticed it," admitted Sugden, gravely.

"Funny, isn't it?"

"Not at all. I think it unfortunate."

"Well," said Mitchell, stabbing a finger at the observing line, "*they* think it's funny."

"Oh, forget it. All animals are curious."

"Curious? Hah!" Lugging off his boots, Mitchell hefted them, swung them around, gauged their weight and handiness. All the time his eyes were on the dromedary. In the end, he changed his mind, cleaned his boots in the sand, then put them on. "They're seeing the world at our expense—and they all look at me when I do this to myself."

"Aw, let's eat," soothed Sugden. "We're hungry, and hunger makes one short-tempered. We'll feel better afterward. Besides, we'll be in Jenkinsville early in the morning."

"Sure, we will. We'll be in Jenkinsville first thing in the morning. We'll offer our junk for all the mallow seeds we can get, and if we don't dispose of the lot—as we probably won't—we'll start another one-hundred-mile hike to Dead Plains to shoot the balance." Mitchell glowered at the cosmos. "If, by some miracle unique in the records of Martian trading, we do switch all we've got, we'll start back on our one hundred fifty

miles of purgatory to Lemport, accompanied by forty-four
camels, forty-four double-humped skunks."

"And one dromedary," Sugden reminded, delicately.

"And one one-humped skunk," agreed Mitchell. He glared
across the sands to where the said skunk was enjoying its own
digestive processes with true Arabian aplomb.

"If you're not going to eat," announced Sugden, "I am!"
He slid another tray from the thermic, stabbed himself a couple
of steaming pinnawursts. He was very partial to minced livers
of the plump and succulent pinna birds.

As the food went cold in the Martian evening, Mitchell
joined in. The pair ate ruminatively, in unconscious imitation
of the camels.

Three hours beyond the flaming dawn the caravan
slouched into the market place in Jenkinsville and unloaded
with many animal grunts and much Terrestrial profanity. Martians came crowding in, more or less ignored the white men,
took a little more notice of Ali Fa'oum, but paid most attention
to the camels. For a long time they looked at the camels and
the camels looked at them, each side examining the other with
the aloofish interest of ghosts discovering fairies.

Mitchell and Sugden let them get on with it. They knew
that in due time, when they thought fit, the natives would turn
to business. Meanwhile, the interim could be used for making
all the necessary preparations, setting up the stalls, displaying
the stocks, getting the books and scales ready. Each Martian
had his hoard of mallow seeds, some small bags, some big bags,
some with two or three.

The seeds were what the traders were after. From this
product of the Martian desert mallow could be distilled—a
genuine cure for Terrestrial cancer. This disease would have
been wiped out long ago if only the temperamental mallow were
cultivatable—which it wasn't. It grew wherever it took the
fancy and nowhere else. It didn't fancy anywhere on Earth.
Hence, its short, glossy-leafed bushes had to be searched for,
and Martians did the searching.

In ones and twos, and in complete silence, the Martians
drifted from the camels to the stalls. They were large-eyed beings, with big chests and flop ears, but otherwise human in
shape. Though literally dumb, they were fairly intelligent. Terrestrial surgeons opined that the Martian voice box once had

functioned, but now was petrified by centuries of disuse. Maybe they were right. Mitchell and Sugden didn't know or very much care. The traders high-pressured their clients in deft sign language, sometimes helped out by writing and sketches.

An old Martian got his bag weighed, was credited with one hundred eighty dollars in gold, solid, heavy, international spondulics. Mitchell showed him a roll of batik-patterned broadcloth and a half-plate glossy photograph of Superba de la Fontaine attired in a sarong of the same material. He didn't mention that the fair Superba was originally Prunella Teitelbaum of Terre Haute. All the same, the old chap liked neither. He pulled a face at Mitchell, indicated that both were trash.

"They're getting finicky," complained Mitchell, addressing the God of Commerce. Irefully, he swung a roll of Harris tweed along the roughwood counter, fingered it, smelled it, held it up for his customers to enjoy the heathery odor of the fabric. The customer approved, indicated that he'd take three arm spans of same. Mitchell sliced off the required length, rolled it dexterously, tossed it over.

Way down in the Communal Hall beyond the serried rows of red granite igloos a band of tribal beaters started playing on a choir of gongs. The instruments ranged all the way from a tiny, tinkling silver hand disk up to an enormous copper cylinder twenty feet in diameter. Every note was powerful and pure, but the tune was blatant torture.

Scowling, Mitchell said to the old fellow, "Now how about a watch? So long as you've got the time, you'll never have to ask a policeman. Here's the very one, a magnificent, fifty-jeweled, ten-day chronometer, rectified for Mars, checked by the Deimos Observatory, and guaranteed by Mitchell & Sugden."

He tried to put it all into signs, sweating as he did it. The Martian sniffed, rejected the timepiece, chose five cheap alarm clocks. Moreover, he went right through the stock of several dozen in order to pick himself five with differing notes. Then he selected a gold bangle set with turquoises, a midget radio, an aluminum coffee percolator and a small silver pepper pot into which he solemnly emptied the inevitable packet of Martian snuff.

"That leaves you two bucks seventy," said Mitchell. The old fellow took his balance in cigarettes and canned coffee, toddled back to pay his respects to the camels. There was still a gang busy soul-mingling with the animals. "Damn the stinkers!" Mitchell heaved a huge bag of seeds onto the scales. The needle swung around. "Seven hundred smackers," he breathed. He scrawled the amount in big figures with a blue pencil, held it out to the new customer.

This one was a young Martian, taller than the average. He nodded, produced a five-year-old catalogue, opened it, pointed to illustrations, conveyed by many signs that he wanted the cash put to his credit until he had enough to get an automobile.

"No use," said Mitchell. "No gasoline. No go. No soap!" He made snakes of his arms in his efforts to explain the miserable and absolute impotence of an automobile sans juice. The Martian watched gravely, started to argue with many further references to the catalogue. Mitchell called in Sugden to help.

After ten minutes, Sugden said: "I get it. He wants a heap with a producer-gas plant. He thinks he can run it on local deadwood."

"For Pete's sake!" groaned Mitchell. "Now they're going Broadway on us! How in the name of the seven devils can we get one here?"

"In pieces," Sugden suggested. "We'll try, anyway. Why not? It may start a cult. We might end up with a million jujubes apiece. We might both be Martian producer-gas automobile tycoons, and be ambushed by blondes like they say in magazines. It'll cost this guy an unholy sum, but it's his sum. Attend to the customer, Jimson, and see that he's satisfied."

With doubtful gloom, Mitchell made out a credit slip for seven hundred, handed it across. Then he took a deep breath, looked around, noticed camels and Martians regarding each other with the same philosophical interest. Some of the animals were munching choice titbits offered them by the natives.

More bags, more weighings, more arguments all through the rest of the day. As usual, the clients didn't want a good proportion of the Mitchell-Sugden stock and again as usual, some of them wanted things not in stock and difficult to obtain.

On the previous trip one Martian had taken a hundred phonograph records and had ordered some minor electrical apparatus. Now he turned up, claiming his apparatus, didn't want another disk, put in an urgent order for a couple of radio transmitter tubes of special design. After half an hour's sema-phoring; he had to draw the tubes before Mitchell understood what was wanted. There was no law against supplying such stuff, so he booked the order.

"Oh, Jiminy," he said, wearily, "why can't you guys talk like civilized people?"

The Martian was faintly surprised by this comment. He considered it solemnly, his big, grave eyes wandering from the liverish Mitchell to the camels and back again. The dromedary nodded, smirked, and let the juice of an overripe *wushkin* drool from its bottom lip. The Martian signed Mitchell an invitation to follow him.

It was on the verge of dusk and time for ceasing opera-tions, anyway. Leaving his exhausted partner to close the post, Mitchell trailed the Martian. Fifteen years before he had trailed one to an illegal still and had crawled back gloriously blotto. It might happen again.

They passed the camels now being groomed by the offi-cious Ali Fa'oum, wandered through the town to a large igloo halfway between the market place and the northern outskirts. A mile to the south the gongs of Communal Hall were sound-ing a raucous evensong. The big tremblor caused dithers in the digestive system.

Inside the igloo was a room filled with a jumble of appa-ratus, some incomplete, some discarded but not thrown out. The sight did not surprise Mitchell, since it was well known that the Martians had scientific abilities along their own peculiar lines. His only emotion was a feeling of disappointment. No still.

Connecting up a thing looking like a homemade radio re-ceiver with a tiny loud-speaker, the Martian drew from its in-nards a length of thin cable terminating in a small, silvery object which he promptly swallowed. With the cable hanging out of his mouth, his big eyes staring solemnly at Mitchell, he fiddled with dials. Suddenly, an inhuman, metallic voice oozed from the loudspeaker.

"Spich! This artificial spich! Just made him. Very hard —cannot do much!"

"Ah!" said Mitchell, faintly impressed.

"So you get me tubes. Do better then—see?"

"Sure," agreed Mitchell. Then the overwhelming thought

struck him that he was the first Terrestrial to hold vocal conversation with a Martian. Front-page news! He was no pressman, but he was trader enough to feel that there ought to be a thousand frogskins in this interview if he handled it right. What would a journalist do? Oh, yes, ask questions. "Why can't you guys speak properly?" he asked, with unjournalistic awkwardness.

"Properly?" squawked the loudspeaker. The Martian was astonished. "We do talk properly. Ten thousand years ago we ceased this noise-talk of low-life forms and talked here"— he touched his forehead—"so!"

"You mean you converse telepathically?"

"Of course—same as camels."

"What?" yelled Mitchell.

"Sure! They are high form of life."

"Like hell they are," bawled Mitchell, his face purpling.

"Hah!" The Martian was amused. "I prove it. They talk here." Again he touched his forehead. "And not here, like you." He touched his throat. "They toil in moderation, eat reasonably, rest adequately, wear no clothes, pay no taxes, suffer no ills, have no worries, enjoy much contemplation and are happy."

"But they darned well work," shouted Mitchell. He smacked his chest. "And for me."

"As all must, high and low alike. You also work for them. Who works the hardest? You see—*glug-glug!*" The loudspeaker gulped into silence. Hurriedly, the Martian made adjustments to the set and presently the speaker came to fresh but weaker life. "Battery nearly gone. So sorry!"

"Camels, a high form of life!" jeered Mitchell. "Ha-ha! I'll believe it when I've got a lemon-colored beard nine feet long."

"Does the delectable pinna know the superiority of our bellies? How can *you* measure the mental stature of a camel where there is no common basis? You cannot talk inside the head; you have never known at any time what a camel is thinking." The loud-speaker's fading crackle coincided with the Martian's patronizing chuckle. Mitchell disliked both noises.

"So long as it knows what I'm thinking, that's all that matters."

"Which is entirely your own point of view." Again the

Martian registered his amusement. "There are others, you know, but all the same—*crackle, crackle, pop!*" The apparatus finally gave up the ghost and none of its operator's adjustments could bring it back to life. He took out the artificial larynx through which he had been talking, signed that the interview was over.

Mitchell returned to the camp in decidedly unsweet humor. Sugden met him, and said, "We shifted sixty percent. That means another hike starting tomorrow morning. A long one, too."

"Aaargh!" said Mitchell. He began to load the thermics. Sugden gave him a look, holed down in his sleeping bag and left him to work it off.

Jenkinsville was buried in slumber and Sugden was snoring loudly by the time he finished. He kept muttering to himself, "Homo saps, huh? Don't make me laugh!" all the while he worked. Then he got the last thermic sealed up, killed a spider he found scuttling around in an empty can, had a last look over the camp.

The camels were a row of blanketed, gurgling shapes in the general darkness, with the nursemaidish Ali Fa'oum a lesser shape somewhere near them.

Looking at them, Mitchell declaimed, "If I thought for one moment that you misshapen gobs of stink-meat knew what I was saying, I'd tell you something that'd take the supercilious expression off your faces for all time!"

With that blood-pressure reliever, he started back to his own sleeping bag, got nearly there, suddenly turned and raced toward the camels. His kick brought Ali into immediate wakefulness, and his bellow could be heard all over the camp.

"Which one of them made that noise?"

"No can tell," protested Ali, sleepily. "Forty-four of them an' dromedary. How tell who makes noise? Only Allah know!"

Sugden's voice came through the night, saying, "Mitch, for Heaven's sake!"

"Oh, all right." Mitchell returned, found his torch. "Telepathic bunk!" he muttered. "We'll see!" By the light of his torch he cut a playing card into forty-five pieces, numbered them with a pencil, shuffled them in the dark, shut his eyes and picked one. *Number twelve.*

Waking again, Sugden stuck his head out and said, suspiciously. "What're you doing now?"

"Crocheting for my bottom drawer," said Mitchell. Ignoring the other, he examined his gun by the light of the torch, found it fully loaded with ten powerful dynoshells. Smiling happily, he murmured, "Number twelve!" and lay down to sleep.

Ali shook him into wakefulness with the first flush of dawn. Sugden was already up, fully dressed and looking serious.

"One of the camels has scrammed," he announced. "Number twelve."

"Eh!" Mitchell shot up like a jack-in-the-box.

Sugden said, "And I don't like that funny look you put on when I told you it was my camel, not one of yours. Have you pinned an abracadabra on it?"

"Me? What, me?" Mitchell tried to look innocent. "Oh, no!"

"Because if you have, you'd better unhex it mighty quick."

"Oh, we'll find it," comforted Mitchell. He got dressed, stowed away his gun, made the mental reservation that he'd do nothing about number twelve, nothing at all. He made the thought as powerful as he could.

The missing animal was waiting for them beside the trail one hour out from Jenkinsville. It took its position in the string as of old habit. Nobody said anything. It was a long time since Mitchell had been so quiet.

After a while, Sugden's dromedary turned its neck and made a horrible face at Mitchell riding right behind. He still said nothing. Deliberately, the caravan swayed on.

The Timid Tiger

*V*AST AND TROPICAL WAS THE HOME OF THE TIMID tiger. There, the heat was oppressive, and moisture fell in great blobs, and only a fantastic light seeped past the mighty trees. The trunks of the trees were tremendous columns soaring up and into the ceiling of thick, ever-present mist, and between them the vari-colored grasses made a rich carpet along the jungle aisles.

In one of these aisles, as in the nave of a woody cathedral, dwarfed by vegetable immensity, Sam Gleeson knelt hip-deep in the carpet and poured a few more drops of ammoniated tincture of quinine between the lips of a prostrate Greenie. Four taller, lankier Greenies stood behind him watching gravely. The one he was ministering was female and below puberty. By Venusian standards, a moppet. Somebody's kid sister. He wondered whether she'd yet learned to write.

The patter of drops sounded constantly as the mist condensed and dripped down. The prostrate one licked her lips and shivered. The watching quartet leaned on their long blowpipes, their eyes intent, and the tiny green figure shivered again. She opened her eyes, revealing great, brilliant orbs like those of a cat. Her hand smoothed her grass skirt and she struggled to sit up.

"She'll be all right now," asserted Sam. He signed to one of the natives. "Sit down with your back to hers to give her support. Let her rest thus for the period of one cigarette-smoke. Then give her this—all of it." He handed over a small phial. "It will do her good. When she has taken it, bear her home that she may sleep."

His knee joints creaked a little as he came erect. Closing his satchel, he hooked it on his cross-strap, swung it round behind him. Perspiration glossed his wizened face and beaded his white, goatee beard. Microscopic pearls of moisture shone in his bleached hair which had never known a hat.

One of the Greenies said, in his swift and liquid tongue, "For this, Earthman, you shall be the little one's father's father's father. The singing reeds shall tell of you to the trees."

"It is nothing," smiled Sam. "I become a great grandfather about once a month. Kids will be kids right across the Milky Way."

They made no reply to that. They had sudden taciturn moments that were disconcerting. Leaving them, he tramped along the glade, on through the welter of the rain forest. He was following an almost indiscernible path which, in an hour's walking, should bring him to his solitary cabin.

A shrill whistle sounded back in the glade now cut off from view by massive trunks. Without looking round he listened for an occasional swish of grass behind and to either side of him. Presently, it came, faint but persistent. He knew it would accompany him all the way home and he made a great pretense of being completely unaware of it. That pretense was proper. It was the polite thing for him to do—just as it was polite of them not to permit a friend to travel alone, without a bodyguard.

From the dark interior of his cabin he looked through his window hoping to catch a glimpse of his escort. It was their habit to circle his shack until his light went up. Once only he'd seen them, vague, shadowy figures gliding swiftly between trees. But he couldn't spot them this time. Sighing, he lit his kerosene lamp. Then he dug out his report book, made an entry in a clear, firm hand.

Again this afternoon I found one standing before my window. He was waiting with the solemn patience of a green statue. I cannot persuade them to knock on the door and come straight in—they remain convinced that that would be insolent. So they stand and wait some place where I'll see them. This one said that an hour to the north was a little girl with a curse in her belly. Of course, it was Raeder's Fever. I reached her in plenty of time and a stiff dose of quinine did the rest.

He stopped writing, gazed thoughtfully at the wall, stroked his goatee while murmuring to himself:

"No use mentioning that this is the seventh case in a child.

It's not important, and it's already on the records. I still think Old Ma Nature has a remedy for everything and that somewhere on this planet is cinchona or a good Venusian substitute."

Putting away his book, he stood at the window and looked out again. The half-light that was day slowly faded to the luminous dark that was night. A mellow warbler began to flute five hundred feet up. There was a smell of trodden grass and of slumbering trees. He turned the lamp up a little more, went to his bookshelf, studied the small row of tomes. Howard Sax's "Medicinal Flora," Professor Wentworthy's "Root Of All Good," Gunnar Hjalmsen's "Natural Drugs," Dr. Reilly's "Hahnemann's Theory" and a mere dozen more. He'd read them all, and again and again. Finally, he selected Walter Kayser's "How To Eat A Cannibal" and settled down with it.

> In dealing with primitive peoples it is essential to establish complete mastery from the start, to establish it firmly, without equivocation, and thereafter to maintain it by reacting sharply to anything which may be construed as a challenge. This means that while being fair, one must be firm; one must be harsh if circumstances so warrant, even brutal if necessary. The savage understands savagery if nothing else, and it is not for the club habitué in New York or London, but the administrator on the spot, with a heavy burden of responsibility upon him, to determine precisely how and when—

Sam frowned as he always did at this point. He had an intense admiration for Kayser, one of Earth's ablest men. This Kayser was now East Indies Controller of Native Peoples, an important post of high honor. It ill became one to disagree with a man of such eminence, but some of Kayser's views made him very fidgety.

> As for missionaries, they are good men oft made injudicious by their own enthusiasms. I like to see them—but not in lawless territory. One has only to consider the list of these brave men slaughtered by Dyaks in the Fly River area of

Borneo alone to realize that they should time their arrivals a little later, when the country has settled down. Wild and bloody aborigines must be taught to fear God before they're invited to love Him.

Well, it was an old book, written when Kayser was young and somewhat fiery. Perhaps he'd changed now. Men usually changed with the passing years. Maybe he'd mellowed into gentler wisdom like Victor Hearn, the famous Consul of Luna, or Jabez Anderson, the equally great Consul of Mars. They were all very great men, able men, worthy pillars of the civilization which, having covered the Earth, had spread to the heavens.

With which concluding thought, Sam Gleeson went to bed.

All day he had plenty to occupy his mind and keep his hands busy. Besides the cooking of his own meals and various household chores there was the pressure of getting things ready in time for the next flight to Earth due in less than three weeks. When flights were timed as far apart as eight months, you just couldn't afford to miss one, and he'd a lot of stuff to consign to Terra.

Most of it was packed in readiness, some had still to be prepared. Those eight fine samples of *odontoglossum venusii* would have to be color-photographed, sketched, dried out and packed before they wilted. He had seventeen samples of bark and a report on one saying that natives distilled from it a crude exhilarant similar to cocaine. In his simple cabin were no facilities for doing fractional analyses and he wasn't a qualified chemist anyway. He was merely a field explorer for the National Botanical Institute and they'd do all the laboratory work.

His water-color sketches of the flowers were talented, but no collector would ever go searching for genuine Gleesons. Packing his sketches along with the spectochromes, he put the flowers deep in eight little fused-quartz bowls, sprinkled fine silver sand over them until they were covered, slid the bowls into a small oven. Leaving them to dry out, he went to the door and opened it. A Greenie was standing outside. The native posed a dozen feet from the door, his long blowpipe in one hand, an expression of ineffable patience on his sharp features.

"Well?" said Sam.

"Earthman, the Voice of my people would talk with you."

Sam looked around, stroked his beard worriedly. More natives waited between the trees. A bodyguard again.

"I am sorry, but I cannot come. I am extremely busy." He looked straight into the other's great cat-eyes. His voice was gentle. "I am very sorry." He went inside and closed the door.

The *odontoglossum venusii* dried out nicely and he repacked them and marked each sample box carefully. Sultriness had got him sweating again, and the beads of it collected in the myriad wrinkles at the corners of his eyes. Finishing the job, he ate, pondered awhile, then opened the door. Two hours had passed but the Greenie still stood there and his fellows still lurked in the background.

"I told you I could not come."

"Yes, Earthman."

Sam felt slightly confused. His mind was full of flowers and herbs and barks, not to mention the urgency of catching the coming flight.

"Why does the Voice want me?" he asked in an effort to clarify the situation.

"Lo, there is death over the mountains and six have died by each other's hands, three of our people and three of yours. Therefore the Voice has said that he must have word with the Gray Chanter or with you. 'Be ye fleet of foot,' he said, 'that I may speak with one.'"

"Hmph!" He stewed it over in his mind. Four years had he lived among the Greenies, but never had he met a Voice. Now was a mighty poor time to make up the deficiency. It would cost him a week. He could ill spare a week. "Did you speak with the Gray Chanter?" he asked.

"Earthman, we have seen him."

"And wouldn't he go?"

"He tried to. He came a little way. Then he struggled with his ghost and came a little further, but his feet were weary within a hundred paces."

"What, is he, too, cursed?" Sam was alarmed at the thought of Father Rooney sick in his solitude sixty miles to the south.

"He said, 'Alas, I am old and feeble, and my ancient bones

refuse to be dragged. Seek the Wizened One and tell him that my ghost is willing but my carcass mutinies.'"

"Wait," said Sam. He went inside, tidied up swiftly, got his satchel, saw that it held all he required. He'd no hat to put on and had never owned a gun. In all probability, he and Father Rooney were the only ones unarmed of the two thousand Terrestrials on Venus.

Before leaving, he took up an old letter, scanned it for the hundredth time. His beard bristled as he murmured its phrases. "You are employed for botanical and not for sociological research . . . expected to devote more time to flora and less to fauna . . . native welfare belongs to the proper department . . . last warning . . . your resignation—" He tore up the letter, stuffed its pieces into the embers beneath the oven, went out. His goatee was cocked defiantly as he emerged from the cabin.

A call good enough to arouse the aged priest was good enough to be answered by him. And besides—it was imperative that Terra should know the tiger, to walk in peace.

The native with whom he'd talked glided along in the lead and Sam followed at a steady, determined pace. The others shadowed silently behind. In single file they slipped through the half-light and the grasses while the mist swirled round the treetops and the dew dripped steadily down.

To reach a village they marched far into the night, with luminous herbs glowing pinkly in the growth through which they trod, and an occasional beacon tree shining like a giant specter between other darker trunks. Only one incident caused a momentary pause in their progress, this being when they found an immense constrictor lying across their path.

The reptile had a body three feet thick and its head and tail ran far away among the trees on either side. Its hide was an even dull-gray, and in the night time darkness that was never dark Sam could see the rise and fall of its sluggish breathing. It was asleep. They jumped it in rapid succession, then ran for a mile. So long as a man saw a constrictor before it saw him, he was safe—he could just outpace it.

A tiny village of lattice huts gave them food and shelter for the remainder of the night. They breakfasted on baked fish, *maro* roots and heavy bread washed down by genuine coffee. The latter had been the first discovery on Venus, and one regarded as sensational by Terrestrial botanists. This, together with the similarity between Venusians and Terrestrials, suggested parallel development of the two planets, producing many things of mutual resemblance, perhaps some identical. Sam was alone in thinking that parellelism somewhat askew. He knew the Greenies!

They were away before the first fishers set out to bait the roaring streams, before the first wild turkey could utter its eerie whistle to the dawn. Still in single file, they glided like phantoms through the rain forest which seemed never-ending, and late in the afternoon of the third day they slipped from a spur of immense trees and found themselves near to the mountains. One couldn't see the mountains, for they were deeply buried in the clouds, but one could see partway across a gradually rising plain which eventually met the mist at an elevation of more than a thousand feet—tree height.

Before them stood the village of the Voice, a large conglomeration of squat, rock-built houses. Their roofs were of pale slate, their windows of laminated quartz. The place stood in amazing contrast with the flimsy lattice hamlets deep in the forest. Around lay small, cultivated fields through which two narrow and noisy mountain streams pounded in liquid ecstasy. Sam had never seen anything like this, though he'd heard of it. The Greenies went up another notch in his estimation.

He found the Voice sitting on a stool in the main room of the central house. The chief proved to be a tall, slender native of well-preserved middle age. His green face was narrow and sharp and bore the peculiar pineapple marking of his kind. Like all Venusians, he was completely hairless and possessed great yellow eyes with slotted, catlike pupils.

Sam gave him a precious cigarette, lit it for him, sat on the stool facing him. There were no salutations among the Greenies. The chief stared at him imperturbably and dragged at his cigarette. After a while, he spoke.

"I am the Voice of my people."

Sam went through the polite routine of affecting dumfounded surprise. Dipping into his satchel, he produced a full pack of cigarettes, gave them to the other. The chief accepted them graciously.

"You do not smoke?"

"I am awaiting your permission," said Sam.

The feline pupils widened as he studied Sam for a long time. The stare was unblinking.

"Smoke!" said the Voice.

Digging out a pellet, Sam lit up. No use hurrying the chief. He'd take his own time and, probably, there'd be the usual cross-examination before he got down to business.

"You speak with my mouth, as does the Gray Chanter," the chief remarked. "Other Earthmen do not, and content themselves with childish signs and gestures. Why?"

Sam fidgeted while he considered the matter. In the outlands, one had to be a diplomat among other things.

"My work," he explained carefully, "keeps me among your people. It is the same with the Gray Chanter. How can we acquire friends and neighbors if we speak not with their mouths? Would you that I sat among the trees and nursed a lonely ghost?" Sam paused inquiringly, but the chief said nothing, so he went on. "Therefore I learned so to speak, as did the Gray Chanter."

"And what of the others?" asked the chief, his great orbs still fixed and blinkless.

"Other men have other tasks. They work together and are not alone. Many work harder and longer hours than I do, and they have not time to acquire other mouths. Some have not the ability because their virtues lie elsewhere. For me, it was easy. For the Gray Chanter it was not so easy. For others it may be hard."

The chief made no comment. He spurted a stream of smoke from between thin lips while his eyes did not shift a fraction. It didn't worry Sam. He'd got used to cat-eyes and to cat-stares, as one did after a while. Fifty months in the rain forest, and you began to understand Greenies—but only began! While he smoked and waited for the next question, he thought idly of Burrough's description of the first Venusian seen by a Terrestrial: physically four-fifths human and one-fifth heaven-knows-what; mentally four-fifths human and one-fifth cat. There was certainly a touch of cat behind their feline eyes; moments of drowsy thoughtfulness, moments of enigmatic stares. They had all the patience of cats, and often the same quiet dignity.

"I am what I am," said the chief suddenly, "and all my people are even thus. There are no differences, neither here,

nor across the mountains, nor on the other side of our world.
Yet you, an Earthman, have a countenance brown and wrinkled
and moss-grown like the bark of an old *radus* tree, while the
Gray Chanter, also an Earthman, is smooth and pale with the
lightness of dawn."

"There is Cherokee in me," said Sam uninformatively.
Then added, "There are men of many colors on Earth, some
white, some red, some black, brown or yellow."

"Ah!" The chief was interested. "And any—green?"

"No, there aren't any green ones on Earth." His tongue
got ahead of his mind as he commented, with a grin, "There
are some said to be green." Then he frowned, put in hastily,
"But they are not."

He wished it could have been unsaid even as the other
pounced on it. He should have known the direct Venusian
mind well enough not to have made such a slip.

"If they are not green," demanded the chief with perfect
logic, "why call them green?"

The smile had vanished from Sam's face and the brilliant
eyes were still upon him while his mind searched frantically for
an explanation which would satisfy the literal-minded Venusian
without hurting his feelings.

Finally, he said, "They are people who're honest, straight-
forward, without guile. Those are thought to be the virtues of
green ghosts. Therefore they are said to be green."

The chief let it pass unchallenged, and still his eyes neither
blinked nor shifted their steady gaze. The way they timed their
silences added greatly to difficulties of conversation with Venusians, for you could never tell whether you'd convinced them
or not. They had an embarrassing habit of asking pointed
questions, and their usual response to an answer was another
and more awkward question. This silence was a long one and
outlasted the chief's cigarette.

In the end, the chief said, "I know many tales of you,
Wizened One, for my mind does not miss the slide of a dew-
drop down a leaf. I know that you are good." He paused
a moment. "Some are good, some are not good. But of you
and the Gray Chanter I know naught but good."

This, uttered in a level voice and accompanied by that
hypnotic stare, made Sam feeble. He waved a hand in futile
dismissal, sought words adequate to the occasion. A halo ill-

became his grizzled pate and he'd feel better without it. From his viewpoint, he'd done nothing but lend an occasional helping hand and mind his own business. Back home in Neosho they called it being neighborly, and they spoke well of you for it, but handed out no diplomas. Before he could find anything to say, the chief went on.

"Now there is great trouble between your people and mine, and death stalks across the mountains. It is an evil thing, for it may spread as the waters spread when they break their bounds. I do not wish to see our forests sheltering only the hunters and the hunted—with no man daring to withhold death from the good lest the good prove bad."

Sam leaned forward, his leathery features intent, the crinkles deepening at the corners of his eyes. There had been trouble, mild trouble, between men and Greenies in the first months of settlement five years ago. Wisdom on both sides had abated it and there'd been no more since. But always it was feared. As Terrestrials gradually grew in numbers so also grew the risk that somebody might start something that couldn't be stopped. He didn't want that. Nobody in full possession of his senses wanted it.

"I am called Elran the Older," continued the chief. "Over the mountains are the people of Elran the Younger. He is my brother. And beyond his lands lie the pastures of the people of Mithra the Silent. My mate is Mithra's sister, and he is my brother-by-bond."

"So?"

"On Mithra's lands are Earthmen. They have been there nearly a year. They have been cutting into his land for some precious mineral, and Mithra approved because he had made a treaty with them. Now a difference has arisen. The Earthmen waxed arrogant and threatening. They brought out their fire weapons." His great eyes lidded for a fraction of a second. "They killed three of Mithra's people."

Sam sucked in his breath, then asked, "And what did Mithra do?"

"He took three for three. By patience and by craft he snared them. They bristled with darts as a tree bristles with leaves and they'd lost their ghosts before they hit the ground. With darts and cords he struck in the night and pulled down all the wires that stretched across the roof of the Earthmen's far-speaking house, thus preventing them from summoning a blast-ship to their aid. Now the Earthmen are sitting in their house and have made it a fort. Mithra has surrounded it and awaits the decision of our kind—for the cry of evil is answered by the cry of good and our mind has got to tip the balance one way or the other."

"This," said Sam, "is bad."

"In the beginning, when Earthmen came to us out of the mist, there was death. But Vaxtre the Ancient and the Earthman we called Tall One came together in wisdom and made peace. Now I am of a mind, Wizened One, that perhaps you and Mithra can achieve the same before it is too late. If not— as Mithra does we shall all do, here and everywhere. A stifled scream is unheard in the glades."

"I shall see Mithra," promised Sam. "I shall go to him at once."

He was off again within the hour. Three days would bring him to the seat of the trouble: one day through the Great Valley and into the land of Elran the Younger, two more days to reach Mithra. That made a total of six days from the cabin to his destination and six days back. If he got stuck too long wherever he was going, his consignment would miss the ship. It required four days to transport it from the cabin to the spaceport. The margin was small.

His face was grim as he thought of that letter. "Native welfare belongs to the proper department." There wasn't a proper department on Venus. There wasn't even a Consul yet! There was only a spaceport still under construction and few Terrestrials outside of it; the majority clung together against the time when their numbers would be more. Those armchair warmers back on Earth ought to be exported and given a taste of forest life. They'd see things differently, after that. "Last warning . . . your resignation may be required." What did they think he was—a root-grubbing automaton?

The Greenies in front seemed to sense his urgency, for he loped along at top pace. The daylight, poor and inadequate by Terrestrial standards, didn't bother the native in the least, and neither did the fall of night. Daytime or night, it was all the same to these people. They could see equally well in either.

Ground rose up and the mist lowered. They were barely

beneath the swirling canopy as they sped through the valley. It was a nuisance, that everlasting fog and, but for radar, would have made all spaceship landings impossibly dangerous. It hung over them like a perpetual shroud, and rays from the invisible sun struggled through so diffused that they threw no shadows.

Mid-afternoon of the second day brought them to the verge of the rain forest which encroached halfway across the lands of Elran the Younger. They plunged into it. That night they ate well, for an incautious turkey forgot to freeze in the gloom as they went past and a blown dart brought it down. The thing was featherless, reptile-skinned and bore no resemblance to a bird except that its cooked flesh was indistinguishable from that of roasted turkey.

Mithra's village was reached a couple of hours ahead of estimated time. It, too, proved to be stone-built, a little smaller than that of Elran the Older, and it was built upon a knoll from which the eternal forest had retreated in all directions. Within a radius of three miles the ground was clear of giant timber and well-tilled.

The Voice himself talked first with the escort, then summoned Sam. The latter found Mithra to be another middle-aged Greenie, shorter and stockier than Elran the Older, and with eyes of light amber.

"I am the Voice of my people," he said formally. Sam offered no reply, knowing that none was expected, but put on the usual surprise act. The chief came quickly to the point, showing himself more abrupt than his distant brother-by-bond. "I know of you as all know of you. Here, you are welcome— but I know not what you can do."

"What happened?" inquired Sam.

"An Earthman came when the life-tide was rising in the trees and stayed until it ebbed. He talked not with our mouth and spoke only by signs and picture writing. We gave him room and nourished his belly, for he was of our shape and alone. For many days he sought among the rocks, along the earthcracks and the chasms, until one day he came to me with his ghost a-dancing and said he'd found that which he'd been seeking. It was merely a vein of *rilla* metal which is of no use to man or beast."

"It hardens and toughens steel beyond belief," Sam told

him. "There is none on Earth. We can use it in constructing spaceships."

"I made a treaty with him," the chief went on, "whereby he could dig up all the *rilla* metal within one hundred man-lengths of his discovery. He went away. A long time later, he came back with five others. My people helped them build a rock house. Over this house the Earthmen put a web of wires and through it they talked to a blastship and brought it down to them through the mist. Twenty more Earthmen came from the ship, with much machinery. The ship departed. Those left behind used the machinery to dig up and melt the *rilla* metal. They worked for almost a year and sent away much of it until there was no more." He hooded his eyes in thought while Sam waited for him to continue.

"Then they came and told me that there is a lot more *rilla* metal within this hill. They said they must have it, village or no village, and that I must make another treaty. I refused. They grew wrath and threatened to release my ghost. One of my people raised his blowpipe and they turned their weapons on him. We buried him in the dark. The Earthmen ran back to their house with many of my young men following in their tracks. We buried two of those also! The next night we trapped three Earthmen and appeased our dead. We also tore down the web of wires above the house and surrounded the place with warriors. Since then, they have not dared to come out and we have not dared to go in."

"May I speak with these Earthmen?" Sam asked.

The chief didn't hesitate, and said, "You shall be conducted to them whenever you wish."

"In the morning, then. I would first like to look around the village and the hill, also examine the place from which the *rilla* metal has been taken."

The building that had become a fort rested alongside another knoll a mile and a half to the south of Mithra's place. It squatted dull and menacing in the poor light of morning.

Countless Greenies prowled phantomlike in the nearest spurs of the rain forest. Some had huge, multi-mouthed blowguns which needed the simultaneous impulse of six men but could throw heavy darts more than two hundred yards. Others bore accurate and vicious arbalests fitted with heavy metal springs and low-geared winders—a weapon Sam had never seen before.

Although he did not come across any on his way to the fort, Sam knew that the Venusians also possessed flame throwers of alarming efficiency. The entire horde kept to the fringes of the forest, well out of range of the fort, and were content to wait. If you crouch by a water hole long enough, the trembling roebuck is bound to appear.

He tramped toward the house with his hands in his pockets, his goatee bristling, and an air of confident nonchalance which might serve to stay any itchy trigger-fingers behind those walls. In the bad illumination Earth-eyes couldn't distinguish friend from foe at any range greater than a voice could carry. The Greenies knew no such handicap. Folks back on Earth who blandly assumed that on any new world one automatically fitted in just couldn't realize the toughness of little things, such as being, by comparison, half-blind. It was always the little things that proved tough. Not the big ones. A bullet in the abdomen was only a little thing. His stomach jumped at the thought.

But no shot sounded. Within fifty yards of the house he passed a board crudely lettered:

TERRALOID

CORPORATION

That wasn't so good. Terraloid were big and powerful and not in business for the sake of their health. Their reputation wasn't evil, and they'd never been known to pull a deliberate swindle, but they were gogetters, efficient, impatient, unwilling to bide their time. Commercially, they were short-cut artists and more than once they'd fallen foul of consuls by their eagerness to march too far in advance of events.

A big, beefy man opened the door, growled, "How the blazes did you get here without masquerading as a pincushion? Don't you know there's plenty trouble hereabouts?"

"That's what I've come to discuss with you. Mithra sent me."

"Ho-hum, a dove of peace!" rumbled the other with a trace of sarcasm. He conducted Sam to an inner room in which were a dozen men, some cleaning and adjusting weapons, others busily completing a new web antenna. "Boys, here's a negotiator." They looked up disinterestedly. The big man sank into a chair which creaked under his weight, said to Sam, "I'm Clem Mason, manager of this outfit. Who're you, why did Mithra pick you out, what's he want to say, and what authority have you got—if any?"

"I'm Sam Gleeson. I'm merely a fieldman for the National Botanical Institute—for as long as that job lasts, which won't be long!" replied Sam evenly. "I've got as much authority as that gives me, which is none whatever. As for the reason why Mithra called me in, I guess it was because I speak his language and know his people." As an afterthought, he added, "And probably because Father Rooney couldn't come."

"Father Rooney!" Clem Mason scowled. "Never heard of him! But we don't want any priests interfering in this. They tell tales back home and the story loses nothing in the telling. Then boudoir warriors complain to the newscasts and the public tears its hair and the next thing you know we've got to say, 'Yes, sir,' and 'No, sir,' and 'Thank you very much, sir,' to every stinking aborigine who comes our way. Why can't people leave us to do our own dickering?" He glared across at the well-oiled guns. "We know how!"

Sam smiled broadly and said, "Seems it's up to you and me to cool things down before Father Rooney comes along to make more trouble, eh?"

The other thought that one over, then growled begrudgingly, "Maybe you've got something!"

"I've heard Mithra's story about what happened," Sam pursued. "Let me hear yours. Then we'll see what we can do to straighten things out."

"It's simple. We worked out a *rilla* vein which we'd got under covenant with Mithra. It was a tentacle broken off from a mother lode some place. Our instruments found the lode far down under the northward knoll. There's tons of the stuff, and it's needed badly. Then we got all balled up because none of us knows a word of Venusian. We drew pictures and played snake-arms for hours trying to explain to Mithra that we'd found Aladdin's cave way down under his cellar and that we wanted another covenant to get it out. We offered him fair terms, were willing to play square, but the more we argued the tougher he got."

"Go on," Sam encouraged.

"I got riled by his stubborness and cursed him for a skinny green nitwit. I knew he couldn't understand English anyway. After that, it was a case of one durned thing leading to another."

"In what way?"

"A young Greenie among Mithra's crowd lifted his blowpipe. Maybe he didn't like the way I'd said what I'd said. Or maybe he lifted it with nothing in mind. But Fargher was jumpy and taking no chances and popped him on the spot. We beat it back here with a splurge of angry Greenies slinking after us through the night, and we had to blow back at them to hold them a bit. I don't know whether we hurt any more."

"You killed two," Sam informed.

Mason made a negligent gesture and continued, "They were mighty swift to call it quits. They caught Fargher and Meakin and Wills out in the darkness and mauled them in ten seconds flat! They blew cord-carrying darts across the roof and lugged down our web. Since then, we've stuck to the house and tried to call base on our portable, but the range is too long, and intervening mountains blot us out. So we're going to fix up a new web and they had better not try to get *that* down! We'll get a blast-ship here. After that, the fashionable attire for well-dressed Greenies will be sackcloth and ashes!"

"Trouble begets trouble," opined Sam. "I fear me that this is no petty skirmish with a local tribe. It isn't as simple as that. I've been getting the hang of some queer things about these Venusians. They've no tribes, no nations. They've no local patriotisms—but they're Venus-conscious! They've only one color, one language, and one something-else I've not yet been able to identify. But the divide and rule principal just won't work on this planet, for the woes of one are the woes of all."

"Never mind the lectures," put in Mason sourly. "Say what you've got to say and let's go digging."

"The point I'm trying to drive home is that you can't indulge in purely local shenanigans. Even Elran the Older, three days march away across the mountains, knows all that's going on and is ready to do exactly what Mithra does. The alternative to peace is an Earth-Venus war. For all our superior weapons, there are only a couple of thousand of us on the planet. There are umpteen millions of Greenies, and we've got to seek them out, one at a time, every man jack of them, in the biggest jungle in the solar system. Fat lot of use our blast-ships and atomizers will prove in circumstances like that!" He mused a moment. "What's the use of the mightiest power if it can't be applied?"

"We can apply it all right," Mason asserted. "You've sat on your buttocks too long—you've forgotten the planet behind the two thousand!"

"Behind them for three weeks every eight months!" Sam retorted. "You know we're planet-raking before our time. We've not yet developed spaceships good enough to chase a world around its orbit. In another fifty years, maybe—but not yet. That shaves us down somewhat, doesn't it? Earth's in a poor position to conquer Venus by force."

"That's your—" Mason began, but Sam interrupted him.

"Let me go on. You want *rilla* metal. That's all you're here for. If you can get it by cajoling Mithra, it'll come a lot cheaper than by fighting him for it. If you're a shareholder, you should appreciate that. If you're not holding any of their stock, why should you do Terraloid's blood-letting?"

"He's dead to rights there, Clem," put in one of the listening men. "I came here to get on with a job of work and land home with a whole skin and plenty of moola. If there's any pushing around to be done, let 'em call in the marines!" Several others murmured agreement.

"O.K.," said Mason. He hooked big thumbs in the armholes of his vest, tilted backward in his chair. "So we soothe Mithra—how?"

"Can you get out that *rilla* without wrecking his village?"

"Sure we can. It's down deep. We can run side shafts from the base of the knoll. It's dead easy!"

"Did you explain that to Mithra?"

"Goldarn it! That's what we tried to do," complained Mason, his voice rising, "but without his lingo we couldn't make him understand. He's seen what a mess we've made of the surface-vein here and thought there'd be the same upheaval there."

"Naturally?" prompted Sam.

Mason was reluctant, but after a while he gave in with, "Well, I guess so. It was natural. He's no miner or metallurgical engineer."

Sam leaned forward in his seat. "Now can I tell Mithra that the metal will be taken without disturbing one stone or slate within his village, and that after it is done you will leave him fine passages and underground rooms which his people can use for storage?"

"You bet!" The other became amiable suddenly. "We'd even trim up the walls for them."

"Good. I'll go and tell him. I think it'll satisfy him—in fact I'm sure of it."

"Let's hope so." Mason's chair came forward as he sat up. "But there's still one snag."

"What's that?"

"Three of my men died, and don't you forget it! What is Mithra going to do about that?"

Sam rose to his feet in readiness to leave. Now that his mission seemed to be getting some place, he felt tired, thoroughly tired and weary. Too much long distance marching and too little sleep. Six days to get back at the same hurried pace and the spaceship still to catch. This life was punishing to one's dogs.

"Mithra will send you the culprits and you may punish them as you wish."

"Like heck he will," said Mason. "Unless he's nuts."

"Oh, yes, he will—on one condition."

"What condition?"

"That you send him the three who killed his men and leave him to punish them."

"You got me there. It's even-Steven. They're dead, anyway."

"So are Mithra's men," said Sam.

Mithra made the peace, the prowling shadows vanished from the fringes near the fort, the arbalests and flame throwers were put away. No messenger went forth to bear the tidings, a fact Sam noted thoughtfully.

"I can't see what else we can call it but a miserable misunderstanding," said Sam to Mason as he made ready to leave the village. "It's not for me to place the blame, but I reckon it'd be wiser if you gave one of your guys time off to learn the language. When people on Earth can't always make themselves understood, what hopes have you got semaphoring at a Greenie?"

"I'll see what can be done," promised Mason. "And thanks a lot!" He frowned suddenly, and added, "If you meet that

Father Rooney, stall him off for me, will you?"

"I will," agreed Sam, smiling. He hiked his satchel and left.

The same native who'd brought him was his guide on the way back, but the remainder of his bodyguard had increased in number from three to twelve. He was greatly honored, for this was the escort of a Voice. Politeness still demanded that he follow his guide and pretend not to notice the others.

Twelve protecting shadows stayed with him the full length of his journey home and duly circled his cabin before fading away into the heat-haze and the half-light. They'd been phantoms throughout the trip and like phantoms they disappeared.

It was good to be back in the shack, to see the old, familiar fragment of glade through the window, to hear the regular *put-put-put* of moisture falling onto the roof, to have books biding his perusal, a bed waiting for his body.

Morning found him frantically energetic. From Mithra's land he'd plucked a new herb which looked like heather but smelled and tasted like mint. It hadn't wilted during the journey. He sand-dried it, sketched it, photographed it, packed it in a box which he tagged: *erica mithrii.* There were four new roots with which to deal, in addition to the other roots and samples of bark still waiting attention. And a report to write about every one of them. He was still busy in the middle of it when a heavy metallic rattle and the deep roar of a Diesel engine brought him outside. He was just in time to see the caterpillar from Base rumble into the glade. There were four men aboard. The machine was two days early and much of his stuff wasn't ready for it; he stood and watched its approach with mixed feelings.

With a final burst of power that sent curls of thick blue smoke through the grasses and the herbs, the huge machine stopped before his door and its passengers climbed out. The treads had left two enormous weals across the glade to between the farther trees.

He recognized none of the four. The first of these, making no remark, handed him a bunch of mail and strolled into the cabin, the others following. Sam entered last shuffling his mail and feeling ireful.

Inside, he found the first entrant squatting on the edge of his bed; a beefy personage with a thick neck, a florid complexion, and an elusive touch of humor playing around his heavy jowls.

Without preamble, this one said, "Brother Gleeson, you're fired."

Sam tossed the mail unopened onto his bed, seated himself carefully on a sample box. "I've been expecting it."

"So have I," informed the other cheerfully. "I've been trying for months to persuade the Institute to shake you off."

"Indeed?" Sam wrinkled his eyes as he studied the speaker. "Why? What have I done to you?"

"You got me bothered by making me realize how much I've yet to learn." He jerked a brawny thumb to indicate the spectacled, apprehensive young man at his side. "Same with him. He's Jud Hancock, your successor, and he feels apologetic about it."

"All right," said Sam, listlessly. "Guess this is where I pack up and go home."

"Oh, no, you don't!" He leaned forward, rested thick arms on thicker knees. "Earth's decided that now's the time to appoint a Venusian Consul and get things better organized. I have been honored with the task, and I think it's a tough one. What I'm going to need, real bad, will be an adviser on native affairs. That's where you come in."

Sam said, quickly, "What makes you think that?"

"Your reports. I've read 'em all."

"Who are you?"

"Walt Kayser," answered the other.

A wave of embarrassment came over Sam, and he murmured, "You expect *me* to advise *you?*"

"Most certainly! Where the devil can I get advice except from the right people? Who understands Venusians better than you?" He looked up questioningly, his eyes keen and sharp. "For instance, what's all this stuff you've got about what you call 'Venusian auto-rapport'?"

"I don't quite know even now," Sam replied. His hair was standing up and his goatee lying down, and his mind was in a confused whirl. "All I've found out is that as long as things go smoothly for them the Greenies are individuals exactly as we are. But when involved in difficulties great enough to cause mental stress they appear to become part of a communal mind. Immediately a Greenie is in trouble the whole world of Greenies knows about it, discusses it, analyzes it, advises him what to do in some queer mental way, and, if necessary, comes to his aid."

"Telepathy?"

"No, it's definitely not that. It isn't deliberate. It's quite involuntary and automatic and operates only under strain. It's just a peculiar faculty unknown on Earth or Mars." Enthusiasm for his subject crept into his voice. "You know, it means we've got to be almighty careful in our dealings with them. Here, one sucker means a whole world warned. Venus is the wrong place for pulling fast ones. The only way in which we can let them know we're good is by being good all the time. We've got to maintain a code of ethics out of stern necessity."

"Or else?"

"Else they're likely to be tough—maybe too tough for us to handle. It's going to be a long, long time before we get the full measure of their capabilities!" His features grew reminiscent, thoughtful. "Sometimes I find myself quite unable to decide whether the Greenies are genuine individuals or merely independent fragments of some huge, incomprehensible, planet-covering Greenie entity. There are times when they show strange aspects of both. Occasionally I think of them not as a race, but as a being, a sort of timid tiger. It's polite and retiring—and it's wisest to let it stay that way."

"You see!" said Walter Kayser.

"See what?"

Kayser turned to his three companions and said, humorously, "He says, 'See what?' He can't hear himself talk!" He turned back to Sam. "The man who's playmate of a timid tiger is the man I need. What, in your opinion, is our most urgent requirement in creating wider and better contact with the Greenies?"

"Linguists," Sam told him emphatically. He stood up. "That's the only way in which I've gotten to know them."

"The only way?" queried Kayser, lifting an eyebrow.

"Sure!" Sam moved restlessly across the room, the others watching. The swift march of events was still a little too much for his orderly mind. What to do for the best? Wasn't Kayser weighing his friendship with natives a little too heavily? Darn it, all he'd done was learn to talk their own lingo. Any fool could do that if he took the trouble. His preoccupied gaze went through the window, saw a Greenie waiting patiently outside.

"Pardon me," he said to the quartet, opened the door, and went out.

The native leaned on his blowpipe, looked at Sam with great yellow eyes that were grave and brooding. "The Gray Chanter," he said.

"What of him? Is he sick?"

The other nodded. "They say he forbids us to summon you, but it is not good for him to struggle alone. He has spoken gently, saying that we are company enough. Alas, he cannot grasp the mind of his people."

Sam blinked and said, "Wait!"

Returning to the cabin, he snatched up his satchel, slung it over his shoulder. "Father Rooney is ill," he told his surprised visitors. "Unfortunately, you could never cross the ravines and rope bridges in that caterpillar. So this is where I go." With that, he was gone.

The dumfounded four crowded the cabin door and watched him vanish through the trees behind his swiftly loping guide. The last branches rustled behind him, the leaves dripped down and all was silence. Then, suddenly, a dozen stealthy shapes, blowguns in hand, flitted from the trees and entered the invisible path Sam had taken.

"Hey, look at that!" breathed Hancock, grabbing Kayser's arm.

"His escort," murmured Kayser. He shrugged broad shoulders. "And I don't rate one better! Sixty miles—just like that!" He mused a lot, "There was a remark in one of his reports that caused effervescence in my thinkery. He said, 'They've been kind to me.'"

"Humph!" contributed Hancock, looking comforted.

"He didn't take up your offer," one of the other pointed out.

"He will, he will," asserted Kayser positively. "He's constitutionally incapable of refusing."

A Little Oil

HE SHIP HUMMED AND THRUMMED AND DRUMMED. It
was a low-cycle note, sonorous and penetrating like
that produced by the big-pipe octave of a mighty
organ. It moaned through hull-plates, groaned out
of girders, throbbed along nerves and bones, beat upon tired
ears and could not be ignored. Not after a week, a month
or a year. Certainly not after most of four years.

There was no effective cure for the noise. It was the inevitable, unavoidable result of bottling an atomic propulsor
within a cylinder of highly conductive metal. The first ship
had screeched one hundred cycles higher, minute after minute,
hour after hour, and had never returned. Somewhere amid the
waste spaces of the infinite, it might still be howling, unheard,
unheeded, after thirty years.

Ship number two had started out with a slag-wool pad-
ded engine room and silicone-lined venturis. The low note.
The drone of a burdened bee amplified twenty thousand times.
And the bee had not come back to the hive. Eighteen years into
the star field and blindly heading onward for another hundred,
thousand or ten thousand years.

The vessel now thundering along was number three, not
going outward, but on its way back, heading for home. Nosing
toward a not-yet-visible red dot lost in the mist of stars, a
strayed soul fumbling for salvation, it was determined not to
be damned as others had been damned. Ship number three—
that meant something.

Sea sailors cherish sea superstitions. Space sailors coddle
space superstitions. In the captain's cabin where Kinrade sat
writing the log, a superstition was pinned to the wall and functioned as a morale booster.

THIRD TIME DOES IT!

They had believed it at the start when the crew had numbered nine. They would believe it at the finish, though reduced to six. But in between times there had been and might again be bad moments of shaken faith when men wanted out at any cost, even the cost of death, and to hell with the ultimate purpose of the flight. Moments when men fought other men in effort to break loose from audiophobia, claustrophobia, half a dozen other phobias.

Kinrade wrote with the pen in his right hand, a bluedsteel automatic within easy reach of his left. His eyes concentrated on the log, his ears on the ship and its everlasting drumming. The noise might hesitate, falter or cease, and the blessing of its cessation would be equally a curse. Or other sounds might rise above this persistent background, an oath, a shout, a shot. It had happened once before, when Weygarth cracked. It could happen again.

Kinrade was somewhat edgy himself, for he jerked in his seat and slid his left hand sidewise when Bertelli came in unexpectedly. Recovering, he swung his chair round on its socket, gazed into the other's sad gray eyes.

"Well, have they marked it yet?"

The question startled Bertelli. His long, lugubrious, hollow-cheeked face grew longer. His great gash of a mouth drooped at the corners. The sad eyes took on an expression of hopeless bafflement. He was clumsily embarrassed.

Recognizing these familiar symptoms, Kinrade became more explicit. "Is Sol visible on the screen?"

"Sol?" Bertelli's hands tangled together, the fingers like carrots.

"Our own sun, you imbecile!"

"Oh, *that!*" The eyes widened in delighted comprehension. "I haven't asked."

"I thought maybe you'd come to tell me they've got it spotted at last."

"No, Captain. It's just that I wondered whether you need any help." His expression switched from its accustomed glumness to the eager smile of a fool more than willing to serve. The mouth lifted, widened so much that it made the ears stick out and reminded the onlooker of a slice of melon.

"Thanks," said Kinrade, more kindly. "Not right now."

Bertelli's embarrassment came back in painful strength. His face was humbly apologetic for having asked. After shifting around on his big, ugly feet, he went out. As always, he skidded violently on the steel-floored catwalk, regained balance with a clatter of heavy boots. Nobody else slipped at that spot, but he invariably did.

Kinrade suddenly realized that he was smiling and changed it to a troubled frown. For the hundredth time he consulted the ship's register, found it no more informative than on the ninety-nine other occasions. There was the little roster with three names of the nine crossed out. And the same entry halfway down: *Enrico Bertelli, thirty-two, psychologist.*

It was the bunk. If Bertelli were a psychologist or anything remotely connected with scientific expertness, then he, Robert Kinrade, was a bright blue giraffe. For almost four years they'd been locked together in this groaning cylinder, six men carefully chosen from the great mass of humanity, six men supposed to be the salt of the Earth, the cream of their kind. But the six were five men and a fool.

There was a puzzle here. It intrigued him in spare moments when he had time to think with a mind untrammeled by serious matters. It dangled before him tantalizingly, making him repeatedly picture its subject all the way down from sad eyes to flat feet. During rare moments of meditation, he found himself vainly trying to analyze Bertelli and deduce the real reason for his being, concentrating upon him to the temporary exclusion of the others.

As opportunity occurred, Kinrade watched him, too, marveling that any so-called expert could be so thoroughly and unfailingly nit-witted. He studied Bertelli with such intentness that he failed to notice whether the others might be doing the same for similar reasons born of similar thoughts.

Yet this concentration was his answer—and he did not know it.

Marsden was duty navigator and Vail stood guard in the engine room when Kinrade went to lunch. The other three already were at the table in the tiny galley. He nodded briefly and took his place.

Big blond Nilsen, atomic engineer by choice, plus botanist by official coercion, eyed Kinrade skeptically and said, "No sun."

"I know."

"There ought to be."

Kinrade shrugged.

"But there isn't," Nilson persisted.

"I know."

"Do you care?"

"Don't be a sap." Breaking open a packaged meal, Kinrade tossed it into his compartmented plastic plate.

Thrum-thrum went the ship from floor, walls and ceiling.

"So you think I'm a sap, do you?" Nilsen leaned forward, stared with aggressive expectancy.

"Let's eat," suggested Aram, the thin, dark and nervous cosmogeologist at his side. "One bellyache's enough without hunting another."

"That's not the point," declared Nilsen. "I want to know—"

He shut up as Bertelli mumbled, "Pardon me," and reached across him for salt in a container fastened to the other end of the table.

Unscrewing it, Bertelli brought it to his end, sat down, found himself on the extreme edge of his seat. His eyes popped very slightly in mild surprise. He stood, slid the seat forward on its runners, sat again, knocked the salt off the table. Radiating shame and self-consciousness, he picked it up, used it in the manner of one emptying a large bucket, practically lay full length on the table to screw it in its original position. That task performed, he squirmed backward with his behind in the air, gained the seat again.

It was the edge and so near that he began to slide off it. The eyes bulged a fraction more widely than before and once again he went through the seat-sliding performance. Finally he sat down, smoothed out an invisible napkin, favored everyone with a look of abject apology.

Taking in a deep breath, Nilsen said to him, "Sure you wouldn't care for a little more salt?"

Bertelli's eyes dulled under the impact of the problem, sought his plate, examined it with idiotic care. "No, I don't think so, thank you."

Surveying his own plate a moment, Nilsen looked up, met Kinrade's eyes, asked, "What's this guy got that others haven't got?"

Grinning at him, Kinrade replied, "That problem is a corker. I've been trying to figure it out and I can't."

A half-smile came into Nilsen's features as he confessed, "Neither can I."

Bertelli said nothing. He went on with his meal, eating in characteristic manner with elbows held high and his hand uncertainly seeking a mouth it could not miss.

Putting a pencil-tip to the screen, Marsden said, "That one looks pink to me. But it may be my imagination."

Kinrade bent close and had a look. "Too small to be sure. A mere pinpoint."

"Then I'd been kidding myself."

"Not necessarily. Your eyes may be more color-sensitive than mine."

"Ask Goofy here," suggested Marsden.

Bertelli examined the brilliant dot from ten different distances and as many angles. Finally he squinted at it.

"That can't be it," he announced, triumphant with discovery, "because our sun is orange-red."

"The fluorescent coating of the screen would make it look pink," informed Marsden with a touch of impatience. "Does that dot look pink?"

"I don't know," Bertelli admitted miserably.

"You're a great help."

"It's too far away for more than mere guesswork," said Kinrade. "Resolution isn't good enough to cope with such a distance. We'll have to wait until we get a good deal closer."

"I'm fed up waiting," said Marsden, scowling at the screen.

"But we're going home," Bertelli reminded him.

"I know. That's what's killing me."

"Don't you *want* to go home?" Bertelli puzzledly asked.

"I want to too much." Irritatedly, Marsden rammed the pencil back into his pocket. "I thought I'd stand the inward trip better than the outward one just because it would be homeward. I was wrong. I want green grass, blue skies and plenty of room to move around. I can't wait."

"I can," said Bertelli, virtuously. "Because I've got to. If I were unable to wait, I'd go nuts."

"Would you?" Marsden looked him over, the grouch slowly fading from his face. The change went as far as a chuckle. "How much of a trip would that be?"

Leaving the navigation room, he headed toward the galley, still chuckling as he went. Rounding the farther corner, he let out a low guffaw.

"What's funny?" asked Bertelli, vacantly mystified.

Straightening up from the screen, Kinrade eyed him with care. "How is it that whenever somebody starts blowing his—" Changing his mind, he let the sentence die out.

"Yes, Captain?"

"Oh, forget it."

The ship plunged onward, moaning at every plate.

Vail appeared presently, coming off duty and on his way to eat. He was a short man of great width, with long arms and powerful hands.

"Any luck?"

"We're not sure." Kinrade indicated the dot burning amid a confusing host of others. "Marsden thinks that's it. He may be wrong."

"Don't you *know?*" asked Vail, looking at him and ignoring the screen Kinrade was pointing to.

"We will in due time. It's a bit early yet."

"Changing your tune, aren't you?"

"What do you mean?" Kinrade's tone was sharp.

"Three days ago you told us that Sol should become visible in the screen almost any time. That gave us a lift. We needed it. I'm no sniveling babe myself, but I must admit I wanted that boost." He surveyed the other with a touch of resentment. "The higher hopes go, the lower they fall when they drop."

"I'm not dropping mine," Kinrade said. "Three days plus or minus is a tiny margin of error in a return trip taking two years."

"That would be true if we're on correct course. Maybe we aren't."

"Are you suggesting that I'm not competent to work out the proper coordinates?"

"I'm suggesting that even the best of us can blunder," Vail gave back stubbornly. "In proof of which, two ships have gone to pot."

"Not because of navigational errors," put in Bertelli, looking unconvincingly profound.

Pursing his lips, Vail stared at him and inquired, "What the hell do you know about space navigation?"

"Nothing," Bertelli confessed with the air of one surrendering a back tooth. He nodded toward Kinrade. "But he knows enough."

"I wonder!"

"The route for return was worked out in full detail by Captain Sanderson before he died," said Kinrade, his color a little heightened. "I've checked and rechecked at least a dozen times. So has Marsden. If you're not satisfied, you can have the calculations and go through them yourself."

"I'm not a trained navigator."

"Then shut your trap and leave other—"

Bertelli broke in with a note of protest. "But I didn't have it open!"

Shifting attention to him, Kinrade asked, "You didn't have what open?"

"My mouth," said Bertelli. He registered personal injury. "Don't know why you have to pick on me. Everyone picks on me."

"You're wrong," Vail told him. "He—"

"There you are. I'm wrong. I'm always wrong. I'm never right." Emitting a deep sigh, Bertelli wandered out, dragging big feet. His face was a picture of misery.

Vail watched him in faint amazement, then said, "That looks to me like a persecution complex. And he's supposed to be a psychologist. What a laugh!"

"Yes," agreed Kinrade, without humor. "What a laugh!"

Going to the screen, Vail examined it. "Which one does Marsden think is Sol?"

"That one." Kinrade pointed it out for him.

Staring at it hungrily for quite a time, Vail finished, "Oh, well, let's hope he's right." Then he departed.

Left alone, Kinrade sat in the navigator's chair and looked at the screen without seeing it. His mind was on a problem that might be real or might be imaginary.

When does science become an art? Or should it be: when does art become a science?

Aram cracked next day. He got a dose of "Charlie," the same psychotic behavior pattern that had put an end to Weygarth. There was a technical name for it, but few knew it and fewer could pronounce it. The slang term came from an ancient, almost forgotten war in which the rear-gunner of a big aircraft—Tail End Charlie—would think too long of the heavy bomb-load and the thousands of gallons of high octane spirit right behind his perspex parrot-cage, and all of a sudden he'd batter upon the walls of his prison, screaming.

The way Aram broke was characteristic of this space affliction. He sat next to Nilsen, quietly downing his meal, but picking at the compartmented plastic tray as though completely indifferent to food or drink. Then, without a word or the slightest change of expression, he pushed away the tray, got up and ran like hell. Nilsen tried to trip him and failed. Aram shot through the door like a bolting rabbit, raced headlong down the passage toward the airlock.

Slamming his own chair back to the limit of its holding rails, Nilsen went after him with Kinrade one jump behind. Bertelli stayed in his seat, a forkful of food halfway to his mouth, his gaze fixed blankly on the facing wall while his big ears remained perked for outer sounds.

They caught Aram frantically struggling with the airlock wheel and trying to force it the wrong way around. Even if he had rotated it the right way, he wouldn't have had time to open it. His thin features were pale and he was snuffling with exertion.

Reaching him, Nilsen jerked him around by one shoulder, smacked him in the jaw. There was plenty of force behind that blow. Aram, a small, lightly built man, caromed along the passage and ended up as an unconscious bundle by the forward door. Rubbing his knuckles, Nilsen grunted to himself, checked the airlock wheel to make sure it was holding good and tight.

Then he grasped the victim's feet while Kinrade lifted the shoulders and between them they bore the sagging Aram to his tiny cabin, laid him in his bunk. Nilsen remained on watch while Kinrade went for the hypodermic needle and a shot of dope. They put Aram out of the running for the next twelve hours. This was the only known countermeasure: an enforced sleep during which an overactive brain could rest and strained nerves recuperate.

Returning to the galley, Nilsen resumed his interrupted meal, said to Kinrade, "Good thing he didn't think to swipe a gun."

Kinrade nodded without answering. He knew what the other meant. Weygarth had tried to hold them off with a gun while he prepared his dash to false freedom on a blast of air. They could not rush him without risking serious loss. They'd had to shoot him down quickly, ruthlessly, before it was too late. Weygarth had been their first bitter casualty only twenty months out.

And now they dared not suffer another loss. Five men could run the ship, control it, steer it, land it. Five represented the absolute minimum. Four would be damned forever to a great metal coffin thundering blindly amid the host of stars.

It brought up yet another of the problems that Kinrade had not been able to resolve, at least to his own satisfaction. Should an airlock be fastened with a real lock to which only the captain held the key? Or might that cost them dear in a sudden and grave emergency? Which was the greater risk, lunatic escape for one or balked escape for all?

Oh, well, they were homeward bound, and when they got back he'd hand over the log and the detailed reports and leave the big brains to work it out for themselves. That was their job; his to make landfall safely.

Kinrade glanced at Nilsen, noted the introspective frown on his face and knew what he was thinking of Weygarth. Scientists and top-grade technicians are people with highly trained minds, but that does not make them less or more than other men. Their status does not keep them in splendid isolation from humanity. Outside of their especial interests, they are plain, ordinary folks subject to the strains and tensions of every man. Their minds are not and cannot be solely and ever-lastingly occupied with one subject. Sometimes they think of other men and sometimes of themselves. Nilsen's was a trained mind, intelligent and sensitive, therefore so much the more liable to crack. Kinrade knew instinctively that if and when Nilsen made a break for the lock, he would not forget the gun.

It took less intelligent, less imaginative types—the cow-mind—to endure long incarceration in a huge steel boiler on which a dozen devils hammered hour after hour, day after day, without cease or let-up. There was another problem for Earth's bigbrains to mull a while: dull-witted people were tops for endurance, but useless functionally. Bright minds were essential to run the ship, yet somewhat more likely to go *phut*, even though only temporarily.

What did this add up to? Answer: the ideal space crew

should be composed of hopeless dopes with high I. Q. A contradiction in terms.

Now that he came to consider it, the thought struck him that here might be the solution to the mystery of Bertelli. Those who had designed and built the ship and hand-picked the crew were people of formidable craftiness. In was incredible that they'd dig up a gormless character like Bertelli in a spirit of not giving a damn. The selection had been deliberate and carefully calculated, of that Kinrade was certain. Perhaps the loss of two ships had convinced them that they'd have to be more modest in their choice of crews. Maybe Bertelli had been planted to test how a dope made out.

If so, they had something—but it wasn't enough. Without a doubt, Bertelli would be the last to crack, the last to race for the airlock. Beyond that, nothing could be said in his favor purely from the technical viewpoint. He knew little worth knowing and that he had learned from the others. Any responsibility with which he was entrusted invariably got fouled up in masterly style. Indeed, with his big, clumsy mitts on any of the controls, he would be a major menace.

He was liked, all right. In fact, he was popular in a way. Bertelli had other accomplishments about as genuinely useful on a spaceship as a skunk's smell-gun at a convention. He could play several musical instruments, sing in a cracked voice, mime in really funny manner, tap-dance with a peculiar sort of loose-jointed clumsiness. After they'd got over their initial irritation with him, they had found him amusing and pathetic—a bumbler they were sorry to feel superior to, because they couldn't think of anyone who wouldn't be superior to him.

The schemers back home would learn that a spaceship is better without non-technical thickheads, Kinrade decided rather uncertainly. They had made their test and it hadn't come off. It hadn't come off. It hadn't come off. The more he repeated it to himself, the less sure he felt about it.

Vail came in, paused at the sight of them. "I thought you'd finished ten minutes ago."

"It's all right." Nilsen stood up, brushed away crumbs, gestured toward his chair. "I'll go watch the engines."

Getting his tray and meal, Vail seated himself, eyed the others. "What's up?"

"Aram's in bed with Charlie," Kinrade told him.

Not the flicker of emotion crossed Vail's face. He made a vicious stab at his food, said, "The Sun would bring him out of that condition. That's what we all want, a sight of the Sun."

"There are millions of suns," informed Bertelli, eagerly offering the lot.

Leaning his elbows on the table, Vail said in a harsh voice and with great significance, "That is precisely the point!"

Bertelli's eyes dulled into complete confusion. He fidgeted with his tray, knocked his fork around without noticing it. Still looking at Vail, he felt for the fork, picked it up by the prongs, absently poked at the tray with the handle. Then he lifted the handle toward his mouth.

"I'd try the other end," advised Vail, watching with interest. "It's sharper."

The eyes lowered, studied the fork while gradually they took on an expression of vacant surprise. He made a childish motion indicative of helplessness. Finally he bestowed on both his usual apologetic grin and at the same time gave a casual twitch of finger and thumb that landed the handle smack in his palm.

Kinrade noticed that flip. Vail didn't, but he did—and for once he got a strange, uncanny feeling that Bertelli had made a very small mistake, a tiny error that might have passed unseen.

When Kinrade was in his cabin, the intercom called on the desk and Marsden's voice said, "Aram's just come out of it. He's got a sore jaw, but he seems cooled down. I don't think he needs another shot—yet."

"We'll let him run loose, but keep an eye on him for a while," Kinrade decided. "Tell Bertelli to stick close. He has nothing better to do."

"All right." Marsden paused, added in lower tones, "Vail is pretty surly lately. Have you noticed?"

"He's okay. Just gets jumpy now and again. Don't we all?"

"I suppose so." Marsden sounded as if he'd like to say more, but he didn't. He cut off and the intercom went silent.

Finishing the day's entry on the log, Kinrade examined himself at the mirror, decided he'd put off a shave a little longer. This was his idea of petty luxury; he disliked the chore, but lacked the courage to grow a beard. Other men, other notions.

He lay back in his chair and enjoyed a quiet think, first about the planet called home, then the men who had sent this ship into space, then the men who were flying it with him. They'd been trained for the job, these six who, for the first time, had reached another star, and their training had incorporated a certain amount of useful flexibility. The three spacemen among them had been given superswift education in some branch of science. The scientists had undergone courses in space navigation or atomic engineering. Two aptitudes per men. Then he thought again and eliminated Bertelli.

Pre-flight education had gone further than that. A baldheaded old coot who bossed a lunatic asylum had lectured them on space etiquette with every air of knowing what he was talking about. Each man, he had explained, would know only three things about his fellows, to wit: name, age and qualification. No man must ask for more nor seek to pry into another's private life. Unknown lives provide no basis for irrational prejudices, antagonisms or insults, he had said. Empty personalities don't clash so readily. So it was established that none might urge another to reveal what made him tick.

Thus Kinrade could not probe the reasons why Vail was irritable above the average or what made Marsden more impatient than others. He could not determine from past data why Nilsen potentially was the most dangerous or Aram the least stable. Neither could he insist that Bertelli explain his presence in understandable terms. Pending successful completion of the flight, each man's history remained hidden behind a curtain through which, from time to time only insignificant items had been glimpsed.

After most of four years existing cheek by jowl with these people, he had come to know them as never before—but not as he would know them some day in the green fields of Earth when the flight was a bygone event, the tabu was broken and they had memories for free discussion.

He liked to muse on these matters because he had developed a theory that he intended to dump right in the laps of the experts. It concerned lifers in penitentiaries. Not all criminals are stupid, he believed. Many might be intelligent, sensitive men somehow pushed or kicked off the path called straight and narrow. Walled up, some of them would get a dose of Charlie, try to bust out, beat up a warder, anything, *anything* to escape

—and be rewarded for their efforts with solitary confinement. It was like treating a poisoned man with an even more powerful dose of what made him ill. It was wrong, wrong. He was convinced of that. There was a reformist streak in Kinrade.

Upon his desk he had a neatly written scheme for the treatment of lifers likely to go psycho. It involved constant individual observation and the timely use of occupational therapy. Whether or not it was practical, he didn't know, but at least it was constructive. The plan was his pet. He wanted leading penologists to play with it, give it a serious tryout. If it worked—and he felt that it should—the world would have derived one benefit from this flight in a way not originally contemplated. Even that alone made it profitable.

At that point, his thoughts were brought to an abrupt end by the arrival of Nilsen, Vail and Marsden. Behind them, waiting in the doorway, but not entering, was Aram with Bertelli in attendance. Kinrade braced himself in his seat and spoke gruffly.

"This is great. Nobody at the controls."

"I switched on the autopilot," Marsden said. "It will hold her on course four or five hours. You said so yourself."

"True." His eyes examined them. "Well, why the scowling deputation?"

"This is the end of the fourth day," Nilsen pointed out. "Soon we'll be into the fifth. And we're still looking for Sol."

"So?"

"I'm not satisfied that you know where we're going."

"I am."

"Is that a fact or more face-saving?"

Kinrade stood up, said, "For the sake of argument, suppose I admitted that we're running blind—what could you do about it?"

"That's an easy one." Nilsen's air was that of one whose suspicions have almost been confirmed. "We picked you for captain after Sanderson died. We'd withdraw the vote and choose somebody else."

"And then?"

"Make for the nearest star, hunt around for a planet we can live on."

"Sol *is* the nearest star."

"It is if we're heading right," Nilsen retorted.

Sliding open a drawer in his desk, Kinrade took out a large roll of paper, spread it across the top. Its multitude of tiny squares bore a large number of dots and crosses amid which a thick, black line ran in a steady curve.

"This is the return course." His fingers indicated several crosses and dots. "We can tell by direct observation of these bodies whether or not we are on course. There's only one thing we can't check with absolute accuracy."

"What's that?" inquired Vail, frowning at the chart.

"Our velocity. It can be estimated only with a five per cent margin of error, plus or minus. I know we're on course, but not precisely how far along it. Hence the four-day lag. I warn you that it can extend to as much as ten."

Nilsen said, heavily, "They took photos of the star formation on the way out. We've just been putting the transparencies over the screen. They don't match."

"Of course they don't." Kinrade displayed impatience. "We're not at the same point. The star field will have circumferential displacement."

"We aren't without brains despite not being trained navigators," Nilsen gave back. "There is displacement. It progresses radially from a focal point that is not the pink spot you claim is Sol. The point is about halfway between that and the left edge of the screen." He gave a loud sniff, invited, "Can you talk yourself out of that one?"

Kinrade sighed, put a finger on the chart. "This line is a curve, as you can see. The outward course was a similar curve bending the reverse way. The tail camera focused along the line of the ship's axis. A few thousand miles out, it was pointing sunward, but the farther the ship got, the more its axis pointed to one side. By the time we crossed the orbit of Pluto, it was aiming to hell and away."

Peering at the chart, Nilsen thought a while, asked shrewdly, "If you are sincere, what's the absolute margin of error?"

"I told you—ten days."

"Nearly half of those have gone. We'll give you the other half."

"Thanks!" said Kinrade, faintly sarcastic.

"After which we'll either see Sol and identify it beyond doubt or we'll have a new captain and be heading for the nearest light."

"We'll draw lots for captain," suggested Bertelli from the back. "I'd like the chance to boss a ship."

"Heaven help us!" exclaimed Marsden.

"We'll pick the man best qualified," said Nilsen.

"That's why you chose Kinrade in the first place," Bertelli reminded him.

"Maybe. But we'll find someone else."

"Then I insist on being considered. One dope is as good as another for making a mess of things."

"When it comes to that, we're not in the same class," replied Nilsen, feeling that his efforts were being subtly sabotaged. "You can out-boob me with your big hands pinned to your big ears." He looked over the others. "Isn't that so?"

They grinned assent.

It wasn't Nilsen's triumph. It was somebody else's.

Merely because they did grin.

Bertelli organized another party that night. For once his birthday was not the pretext. Somehow he'd managed to celebrate seven birthdays in four years without anyone seeing fit to count them all. But an excuse can be overdone, so he announced his candidacy for the post of captain, explaining that he wished to curry favor with voters. It was as good as any.

They cleared the galley as they'd done a score of times before. They broke a bottle of gin, shared it between them, sipped with introspective glumness. Aram did his party-piece by bird-calling between two fingers, received the usual polite applause. Marsden recited something about the brown eye of the little yellow dog. By that time Nilsen had warmed up sufficiently to sing two songs in a deep, rich bass. He gained louder applause for having varied his repertoire.

Weygarth, of course, wasn't there to do his sleight-of-hand tricks. Sanderson and Dawkins were also missing from the bill. Temporarily, their absence was forgotten as the tiny audience awaited the star turn.

Bertelli, of course. This was the sort of thing at which he excelled and the chief reason why a major nuisance had become tolerated, liked, perhaps loved.

When they'd held the alien landfall spree, he'd played an oboe for most of an hour, doing more things with the instrument than they had believed possible. He had ended with a sonic impression of an automobile collision, the agitated toot of horns, the crash, the heated argument between oboe-voiced drivers that finished with decidedly rude noises. Nilsen had almost rolled out of his seat.

On the way home, there had been a couple more whoopees arranged for no particular reason. Bertelli had mimed for these, his dental plates removed, his features rubbery, his arms like snakes. First the eager sailor leaping ashore and seeking feminine company. The search, the discovery, pursuit, encounter, rebuff, the persuasion, the going to a show, the strolling home, the pause on the doorstep rewarded with a black eye.

Another time he'd reversed the role, become a plump blonde followed by an eager sailor. Wordlessly, but with motions, gestures, posturings and facial expressions equal to if not better than speech, he had taken them on the night's prowl ending with the fight on the doorstep.

This time he pretended to be a bashful sculptor shaping a statue of Venus de Milo with invisible clay. Piling up a column of what wasn't there, he hesitantly stroked it, nervously patted it, embarrassedly smoothed it into near-visible form. He rolled two cannon-balls, plonked them on her chest while covering his eyes, rolled two pills and shyly put them on top, delicately molded them into shape.

It took him twenty hilarious minutes to make her almost, but not quite, complete, at which point he took idiotic alarm. He scanned the horizon, looked out the door, peered under the table to insure that they two were alone. Satisfied, yet full of embarrassment he made a faltering approach, withdrew, plucked up fresh courage, lost it again, had a spasm of daring that failed at the critical moment.

Vail offered pungent advice while Nilsen sprawled in the next seat and held an aching diaphragm. Summoning up everything he had in an effort to finish the job, Bertelli made a mad rush at it, fell over his own feet, slid on his face along the steel floor-plates. Nilsen made choking sounds. Stupidly enraged with himself, Bertelli shot to his feet, drew his bottom lip over the tip of his nose, waggled his bat-ears, closed his eyes, made one violent stab with a forefinger—and provided Venus with a navel.

For days afterward, they chuckled over that performance, making curvaceous motions with their hands or prodding each other in the paunch at odd moments. The ghostly Venus stayed good for a laugh until . . . the Sun came up.

Making another of his frequent checks late in the eighth day, Marsden found that one of the transparencies now coincided dot for dot with focal point two inches leftward of an enlarged pink glow. He let go a howl that brought the rest of the crew racing to the bow.

Sol was identified. They looked at it, licked lips over it, looked again. Four years in a bottle is like forty years in the star fields—and they had been bottled too long. One by one they visited Kinrade's cabin and exulted over the superstition on the wall.

THIRD TIME DOES IT!

Morale boosted way up. The ship's drumming and thrumming somehow lost its hellishness and took on a heartening note of urgency. Jangled nerves accepted the new and different strain of anticipation right to the glorious moment when a voice from Earth came feebly through the radio receiver. The voice strengthened day by day, week by week, until finally it bawled from the speaker while the fore observation-port was filled with half a planet.

"From where I'm standing, I can see an ocean of faces turned toward the sky," said the announcer. "There must be half a million people present, sharing the most eventful hour in history. At any moment now, folks, you will hear the distant drone of the first spaceship to return from another star. I just can't tell you how much—"

What followed the landing was the worst part. The blaring bands, the thunder of cheers. The handshakes, speeches, the posing for press photographers, newsreels, television scanners, the cameras of countless frantic amateurs.

It ended at last. Kinrade said farewell to his crew, felt the beartrap grip of Nilsen's hand, the soft, frank clasp of Aram, the shy, self-conscious touch of Bertelli.

Looking into the latter's mournful eyes, he said, "The authorities will now start howling for all the data we've got. I suppose you've finished your book."

"What book?"

"Now, now, don't kid me." He offered a knowing wink.

"You're the official psychologist, aren't you?"

He didn't wait for an answer. While the others busied themselves collecting personal belongings, he got the log and the file of reports, took them to the Administration Building.

Looking no different for the passage of time, Bancroft sat paunchily behind his desk, said with satirical satisfaction, "You are now looking at a fat man wallowing in the joys of promotion and higher salary."

"Congratulations." Kinrade dumped the books and sat down.

"I would swap both for youth and adventure." Casting an anticipatory glance at what the other had brought, Bancroft went on, "There are questions I'm bursting to ask. But the answers are hidden somewhere in that pile and I guess you're in a hurry to go home."

"A 'copter will pick me up when it can get through the overcrowded air. I have twenty minutes to spare."

"In that case I'll use them." Bancroft leaned forward, eyes intent. "What about the first two ships?"

"We searched seven planets. Not a sign."

"They hadn't landed or crashed?"

"No."

"So they must have gone on?"

"Evidently."

"Any idea why?"

Kinrade hesitated, said, "It's a hunch and nothing more. I think their numbers were reduced by accident, sickness or whatever. They became too few to retain control of the ship." He paused, added, "We lost three men ourselves."

"Tough luck." Bancroft looked unhappy. "Who were they?"

"Weygarth, Dawkins and Sanderson. The first died on the way out. He never saw the new sun, much less his own. The story is there." He gestured toward the reports. "The other two were killed on the fourth planet, which I've established as unsafe for human habitation."

"What's wrong with it?"

"A big and hungry life-form exists under the surface, sitting with traps held open beneath a six-inch crust of soil. Sanderson walked around, fell into a red, sloppy mouth four feet wide by ten long. He was gulped from sight. Dawkins rushed to his rescue, but dropped into another." His fingers fumbled with each other as he finished, "There was nothing we could do, not a damned thing."

"A pity, a great pity." Bancroft shook his head slowly from side to side. "How about the other planets?"

"Four are useless. Two are made to measure for us."

"Hah, that's something!" He glanced at the small clock on his desk, continued hurriedly. "And now the ship. Doubtless your reports are full of criticisms. Nothing is perfect, not even the best we've produced. What do you consider its most outstanding fault?"

"The noise. It could drive you out of your mind. It needs cutting out."

"Not completely," Bancroft contradicted. "There is psychic terror in absolute silence."

"All right. Then it needs cutting down to more endurable level. Try it yourself for a week and see how you like it."

"I wouldn't. The problem is being beaten, although slowly. We have a new and quieter type of engine already on the test-bench. Four years' progress, you know."

"We need it," said Kinrade.

Bancroft went on, "And what do you think of the crew?"

"Best ever."

"They ought to be. We skimmed the world for the cream —nothing less was good enough. Each man was tops in his own particular line."

"Including Bertelli?"

"I knew you'd ask about him." Bancroft smiled as if at a secret thought. "You want me to explain him, eh?"

"I've no right to insist, but I'd certainly like to know why you included such a dead weight."

"We lost two ships," said Bancroft, looking serious. "One could be an accident. Two were not. It's hard to believe that an exceptional kind of breakdown or a collision with a lump of rock or some other million-to-one chance would occur twice running."

"I don't believe it myself."

"We spent years studying the problem," Bancroft continued. "Every time we got the same answer: it wasn't due to any defect in the vessels. The cause lay somewhere in the human element. Short of a four-year test on living men, we could do no more than speculate. Then one day the likely solution popped up by sheer chance."

"How?"

"We were in this very room, beating our brains for the hundredth or two-hundredth time, when that clock stopped." He indicated the timepiece facing him. "A fellow named Whittaker from the Space Medicine Research Station wound it up, shook it, got it going. Immediately afterward a brainwave hit him, kerplonk!"

Picking up the clock, Bancroft opened its back, turned it toward his listener.

"What do you see?"

"Cogs and wheels."

"Nothing else?"

"Couple of coiled springs."

"Are you sure that is all?"

"All that matters," declared Kinrade, having no doubt.

"Wrong, dead wrong," said Bancroft, positively, "You have made precisely the mistake we made with ships number one and two. We built giant metal clocks, fitted them with human cogs and wheels accurately designed for their purpose. Cogs and wheels of flesh and blood, chosen with the same care as one would choose parts for a fine watch. But the clocks stopped. We had overlooked something that Whittaker suddenly thought of."

"Well, what was it?"

Bancroft smiled and said, "A little oil."

"Oil?" exclaimed Kinrade, sitting up.

"Our error was natural. In a technological age, we technicians tend to think we're the whole cheese. We aren't. Maybe we're a very considerable slice, but we are not the lot. Civilization is composed of others also, the housewife, the taxi driver, the dime store salesgirl, the postman, the hospital nurse, the corner cop. It would be a hell of a civilization built solely on boys pushing studs of computor-machines and without the butcher, the baker, the candlestick-maker. That's a lesson some of us needed to learn."

"You've got something," Kinrade agreed, "but I dont know what."

"We had another problem in our laps," said Bancroft. "What sort of oil must you use for human cogs and wheels? Answer: human oil. What kind of individual specializes in being oil?"

"And you dug up Bertelli?"

"We did. His family has been oil for twenty generations. He is the present holder of a great tradition—and internationally famous."

"Never heard of him. I suppose he traveled with us under a false name?"

"He went under his own."

"I didn't recognize him," Kinrade persisted. "Neither did anyone else. So how can he be famous? Or did he have his face altered by plastic surgery?"

"He changed it completely in one minute flat." Getting up, Bancroft lumbered to a filing cabinet, opened it, sought through several folders. Extracting a full-plate glossy photograph, he slid it across the desk. "All he did to his face was wash it."

Picking up the picture, Kinrade stared at the chalk-white features, the cone-shaped hat set rakishly on a high, false skull, the huge eyebrows arched in perpetual surprise, the red diamonds painted around the mournful eyes, the grotesque, bulbous nose, the crimson ear-to-ear mouth, the thick ruff of lace around the neck.

"Coco!"

"The twentieth Coco with which this world has been blessed," Bancroft confirmed.

Kinrade had another long look. "May I keep this?"

"Certainly. I can get a thousand more copies any time I want."

Kinrade emerged from the Administration Building just in time to see the subject of his thoughts in hot pursuit of a ground-taxi.

With a shapeless and hurriedly packed bag swinging wildly from one hand, Bertelli went along in exaggerated, loose-jointed bounds with big boots rising waist-high, while his long neck protruded forward and his face bore a ludicrous expression of woe.

Many a time the onlooker had been puzzled by the fleeting familiarity of one of Bertelli's poses or gestures. Now, knowing what he did know, he recognized instantly the circus jester's classic anxiety-gallop across a sawdust ring. To make it complete, Bertelli should have been casting frightened glances over one shoulder at a floating skeleton attached to him by a long cord.

Bertelli caught up with the taxi, bestowed an inane smile, slung his bag inside and clambered after it. The taxi whirled away with twin spurts of vapor from its underbody jets.

For a long minute, Kinrade stood looking absently at the poised spaceships and the sky. His mind was viewing the world as a gigantic stage on which every man, woman and child played a wonderful and necessary part.

And holding the whole show together with laughter, exaggerating temper and hostility and conflict into absurdity, was the clown.

If he'd had to assemble the crew, he couldn't have picked a better psychologist than Bertelli.

Rainbow's End

THE TRAP WAS ANYTHING BUT APPARENT. IT WAITED with an air of complete innocence. Victims walked into it confidently, willingly, even eagerly—and never knew what hit them.

About the confidence, willingness and eagerness of the four-man crew of scout-vessel 87D there could be no doubt whatever. They made it obvious with the way they came down. Out of a clear blue sky they swooped in their golden vessel with a crimson trim along its sides and its number writ large upon its pointed prow. Thunder poured from its tail in rhythmic bursts of sound so violent that leaves quivered on trees for miles around and birds were shocked to silence.

With aggressive self-assurance they dumped the ship on a grassy flat and scrambled out while yet the noise of their arrival continued to echo and re-echo over hills and dales. They made a tough, space-hardened group outside the main port, greeting fresh air and solid earth with the grim satisfaction of those who have been without either for far too long.

Reed Wingrove, the astrogator, said gleefully, "Gee whiz! What a sweet little lump of plasma. They should make us space-commodores for discovering this one." He was young, tall, fresh-featured and nursed the hope that he might be suitable material for big brass.

"More likely they'll toss us in the clink," thought Jacques Drouillard, his black eyes taking in the surrounding scene. "We've overshot official limits by a slice of a lifetime. We had no right to come so far. They'll have written us off for dead by the time we get back."

"Or as deserters," suggested Bill Maguire.

"I take all responsibility for where we go or do not go,"

reminded Captain Walter Searle. A big, slow-speaking man, he spent much time with his thoughts.

"Jacques can hear the awful sound of the years rushing past," Bill Maguire explained. There was a good-natured grin on his freckled Irish pan as he eyed the contrastingly swarthy Drouillard. "He never forgets that time and fair ladies wait for no doddering space-jerk."

"Maybe he's got something there," put in Reed Wingrove sobering a lot. He pointed southward. "There's uranium under those hills. The frenzied way the counters clicked as we shot over them suggests that they're solid with the stuff. It might be the strike of the century, right where it's most needed, just beyond the exploratory rim. It's to be had for the taking, no price asked." He looked them over, added, "That is to say, no price other than the best years of our lives."

Maguire met him eye for eye and said, "We've been shaken up together in a hot and noisy bottle for months and months and months. We're due for an equally long dose of the same medicine before we get back. Isn't that all the more reason for being happy now?" Smoothing his red hair, he sniffed appreciatively at the atmosphere, worked his boots around in the long, soft grass. "C'mon, let's get rid of the space-heebies and enjoy life between the spells of misery."

"What makes you think you suffer?" asked Captain Searle, looking at each in turn. "You signed on for ten years, with your eyes wide open."

"I got kidded by all that stuff about celestial Callisto," grumbled Drouillard. "Thought I'd get about twenty jaunts there and back. I didn't bargain for spending most of my term on one long trip. Thirty months to get here, thirty to return, plus the twelve we'll have to stay put while waiting for favorable planetary setups. That makes six years at one go. Six years is a heck of a long time." He rubbed his blue chin, making rasping sounds. "Too much to give for a hunk of uranium, large or small."

"*If* we can give it," said Maguire. "It may belong to somebody else who doesn't want to sell." He gestured to one side, added, "I'm inclined to think so because here comes somebody else!"

Leaning against the rim of a warm propulsion tube, he

eased his gun in its holster, chewed a juicy stem of grass, and watched the newcomer's approach.

The others reacted similarly, holding themselves prepared, but not alarmed. There was nothing frightening about the appearance of this world's highest life-form. Besides, they had complete confidence in their own power, an assurance born of human settlement of many scores of worlds, some hostile, some merely eerie. And, of course, they were blissfully unaware of the trap.

The arrival was a half-pint humanoid, a fact that surprised them not at all. Grabbing the cosmos brings a sudden surfeit of surprises, after which one loses the capacity for amazement. One learns to expect anything, even a midget mock-up of oneself, and remains phlegmatic. So no eyebrows were lifted as this world's first representative came near.

He got right up to them, displaying no fear, but examining them with a certain childish naivete. Small, no more than three feet in height, he had perky, birdlike features and sharp, quickly darting eyes. A cone-shaped felt hat of vivid crimson sat on his head and was pulled so far down that it made his pointed ears stick out. His clothes were an equally vivid green with silver trimmings. His long, narrow, green shoes bore silver buttons. His only weapon was a gnarly stick upon which he leaned while he surveyed them with brilliant and beady optics.

"They're tiny," murmured Wingrove to the others. "We could have guessed it from that toy-town we spotted just before we dived." Offering the dwarf an ingratiating smile, he pointed to himself and said, "Reed Wingrove."

Giving him a quick, piercing glance, the other made no response. They broke the embarrassing silence by introducing themselves one by one. Motionless except for his continually shifting orbs, the dwarf leaned on his stick and ruminated.

After a while he said, "Rifkin," in a small, reedy voice.

"He *can* speak, anyway," commented Drouillard. "That is something! We won't have to go double-jointed trying to make sign-talk. It's mighty tiring playing snake-arms. Now we can learn his language or teach him ours."

"I fail to see," said Rifkin, in perfect English, "why that should be necessary."

The effect was electric. Space-born phlegmaticism got

thrown to the winds. Drouillard jumped a foot. Captain Searle pulled his gun, shoved it back, scowled around in search of the suspected ventriloquist. Maguire hastily unleaned from the propulsion tube, carelessly braced himself on the hotter part, farther back, burned his hand and yelped with pain.

Taking a firm grip on himself, Wingrove asked, "You understand our mode of talk?"

"Of course," said Rifkin, with disarming casualness. He used his gnarly stick to behead something like a daisy.

"How the deuce—?" began Captain Searle, still watching the others for suspicious mouth-movements.

Ignoring his commander, Wingrove went determinedly on. "Is English spoken here?"

"How silly!" remarked Rifkin.

There didn't seem to be a satisfactory retort to that one. It was too obvious for adverse comment. In fact "silly" was an understatement—it was downright ridiculous.

Wingrove sought around for another angle, said, "Then how do you know it?"

"I can *fahn* it," informed Rifkin, much as one would mention the obvious to a child. "Surely you know that? How can people communicate if they cannot *fahn* one another's speech-patterns?"

"*Morbleau!*" Drouillard ejaculated. He stared around suspiciously, in unconscious imitation of Searle. "*A chaque saint sa chandelle!*"

"*Si chacun tire de son cote!*" agreed Rifkin with devastating impartiality.

Drouillard pulled out lumps of hair, then squatted on his heels and began to eat grass. He appeared to be working off something in the way of feelings. With mounting irritation, Captain Searle watched him for a while, then couldn't stand it any longer.

"Stop . . . *doing* . . . THAT!" he bawled, with pauses for emphasis. He nudged the other with a heavy boot. As Drouillard came erect, Searle demanded, "Now, what was all that double-talk you just pulled?"

"French," said Drouillard dreamily. "They speak it where I come from, in Canada." He bleared at the dwarf. "And *he* knows it!"

"How can I possibly *know* it?" Rifkin contradicted. "One cannot *know* what has never been learned!" He made a sniff of disgust. "I *fahned* it."

"I'll take you up on that," Searle snapped back at him. "How do you *fahn* it?"

"There is a prize question," decided Rifkin, twitching his pointed ears. "A veritable conundrum because if you do not know the answer, it is evident that you cannot *fahn* a speech-pattern yourselves."

"Would I ask, if I could?" inquired Searle.

"And if you cannot do it yourself," Rifkin went on, "there is no way in which I can explain it to you." His piercing little eyes met Searle's. "Could you make an earless stone appreciate your playing on a flute?"

"No," Searle admitted.

"Well, then, there you are!" Rifkin leaned his slight weight on his crooked stick. "I doubt whether Mab herself could explain it. Or Morgaine either, for that matter. You have asked me the impossible."

"Let's leave it at that and consider ourselves lucky," Wingrove suggested to the dissatisfied Searle. "Here we are, landed undamaged, and in communication with the inhabitants, all within one hour. I bet we've busted a record."

"Leave this to me," Searle ordered. He turned to Rifkin. "We are anxious to learn as much as possible about this world of yours and—"

"Why?" asked Rifkin.

Was there shrewd understanding in those sharp little eyes? A sparkle of cynicism, a depth of guile? No way of telling.

Searle went patiently on, "Mutual understanding is the basis of friendship which is essential if we are to maintain contact to our common profit." He waited for an effect that did not prove visible. "Now if one of my men could pay a courtesy call to your nearest town—"

"He will be quite welcome," assured Rifkin. As an afterthought, he added, "In Ballygullion."

"*Where?*" screamed Maguire, his red hair standing up like a brush.

"Ballygullion," repeated Rifkin.

"What's wrong with that?" demanded Searle, staring hard

at Maguire.

Pop-eyed, Maguire said, "Jeepers, that's where I was born!"

"Natch!" observed Rifkin, airily treating the incomprehensible as obvious.

Bunching his hands until the knuckles were white, Searle said to Rifkin, "Why the natch? How can he have been born here? This planet was completely unknown to us before our arrival." He let a puzzled and wary gaze run over the general scene. "There is something decidedly off-the-orbit about this place."

"The town has any name one cares to give it," Rifkin explained, again in the manner of tutoring a kindergarten. "Some call it this, some call it that. It can have one name today, another name tomorrow. I can recall a rare occasion when three persons referred to it by the same name for a whole week, they being lazy-minded."

"Pinch me awake," Drouillard requested, offering an arm to Wingrove.

"What does it matter?" Rifkin asked. "One can easily *fahn* the name given to it by any person at any moment."

"So now, being Wednesday, it is Ballygullion?" Maguire asked weakly.

"If you like the name. You ought to like it. I *fahned* it when I looked at you and knew it should please you."

"That settles it," snapped Searle. He gave Maguire the cold, authoritative eye. "Somebody's got to stick out his neck and get us the dirt. Who could be better than a native by birth? I accept your offer to go."

"Who?" said Maguire, dazed. *"Me?"*

They all chorused, "You!"

Rifkin's eyes glittered as he took him away.

It was ten days before Bill Maguire returned to find the crew preparing themselves for action. Struggling in through the main port, he breathed heavily, stared down at the ladder up which he had climbed.

"Who's been stretching the stairs?"

Putting down the gun which he had just oiled, Captain Searle glowered at him. "You're in the nick of time. We were about to set out and pull that midget burg apart until we found either you or your body."

"Didn't know I was so much appreciated," said Maguire.

"One man is a quarter of my crew," Searle went on, remaining severe. "I don't lose a man without making someone pay. What the heck detained you?"

"Wine, women and song," informed Maguire blissfully.

"Huh?" Reed Wingrove dropped what he was doing.

"Eh?" Drouillard stood up, snapped his fingers. He had the expression of one who wasn't there when the manna fell.

"Sit down!" rapped Searle. He returned his attention to the impenitent prodigal. His voice was slightly acid. "I don't suppose the real purpose of our mission ever crossed your mind?"

"Not while I could help it," Maguire agreed, displaying complete lack of shame. "Who'd bother about new frontiers, territorial developments or mineral deposits while roaming around with Mab?" Pursing his lips, he gave a low, ecstatic whistle. "She is tall, dark-eyed, sylphlike and gives me fizzy feelings all over. She makes me want to stay here for keeps."

"What have they been pouring down your neck?" inquired Captain Searle, studying him closely.

"Stuff called mead. It's made with honey, herbs and dew fresh off the grass. It's the most wonderful—"

"There can't be honey without bees," Wingrove chipped in. "Are you trying to kid us there are bees here too, same as on Earth?"

"Millions of them," declared Maguire. "Herds and herds of them. Big, fat, busy ones, all as tame as farmhouse cats. The local folk talk to them and the bees talk back. They can *fahn* each other, see?"

"I don't see," said Searle, motioning Wingrove into silence. "Neither do I care." His gaze was still penetrating as he kept it on Maguire. "Who is this Mab who has watered down the goo you use for brains?"

"One of Rifkin's twin daughters." Plainly, Maguire was too bemused to take umbrage. "The best of two pips. The other one is Peg, and she's something too! If it weren't for my civilized upbringing I could—"

"Oh, no you couldn't. One is too much for you, let alone

two." Searle scowled at the metal bulkhead and muttered to nobody in particular. "Looks like we blundered when we picked this red-headed romantic. Now what?"

"Let me go," suggested Drouillard, eagerly. His dark eyes were aflame with the zeal of a man offered a grab at lost opportunities.

Maguire bridled at him. "Lay off, Casanova. *You're* not taking the girls back home." Defiantly, he leaned on the rim of a desk, then frowned in puzzlement and bent over to scan the floor. "Who's been raising the furniture? Couldn't you find anything better to do?"

"Nobody's touched that desk," Wingrove told him. "It seems bigger because you are shorter. I noticed you looked slightly trimmed down the moment you came back. Reckon you've worn two inches off your heels in hot pursuit of everything but what you came here for."

"Nothing wrong with my heels," denied Maguire, raising a leg to examine his boot. "This desk has been upped an inch or two."

"Sober yourself," Wingrove retorted. "You overdid the mead stuff. You didn't have to be greedy."

Searle chipped in with impatience. "Quit arguing." He regarded Maguire with authorative disapproval. "What was that you said about taking these females *back?*"

"They came along with me, just for the jaunt. I left them outside. Told them I wouldn't be long."

"Holy smoke!" Drouillard made for the lock, moving fast to beat the others and get out before Searle could think up a contrary command.

They heard him scramble hurriedly down the ladder. There came a brief chatter during which his deep tones underlay a pair of tinkling voices like little bells. More ladder noises. Drouillard reappeared, conducting his visitors with unwarranted proprietorship.

"Here they are, Cap." He had the excitement of one suddenly endowed with a new interest in life.

Searle looked them over slowly, methodically and with much of the suspicion of an elephant testing a pitfall. They were a pair of ash-blondes, curvaceous, tiny, and as alike as mirror-images of each other. He estimated their height as no more than thirty inches. Both wore crimson caps and bright green clothes trimmed with silver. Holding hands as they posed side by side, they regarded him with tip-tilted eyes, large, blue and guileless. There was a peculiar quality about those eyes and he had to think a while before he found a word to describe it: elfin.

"Which is Mab?" he inquired.

"Me." The one on the left dimpled at him.

Leaning back on his chair, Searle sighed and said to Maguire, "So she is tall and dark-eyed?"

"Well, isn't she?" Maguire pointed at the evidence, indicating the incontrovertible.

They all had another look at Mab, a long, careful look. Manifestly she was blue-eyed and very small. Her dimples deepened.

After a while, Searle uttered an emphatic, "No!"

"All right," said Maguire. "Either you're blind or I'm nuts."

Mab laughed in tiny tinkling tones.

"He's nuts," opined Drouillard. "Space-happy and gone to seed." His own gaze nailed itself firmly on Peg. "But I don't blame him. I could go a bit nuts myself for that green-eyed one with the long chestnut locks." His gaze grew bold and ardent. "She resembles my dream girl."

Nudging him, Reed Wingrove asked, *"Which* one with the long chestnut locks?"

"Use your peepers," invited Drouillard, continuing to devour the object of his attention.

"I'm using mine," interjected Maguire. "Peg is a blue-eyed blonde."

"G'wan," Drouillard scoffed. "You can't look straight even at your own choice."

Captain Searle breathed deeply, reclaimed his gun, hefted it in his hand to feel its weight and balance. When he spoke it was with the ponderous deliberation of one whose mind is made up.

"Reed, show those two girls the way out. Close the lock behind them and keep it closed." The gun came up as Maguire and Drouillard tensed. "Not you two goofies. Neither of you. You're staying put. That's an order!" As Maguire backed away from him and got nearer to the lock, he added in tight tones, "Be careful, Bill. So help me, if you don't obey I'll let you have it!"

"But you cannot," contradicted Mab in her small, chiming voice. "I have *fahned* that in the last resort you could not bring yourself to do it."

Still holding Peg's midget hand, she exited through the lock, drifting out light-footed, with short, dainty steps. Maguire followed, like a sleepwalker. So did Drouillard.

Silently, introspectively, Reed Wingrove closed the lock behind them. He returned to his place, his tread clanging loudly through the ship's plates. There was a faint, sweet scent in the air, an odor of femininity, beckoning, inviting. Captain Searle had not moved. He was sitting at the table, his unused weapon still in his grip, his eyes staring bleakly at the wall.

The minutes crawled by until Wingrove said, "Did you notice that curious design upon their silver buttons? It was on Rifkin's, too. Like four hearts arranged in a circle with their points brought together. It looked sort of familiar to me, but I'm darned if I can place it."

Searle made no reply. He continued to look blankly at the wall while his mind mulled over the situation.

Three weeks crawled by with no sign of the absentees. Wingrove returned from one of his short walks which had become his habit of late, sat himself on the grass beside the grimly brooding Searle, and enjoyed the cool of the ship's shadow.

"How about letting me visit the town, Captain? I might find something."

"No."

"Why not go yourself, then?"

"No."

"Oh, well." Wingrove lay back, shaded his eyes as he studied the bright sky. "Still stewing the problem?"

"Yes." Searle chewed at his bottom lip. "I have examined it from every conceivable angle and it always gets me the same place—here, for keeps. We can handle the ship with its official minimum of four men; at a pinch, we might be able to manage with three. We can't take it home with two—it's impossible."

"Yes, I know."

"So we're stuck with this planet until one or both of those moon-struck loons sees fit to return."

"We could be pinned down someplace worse," ventured Wingrove, indicating the azure sky, the lush landscape. "The longer I'm here the more homey it looks." Twisting on one side, he plucked a flower, held it out for the other's inspection. "Look—a bluebonnet."

"What of it?" Searle gave it no more than a cursory glance.

"There are bluebonnets way back on Earth."

"Don't remind me,' said Searle, ruefully.

"And there are daisies and buttercups and wild mint. I found them all while mooching around the hills." He gave a short, peculiar laugh. "Fancy a hardened space-jerk taking an interest in daisies and buttercups. Shows how you get after too much of it."

"Too much of what?" asked Searle, frowning at him.

"There was a bird trilling at me by the waterfall," mused Wingrove, ignoring the question. "It had a wonderful song. I found it after a while. It was a bulbul, a thing like a thrush. They're on Earth too, in Persia, I think. Queer, isn't it?"

"Similar conditions might produce similar effects, similar results."

"Maybe," Wingrove conceded. "But I've a feeling that's not the whole story. The similarities are too numerous. Somewhere there's another and better explanation of so many coincidences." He pondered awhile, gnawing a grass-stem, then went on, "I noticed that four-heart sign again today, inscribed in various places, on walls and trees and rocks. Reckon it's some sort of tribal totem. Every time I see it I know it's familiar—but can't place it. Wish I could remember."

"You didn't go anywhere near the town?"

"No, Cap. I kept away, like you said."

"Didn't meet anyone, either?"

"That four-heart thing is a puzzle," said Wingrove, biting the stem. "It's got me worried."

"You didn't meet anyone?" Searle persisted.

"Dozens of times I've seen those four hearts on Earth, but can't pull out of my mind exactly—"

Searle stood up, legs braced apart, and looked at him from beneath heavy brows. "Come on out with it! Let's have no more evasions. You've loped off morning and afternoon for more than a week. You've gone with a gleam in your eyes and come back like a zombie. *Who are you meeting?*"

"Melusine," Wingrove said reluctantly. He sat up, threw away the grass stalk.

"Ah!" Searle screwed his right fist into the palm of his left hand. "Another of these midget charmers?"

"She's charming, but no midget."

"That's what *you* think!" said Searle, bitterly. He paced to and fro. "All this, after I'd warned you. I've told you time and time again of the powers they possess, powers we haven't got and don't properly understand."

Wingrove said nothing.

Ceasing his restless parading, Searle faced him and went on, "You know quite well what this Melusine is doing to you. She is extracting a picture ideal from your innermost mind, focussing it upon herself, fooling your senses, making herself appear the solid, fleshy creation of your own dreams and desires. It's a combination of telepathy and hypnotism, or something akin to both. It's a psychological weapon, a redoubtable one, a formidable one, because it exploits the weakest chink in anyone's armor. It persuades a man to make a fool of himself for the only reason he is willing to become a fool. It is damnable!"

"It is wonderful," said Wingrove, eyeing the sky.

"Are you going to desert me, like the others?"

"Not yet." Wingrove came erect. He picked up the blue-bonnet, twiddled it idly between his fingers. "I'm being pulled two ways. Maybe I'm more stubborn than Bill and Jacques, or better disciplined, or less susceptible. Or maybe Melusine is slower, more gentle, and in no hurry to take me." His eyes met Searle's for the briefest moment. "I don't think she would like you to be left all alone."

"That's mighty white of her," said Searle sarcastically. "Especially since she's no guarantee that sooner or later I might not devise a way of boosting off by myself."

"You could never do that."

"I know it, and so do you. But she doesn't. These folk

want to let their world travel incognito by shutting the traps of everyone who finds it. They've a neat play. No bombs, no bullets, no bloodshed. All they need do is offer a guy his heart's desire—and shut him up by pressure of a woman's lips."

"Ah!" sighed Wingrove. "What a beautiful fate."

"Its not funny," snapped Searle, openly irritated. "It's serious. It's effective sabotage of Earth's plans. You know what is happening and why it is happening. You know you are being grossly deceived—and yet this Melusine still appeals to you?"

"And how!"

"Knowing all the time that she is not exactly as you see her? That what you do see is reflected cunningly from the depths of your own mind?"

"It makes no difference. I can only go by how she looks. There's no other basis for judgment. She looks to me like the epitome of all I've ever wanted, even in her most insignificant habits, her smallest gestures and mannerisms. She couldn't suit me better if specially made to my specification."

"You dumb monkey!" said Searle. "She *is* specially made to your specification."

"I know." Unexpectedly, Wingrove hit back. "Could *you* want anything better than what you want the most?"

"Leave me out of this," Searle countered. "You're the lovesick gump, not me." He resumed his pacing. "By hokey, they are even stronger than I'd thought, cleverer, more cunning, more expert."

"You don't know the half of it," Wingrove assured. "You should try a taste for yourself. Melusine has a friend named Nivetta whom she could bring along to meet you and—"

"So that's why she's been slow and gentle," rasped Searle. "That's why she's let you stick around a bit. She wants both birds! Not just you, but you and me! She'll be content when there's nothing here but an empty ship, rotting like a skeleton under the sun."

"Oh, I don't know, Cap. We're planted for twelve months anyway. After a while, persuasion might work the other way and we can take them—"

"You'll never get them back to Earth," declared Searle, positively. "Nor see it yourself, either. Not ever again." He went closer, speaking earnestly. "Look, Reed, we've found a bonanza loaded with uranium. Discovering such items is our job for which we are equipped and paid. Reporting such a discovery to Earth is our bounden duty. If we fail, if we lose ourselves and never turn up, it may be anything from fifty to five hundred years before another Earth ship rediscovers the place. You realize all that?"

"You bet I do."

"Then you will also realize that since these half-pints can *fahn* our speech-patterns—whatever that may mean—and discern our mind-pictures, they can also detect our purposes, our motives. If they don't approve of them, as well they may not, their best move is to destroy us or, at least, prevent our return. A ship is of no use without its crew. They have only to take away the crew—and the ship becomes a lump of junk corroding somewhere in the cosmos. It rots away and Earth's schemes go with it."

"Better for the ship to rot rather than its crew," contributed a voice.

Searle whirled around on one heel.

It was Maguire, red-capped, green-clothed and slightly over four feet high.

There were a dozen shorties with Maguire, some male, some female. Searle recognized Rifkin standing at one side of the group, also Mab clinging possessively to Maguire's arm. The entire bunch now came almost up to Maguire's shoulders instead of a little above his waist as formerly.

Two liquid-eyed creatures on the left went toward Wingrove, moving with the sprightly grace of ballet dancers. One put her tiny hand in his huge paw.

"Melusine," said Wingrove, looking at Searle.

Searle took no notice. Edging closer to the ship's airlock, he spoke to Maguire. "You've shrunk. You're still shrinking. You're going down into your boots."

"I know it," said Maguire. "This world does things to you if you aren't shielded by metal most of the time." He shrugged his indifference. "Do I care? I do not! I'm being reduced to proper size instead of staying big and ugly. So is Jacques. So is Reed. So are you as long as you hang around outside the ship."

Putting a careful foot on the bottom rung of the ladder, Searle readied himself for a quick move.

"I'm having fun while I'm young enough to enjoy it," Maguire went on. "It's doing me good and it's doing nobody else any harm, so I'm going to keep on having it. Just for a start I've become engaged to Mab."

"Congratulations," said Searle, sardonically. His mind busied itself with the question of whether he could take Maguire in one swift snatch, toss him headlong through the lock and into the ship. Also whether he could trust Wingrove to follow of his own accord. Three would be enough to get the boat home. The missing Drouillard could be dug up by some later vessel and frogmarched out of the mess. His big hand tightened on an upper rung.

"He schemes to grab you!" warned Rifkin.

Maguire grinned and asked Searle, "What's the use of plotting when they can *fahn* you all the time?"

Relaxing his grip, Searle growled, "What have you come for?" He kept his attention on Maguire, avoided looking at the others.

"Jacques has got engaged too. So we're having a celebration. Having celebrations is a frequent amusement here. We want you along."

"Why?"

"Why not? No sense in you squatting in the ship holding communion with yourself while everyone else is swimming in joy. What good will that do you? Come on, Cap, we want you along, so how about—?"

"I want you two along," Searle interjected. "And you'd better come fast. I can still be persuaded not to make entries in the log that'll cause both of you to be shot out of the service—but my patience is running dry."

"Now there's a real threat," Maguire scoffed. "I can be drummed out of the ranks. The mere thought of it grieves me. It will grieve Jacques as much—or as little. He's planning to marry Peg and run a little joint called Cookery Nook. We're going to eat fresh food instead of powdered proteins and vitamin pills. We're going to drink mead instead of distilled water. We're going to sing songs and forget all about scout vessel 87D." His eyes slid sidewise at Wingrove. "So will Reed before long, if he knows what's good for him." The eyes returned to Searle. "Give up the fight, Cap, and be a willing loser."

"You can go to blue blazes!" declared Searle.

A dozen pair of sharp, shiny little eyes went over him before they took him at his word and went away. Sitting on the bottom rung of the ladder, elbows on knees, his head between his hands, he stared fixedly at the grass between his feet and the fading bluebonnet to one side.

Maguire went, and Mab, and Rifkin and the rest. He knew that Wingrove also had gone, with Melusine and her companion. He was alone, terribly alone. With the useless bulk of 87D behind him, he sat there unmoving, a long, long time.

He spent the next twenty-two days in his own company with his dessicated foods, his distilled water and utter silence. He spent most of this time entering the ship's log, mooching around a small radius, meditating bitterly, and playing with a friendly bronze beetle that could neither hear nor speak.

By the twenty-second day he was fed up. He sat in precisely the same position as they had left him many days before, on the bottom rung of the ladder, elbows on knees, head between hands. Even the beetle had gone on some mysterious errand of its own.

A slight rustling in the grass. His eyes raised a fraction, saw pointed green shoes with silver buttons. They were tiny and dainty.

"Beat it!" His voice was hoarse.

"Look at me."

"Go away!"

"Look at me." Her tones did not have the bell like tinkling quality of the other's voices. She spoke softly and tenderly, in a way he had heard before.

"Go away, I tell you."

"You are not afraid of me . . . Walter?"

He shivered as memories flooded upon him. Unwillingly, reluctantly, his eyes came up. His vision became fixed on her tiny figure, her tiny, bright-eyed face, and saw neither as they really were. He saw a honey-blonde, brown-eyed with full, generous lips. He arose slowly, his gaze still locked upon hers. Perspiration was shining on his forehead. His hands were bunched as he held them close at his sides.

"Betty died in a Moon-ship crash. I knew you would look like her . . . exactly like her . . . you witch!" He swallowed hard, trying to let his brain retain command over his eyes. It was not easy. "But I know you are not Betty. You cannot be."

"Of course you know." She moved nearer, slim-thighed, slim-hipped, even her walk characteristic of the walk he once had known. "I am Nivetta—today. But tomorrow my name can be another." Her hand went up to tuck a dark gold curl behind her ear, an old familiar gesture that did things to him. "If I am the picture you retain, the memory you treasure, am I not indeed both the memory and the picture? For always? Am I not . . . Betty?"

He put his hand over his eyes to shut out the sight of her. But then her scent reached him, the scent he knew. His words came out in a flood.

"I did not tell Wingrove. I hoped he would discover it for himself and thus confirm my own ideas. I wandered around a little while he was going on his own walks, and one day I found a dolmen, a great stone fairy-table. The four hearts engraved upon it still showed a stalk from their center. I could see at a glance that it was a four-leafed clover."

Her odor was strong now, and close to him. He was talking like a man fighting for time.

"Then I remembered that Mab and Peg are favored names among your kind, and that Morgaine was better known as Morgan le Fay. I remembered it is legendary among us that in the far-off, almost forgotten times your people went away because they were resented, not wanted. They went away, taking with them the seeds of their herbs, fruits and flowers, their incomprehensible arts, their misunderstood sciences which many still call magic. They went in some strange manner of their own, looking for another friendlier world resembling the one they knew of old, seeking the rainbow's end."

She did not speak as he finished, but there was a butterfly touch upon his hairy hand. Her forefinger linked with his thumb. It was an entirely personal gesture which only he and *she* had known. It was, it must be—Betty!

A rush of nostalgic feeling overcame him. He gave himself up to it because surrender was easier than resistance and more satisfying. His loneliness finished, his solitude ended, he looked straight into her eyes and saw only the eyes so well remembered.

Together they walked through the fields and the flowers,

away from the ship, away from that far distant world of forgotten things.

* * *

About the self-confidence and bumptiousness of the four-man crew of scout vessel 114K there could be no doubt at all. Tumbling hurriedly out of the lock, they sniffed the fresh air, patted the good earth, celebrated their successful landing with raucous shouts and some horseplay.

Two of them found a crumbling pile of metal, vaguely cylindrical in outline, a few hundred yards to the north. They investigated it with no more than perfunctory interest, kicked some of its shapeless, powdery pieces, went leap-frogging back to their ship.

"Man, are we lucky!" exulted Gustav Berners, a big Swede, speaking to Captain James Hayward. He chuckled deep down in his chest as he watched the other two members of the crew indulging in an impromptu wrestling match. "When that space storm tossed us umpteen months beyond the limits of exploration, I thought we were goners. Who'd have guessed we'd fall right into the lap of a world like this? Just like home. I feel at home already."

"Home," echoed Hayward. "The sweetest word in any space-jerk's life."

"Enough uranium to last a million years," Berners went on. "Coming over that hill the counters jiggled like we were already worth a million credits apiece. And it's to be had for the taking. No bullheaded aborigines to fight for it."

Hayward said, "Don't go by first appearances."

"Here's a first appearance," announced one of the wrestling pair, ceasing to maul his buddy.

Excitedly they clustered around the gnome-like figure which had come upon the scene, taking in his human shape, tiny stature, crimson cap, green clothes and silver trimmings.

"They're small," commented Hayward. "Semi-civilized pygmies. I guessed as much from that toytown we glimpsed just before we made our bump." Offering the gnome a cordial smile, he pointed to himself and said, "James Hayward."

Giving him a quick, darting glance, the other made no reply. They filled in the silence by introducing themselves one by one. Motionless except for his bright, agile optics, the other leaned upon his gnarly stick, eyeing them and ruminating.

After a while, he said, "Waltskin," in a thin, reedy voice.

"Hah!" said one of the crew. "Let's call him Walter." With humor unconsciously prophetic, he sang, "Walter, Walter, lead me to the altar."

"He can talk, at any rate," observed Hayward. "Now we won't have to play snake-arms trying to make him understand. We can learn his language or teach him ours."

"Neither will be necessary," assured the newcomer, with perfect diction.

They were mutually dumbfounded.

After they had got over it, Berners whispered to Hayward, "This is going to make things dead easy. It will be like taking candy from a kitten."

"You're getting mixed," said Hayward. "You mean like taking bad fish from a child." He grinned and turned his attention to the dwarf. "How come you know our language?"

"I do not know it. I can *fahn* it. How can people communicate if they cannot *fahn* each other's speech-patterns?"

That was too tough for Hayward. He shrugged it off, saying, "I don't get it. I've been around plenty, but this is a new one on me." He loked hopefully toward the distant town, pondering the chances of a little relaxation. "Well, we'll have a tale to tell when we get back."

"When you get where?" asked Waltskin. The sun glowed on the peculiar four-heart sign ornamenting his silver buttons.

"When we get *back*," Hayward repeated.

"Oh, yes," said the other, with subtle change of emphasis. "*When* you get back."

He used his gnarly stick to decapitate something resembling a daisy and waited for the next conversational move leading toward the inevitable end. And in due time his eyes glittered as he conducted the first victim away.

The Undecided

ETER THE PILOT MADE HIS CRASH LANDING WITH
skill deserving of all the huzzahs he did not get. It
is no small feat to dump a four-hundred tonner after
a flying brick has loused up the antigrav and left
nothing dependable but the pipes.

The way he used those tubes verged on the superhuman.
They roared and thrust and braked and flared and balanced so
that ultimately the vessel hit with no more than a mildly un-
pleasant thump that added nothing to the damage. For the time
being the ship and its eight man crew was safe. Or, to be
more precise, its crew of seven men and one woman were safe—
if there is any safety in an unknown and possibly hostile world.

While the others telepathed their congratulations which
modestly he shrugged off, Peter the Pilot remained in his seat,
locked in the control cabin, and studied what was visible of
this strange planet. The armorglass window mirrored a ghostly
reflection of his blue, thoughtful eyes which were set in a
face queerly suggestive of youth preserved to great age. Even
his hair showed the silky whiteness of the very old, yet somehow remained lush and strong. Making no attempt to get out,
he sat there and thought because it was his duty to think. Subconsciously he was aware that three of his crew already had
left the vessel and that the others were retaining mental contact with them.

They were eight Terrans temporarily marooned far off
the beaten tracks. He wasn't unduly worried about that because
the ship was repairable and they had enough fuel for return.
Moreover, the fact that three had gone out showed that this
world could be endured. It would permit life; a point already
suggested by its superficial resemblance to Terra as seen through

the armorglass. No, the worry was not an immediate one. So far, so good. Sufficient unto the day is the evil thereof. The trouble which most encouraged him to ponder was that repairs take time, a long time, and menacing complications not present today can arrive tomorrow or next week.

The prospective threat he had in mind was that other life-form of shape and powers unknown. They had ships, slow, cumbersome, too short-ranged to overlap the Terran sphere of influence, but still ships. Manifestly they had intelligence of a high order.

For twelve centuries this other-form had chased in fruitless pursuit of every Terran vessel straying within their range and had enjoyed the doubtful pleasure of seeing each one's rapidly diminishing rear end. It is galling to have one's curiosity repeatedly stimulated and left unsatisfied, even more galling to know that the interest is not reciprocated. Peter the Pilot had no notion of what bizarre form this other-life might take but he was willing to gamble that they had no teeth—having ground them away long ago.

Now there was excellent chance of a snoopover and much expressing of resentment if the ship remained pinned by its pants, for misfortune had dumped it right in the other's bailiwick. Not even a Sirian Wotzit, he decided, would resist a sitting duck. Hitching his shoulders fatalistically, he opened his mind to the mental voices of his crew.

Rippy the Ranger was saying, "Found a stream. The water is drinkable."

"*You* found it?" harshed Sammy the Sharpeye. "How do you discover something to which you've been directed like a small child?"

"I went the way you told me and I found it," came back Rippy. "Does that satisfy you? Why don't you trim your nails and take a pill?"

Peter sent out a call, "What do you see, Sammy?"

"Trees and trees and trees. You sure picked a hideout—if it will do you any good." Silence, followed by, "I can also see a strange, repulsive, nightmarish shape lurking by the stream. It is guzzling the water because there's no charge. Now it is scowling horribly and—"

"Leave Rippy alone," ordered Peter. "Where's Kim?"

"Don't know,' admitted Sammy the Sharpeye indifferently.

"He got out fast and vanished some place. You'll hear Hector swearing pretty soon."

"Oh, no you won't," interjected Hector the Hasher, his mental impulses strong because of his nearness within the ship. "I had ten locks on the galley, see? I've made landings before, and with a load of gutsies at that!"

"Kim!" called Peter.

Silence.

"When will that guy learn to keep his mind open and respond," Peter complained.

"When he's hungry," offered Hector morbidly.

A new tone chipped in, hooting with irritation. "Let . . . me . . . *sleep*, willya? I gotta catch up . . . somehow!"

"Nilda the Nightwatcher," sighed Hector. "Nilda the Nuisance I call her. What makes her that way?" He paused, then his thought-form boosted with sudden outrage. "Clobo, take your mitt outa that can! By the—"

Peter cut them off while he writhed out of his seat, had a closer look through the armorglass. He was surveying a tiny portion of a world which itself was small part of an alien system and a corresponding fragment of the great unknown. As a representative of a nearby empire firmly founded upon swiftness and sureness of personal decision, he stood ready with the rest to face decisively whatever might befall. Apprehension was not within him, nor the elements of fear. There was only estimation, calculation, and preparedness to decide.

After one million years of Terran growth and mutual acceptance of the consequence of growth, nobody thought of themselves as peculiarly undecided.

Sector Marshal Bvandt slurged in caterpillarish manner across the floor and vibrated his extensibles and closed two of the eight eyes around his serrated crown and did all the other things necessary to demonstrate an appropriate mixture of joy, satisfaction and triumph.

"One is down." He smacked his lips. "At last. After all these years."

"One what?" inquired Commander Vteish.

"A mystery ship. A sample of those ultra-fast cylinders we've never been able to catch."

"No?" Vteish was astounded.

"Yes! It had an accident, or something went bust. The message had just come in but does not give details of what forced it to land. Zwilther was following it in the CX66, and losing distance as usual, when he saw it go off-curve. It chopped around a bit, still at high clip, then made for Lanta."

"Lanta," echoed Commander Vteish. "Why, that is in our sector."

"A most remarkable coincidence," observed Bvandt sarcastically, "seeing that any emergency message is automatically directed to the marshal in charge of the sector it concerns."

"Of course, of course," agreed Vteish hurriedly. "I overlooked that much in the excitement of the moment." Dutifully he slurged, vibrated and performed the eye-shutting to remind his superior that they were two hearts beating as one. "Now what?"

"Lanta is sparsely settled. Its people are simple scrabblers in the dirt. I have sent an order warning them not to interfere with this alien cylinder, to keep clear of it. We cannot permit a gang of hicks to handle a case of this magnitude. Too much depends upon it and such an opportunity may never occur again. Our best brains are needed to make the most of it."

"Definitely," endorsed Vtish. "Undoubtedly."

"Therefore I am going to deal with them myself," announced Bvandt.

"Ah!" said Vteish, carefully using his speaking-mouth. He had two mouths, one on each side. The penultimate insult was to make eating motions with the speaking-mouth. The ultimate:—to make garbled speech-noise with the eating-mouth. For a moment he had been sorely tempted.

"And you are coming with me," Bvandt went on. "Also Captain Gordd and Captain Hixl. We'll take two ships. We'd take fifty if they were immediately available, but they aren't. However, these two are of our latest, most powerful pattern."

"Couldn't some of the other vessels be summoned?"

"They have been called already, but it will take them some time to reach Lanta. We cannot wait for them, we dare not wait. At any time this alien contraption may be away faster than zip. We have got to deal with it before it becomes too late."

"Yes, marshal," admitted Vteish.

"What luck! What a gift!" If Bvandt had possessed

hands, he would have smacked them together with the acme of delight. So he jiggled his extensibles in the nearest equivalent. "Now is our chance to get the measure of this other-life while leaving it ignorant concerning ourselves. After preliminary study of them we will test their defenses by a light attack. Finally, we'll seize their vessel, dig out the secret of its speed and maneuverability. All that knowledge, my dear commander, will give us our biggest boost in twenty lifetimes."

"A boost in one lifetime is enough for me," said Vteish with unashamed cynicism. "I was peculiarly disinterested before I was hatched and expect to be strangely indifferent after I'm burned." He humped toward the coolness of the wall, leaned against it and mused. "Do you suppose that this other-life might be . . . might be . . . like us?"

"I see no reason why not," declared Bvandt, after some thought. "We are by far the highest form in the known cosmos, therefore any other high form must be similar."

"The logic of that is not evident." Vteish drew a crude sketch on the wall. "They might be like this, for example."

"Don't be stupid. Why should they resemble anything so fantastic?"

"Why not?"

Bvandt said severely: "You are too fond of those dreamplays at the festivals. You have leanings toward mental extravagance. Your brain spends half its time conjuring crazy visions for lack of anything better to do." His rearward pair of eyes examined the time-meter on the wall. "Your cure is at hand—you can get busy right now. The ships will be ready within the hour and I shall tolerate no delay on anyone's part. See that you are packed and on board in good time."

"Yes, marshal. Most certainly, marshal," promised Vteish, again carefully using his speaking-mouth.

From the eastward rise over which the trees marched in solid ranks the Terran vessel could be seen as if lying in a hollow.

Like a big, fat slug, Bvandt stuck sucker-footed to the bole of a tree while he applied a powerful monocular to one eye and closed the others. The field of vision did not shift or tremble, for under the monocular his extensibles were braced together and formed a fulcrum much steadier than Terran hands.

Adjusting his instrument's focus, Bvandt got a clear, sharp view of Peter the Pilot sitting on the bottom rung of his vessel's landing ladder and smoking a pipe. He almost fell from the tree.

"By the egg that held me!" Detaching his optic from the eyepiece, he bugged the others, stared around. "Do you see this thing?"

"Yes," said Vteish calmly. "It has only two legs, longer and skinnier than ours. Only two eyes. Its upper limbs bend always in the same place as if they are hard-cored and jointed."

"I see it, too," put in Captain Gordd, who was high on an adjacent tree. He spoke with a kind of incredulous hush. "It resembles nothing on any of our twenty-four planets."

"The question is," said Bvandt, "how many more of these creatures are inside that ship."

Gordd pondered it, guessed: "Any number between ten and twenty. Possibly thirty, though I doubt it."

Having another long, careful look, Bvandt pocketed his monocular, inched down the trunk, gained the ground. "Hurry up with that pictograph."

One of the men descended from his vantage point, did things to the boxlike instrument he was carrying, eventually produced from it a large photo of Peter complete with pipe.

"Well, we've a record of how they look," grunted Bvandt, studying the picture closely. "I would never have believed it if I hadn't seen for myself. Fancy thousands of things like this!"

"Millions," corrected Vteish joining him.

"Yes, millions, all like this." He handed back the photograph, saying: "Prepare copies for transmission to all sector headquarters." Then to Vteish, "Now we'll find out what they've got." He called a nearby trooper. "Get as near as you can and shoot."

"To kill?" asked the trooper.

"To kill," Bvandt confirmed.

"Is that necessary?" Vteish chipped in, greatly daring.

"It is essential that we have a demonstration of their strongest, most desperate reaction," Bvandt said stiffly. He eyed the trooper. "Well, why do you wait? You have your orders!"

The other shuffled off between the trees and into the undergrowth toward the alien ship. The sound of his passage ceased as he dropped to a cautious creep. Beneath the trees the rest waited for the shot and the resulting uproar. Twelve were high in the trees ready to observe and record the other-life's method of defense.

Sitting mild-eyed and sucking his pipe, Peter the Pilot listened, listened, not with his ears but with his mind. Sammy the Sharpeye's tones were coming to him coolly, without emotion.

"They are in the trees a mile to your front. I've been near enough to make certain that they're still there. Boy, what a gang of slooperoos! They sloop and slurp this way and that. They've eight eyes apiece, all on top, but swiveling independently. They've refused to see me so often that I wonder if I'm getting transparent."

"Not with what you're full of!" cracked Rippy's thought-form.

"Shut up!" ordered Peter. "This is a poor time for cross-talk."

"The trees are the trouble," went on Sammy. "They hide too much. Clobo ought to be able to tell you more than I can."

"So at last it is admitted that Clobo has his uses," interjected that worthy. "Clobo comes into his own—during his bedtime. No sleep for the wicked!" He managed to put over a deep mental sigh. "And tomorrow all will be forgotten."

"What do you see, Clobo?" asked Peter, projecting sympathy.

"They are conferring with ugly mouth-noises. It is evident that they are in no way telepathic."

"If they were they'd have overheard us long ago," Sammy pointed out.

"They appear to have reached some sort of decision and have sent away one who bears an object suspiciously like a weapon," Clobo went on. "This one is edging cautiously toward the ship. Now he sinks low and creeps. I have a strange feeling."

"Of what?" demanded Sammy.

"That he does not desire to blow kisses."

"Ho-hum," said Peter knocking the dottle from his pipe. "I do not think it wise to take action myself until I know for certain whether or not his intentions are honorable."

"If you ask me, I wouldn't trust him with Hector's can-opener," opined Clobo.

"Listen who's talking!" invited Hector.

"Now he has paused by a suitable gap and is pointing his weapon forward. If I could see into his alien mind, I'd find it bloated with mayhem. He is about to fire at you, I think. Rippy is hidden in the grass ten yards to his front."

"I shall now reveal myself," announced Rippy.

"Mind you don't get a slug in your bean," warned Peter. He screwed up his eyes as he tried to spot Rippy amid the vegetation more than half a mile away. Nothing could be seen; the growths were too thick.

Clobo's impulses now became a rapid series of high-pitched mental squeaks as he chattered at top pace like an excited commentator at a champ contest. One got the impression that he was jigging up and down as he broadcast.

"Rippy gets to his feet and stares this guy straight in the pan. The sniper lets out a startled hiss and drops his weapon. Rippy doesn't move. The other recovers. Keeping all eight eyes and the whole of his attention on Rippy, he feels for his gun, finds it, picks it up. What's the use of having eyes all around if you don't use them? He's just leveled the gun as Kim arrives from where he isn't looking and jumps on his back. Whoo! Socko! Kim is tearing off lumps and giving them to the frogs. The other has rolled onto his back, making noises with both mouths and waving his legs in all directions. Kim is now extracting his plumbing and draping it tastefully over the bushes. There's a funny sort of blue goo all—"

Closing his mind, Peter opened his ears. There were faint threshing sounds mingled with queer, unidentifiable noises deep in the far vegetation. He eyed the sky as if searching for something now at too great an altitude to be seen. Pulling out his tobacco pouch, he refilled his pipe, tamped it, sucked it unlit.

". . . leaving only a rank and unappetizing mess," finished Clobo, worn out.

"Soup's ready," announced Hector, unimaginatively choosing the worst of moments.

The three troopers sneaked back with their eyes wary on all sides and especially to the rear. Two told their story while the third worked at his box and gave the resulting pictograph to Bvandt.

"Torn to pieces?" said Bvandt incredulously. They made nervous assent. He stared at the pictograph as it was placed in his gripping extensibles. He was appalled. "By the great, red, incubating sun!"

"Let me see." Vteish had a look over the other's ropey limb. His first, second and third stomachs turned over one by one. "Sliced apart with a thousand knives!"

"They must have been lying in ambush," decided Bvandt, not bothering to wonder how the ambushers had known where to place themselves. "Several of them. They attacked with the utmost ferocity. He never had a chance even to use his weapon." He turned to the silent troopers. "That reminds me—where is his gun? Did you retrieve it?"

"It was not there. It had gone."

"So!" Bvandt became bitter. "Now they have a gun. One of our guns."

"Only a comman hand-gun," soothed Vteish. "We have others bigger and better. They don't know about those."

"What do *we* know?" Bvandt snapped. "Nothing—except that they have knives."

"Super-fast ships and ordinary knives," Vteish commented thoughtfully. "The two items just don't go together. They seem incongruous to me."

"To eternal blackness with the incongruity!" swore Bvandt. "Their sharp blades have proved superior to our guns. They have made a kill while we have not. I cannot tolerate that!"

"What do you suggest?"

"We'll try again in the dark." Bvandt slurged to and fro, his voice irritable. "I do not expect to catch them asleep—if they do sleep—for they will keep watch now they know we're around. But if by any chance they are less accustomed to darkness it will give us some slight—"

He stopped as metallic clangings sounded from the distant ship and one of his treetop observers called urgently. Mounting the bole, he used his spyglass.

Something had emerged from the Terran vessel. It was a bright, new and entirely strange shape bearing no resemblance to the two-legged creature previously observed.

This one was rhomboidal in sideview and shone beneath

the sun. It possessed no legs and appeared to move upon
rotating but unseeable bands, or perhaps on hidden rollers.
Many limbs projected from it at the oddest angles, some mul-
tiple-jointed, some tentacular. Trailing behind it a long, thick
cable which ran back into the ship, this weird object trundled
partway toward the tail end bearing in two of its limbs a large,
curved metal plate.

While Bvandt watched pop-eyed, the newcomer turned its
back on far-off observers, held the curved plate to the ship,
applied something to one edge. An intense and flickering light
bloomed at the end of its extended limb and crawled slowly
up the plate's side.

"Welding!" offered Vteish unnecessarily.

Bvandt scowled, glanced higher up his tree, said to the
pictograph operator above him, "Are you recording this?"

"Yes."

"Make several records while you're at it." He looked downward upon half a dozen fidgeting troopers. "You six go a
quarter circle round while remaining within gun-range of that
vessel. Keep together. Don't separate no matter what happens.
Find a good aiming-stand no nearer than you can help and give
that legless nightmare a volley. See that you hit it—I'll flay
the one who misses!"

They moved off obediently but without eagerness. Bvandt
went a little higher up the tree, squatted in a crotch, kept his
glass centered upon the shining alien which continued to concentrate upon its task as if it had not an enemy in the whole
of creation. Vteish, Gordd and Hixl all had their monoculars
aimed at it. The pictograph operator maintained it in his
screen.

Slowly, uneasily, the troopers crawled round, their senses
alert, jumpy, yet unconscious of other eyes watching, other
minds talking.

To the waiting Bvandt the execution squad seemed to
take an interminable time. He was toying with the morbid
notion that already they had met a silent but terrible end when
the hard cracks of six guns made him jerk in his seat. The
brief swish of the missiles could be heard distinctly, and even
louder were the fierce clunks with which they struck their
target.

The brilliant welding light snuffed out. Its shining operator slid three feet noseward, stood still. Tense seconds went by. Then calmly he applied his limb to the opposite seam, the light spurted afresh and the weld-line crept upward.

There was a word so rarely used that some had never heard it in a lifetime. Bvandt not only employed it, but distorted it with his eating-mouth. Vteish was shocked, Gordd astounded, Hixl filed it for further reference.

Then while they watched, the two-legged, two-eyed thing appeared. It came out of the ship, pipe in mouth, a tiny gadget in its hand. The most that their monoculars could determine was that the strange instrument had a hand-grip topped by a small platform on which a little tube of pencillike proportions pointed upward at a high angle. The two-legger squeezed the handle, the tiny tube spat fire, sprang from its platform and speeded into invisibility. A thin arc of vapor hung high to mark its passage.

Enough silence followed to make this performance seem pointless. It ended with a gigantic thunderclap and a distinct quiver in the ground. Over to the right, where the hidden squad lay low, a great tree sprang five or six hundred feet into the air with a ton of earth still sticking to its roots. Other trees leaned sidewise and toppled as if to provide room for it to fall back.

Of the six troopers there was not even a bluish smear.

Climbing tiredly onto his bunk, Peter the Pilot wound the chronometer set in the wall, looked through the tiny three inch port at the darkness outside, lay back and closed his eyes. Something weightily nonchalant and stone-deep trundled noisily through the ship, made many clatterings and clinkings.

Hector's thought form came through with a touch of exasperation. "Good as he may be, I maintain there's plenty of room for improvement. Why can't he be telepathic? If they'd found some way to make him telepathic, I could put over some choice remarks about juggling hardware in our sleeping hours."

"Anyone who can respond to anxiety about mechanical matters, and jump to the job, is a marvel in my opinion," offered Peter. "Be thankful that he's got a one-track mind and sleeps only when there is nothing to do."

"That's just when *I* want to sleep," complained Hector. "When a lot of bellies aren't hanging around me rumbling for chow." A raucous rattle like that of a pneumatic hammer came from near the tail, and Hector yelped: "Get a load of that! Aren't I entitled to some shut-eye?"

"I don't remember you screaming about my rights when I was fooling around in my bedtime," Clobo's mind put in.

"Bedtime!" scoffed Hector. "Any guy who says daytime is bedtime is too daffy to have any rights."

"The trouble with this ship," interjected Sammy, "is too many incurable yaps. My patience is running out fast. Pretty soon I'm going to give up all pursuit of sweet dreams and go around cutting myself a few throats."

"Bah!" said Hector feebly.

Clank whirr! Nobody took further notice. Closing his eyes again, Peter drifted slowly away. As usual, his astral body beat it back to Terra where—on an average of once a week—it roamed its dream-town and—perhaps once a month—joined its dream-blonde.

This proved to be one of the times when the said blonde was among those present. She was facing him across a table, looking bright-eyed at him over a vase of flowers, when suddenly her conversation made a switch.

"But, dear, if we buy this planetoid just for ourselves, you'll have to leave the service because it doesn't make sense for you to run off and—" She paused, then said sharply, "Peter, you are dreaming! *Wake up!*"

He sat up wide awake, still feeling the shock of it.

"All right, Dozey," came the mental impulses of Nilda the Nightwatcher. "Fun's a coming!"

"I'll say!" endorsed Clobo, with relish.

"What do you see, Nilda?"

"A big gun. They've brought it from one of their ships and are now hauling it up the other side of the rise. Reckon it will take them about an hour to reach the crest."

"Do you think it might be powerful enough to damage our plates?"

"For all I can tell it might be able to splash us over the landscape. It is no toy. It takes about sixty of them to drag it along. The trees are impeding them more than somewhat." She was quiet for a time, gave several little indistinguishable mutterings, then finished: "You're the official thinkbox. What do you want me to do about this?"

"If you gave me the precise range and angle with reference to this ship, I could donate a hoister," he mused. "But that would tell them something about our heavy armament. The light stuff doesn't matter. I'd rather not use the heavy if it can be avoided. Besides, it might shake us to pieces while we're grounded."

"So what?" invited Nilda.

"So I'll leave you a medium disruptor at the bottom of the ladder. You can plant it where it will be most disconcerting."

"All right," agreed Nilda with lack of emotion strange in a female.

Clobo promptly screamed: "Give me time to get clear, you bug-eyed assassin! I'm right in the trees and almost over them!"

"Are *you* calling *me* bug-eyed?" demanded Nilda. "Why, you spook-faced runt, I've half a mind—"

"That's just it—you've half a mind," said Clobo. "Lemme out before it does me damage."

"Give him time to duck out," ordered Peter. "I'll check whether any of the others are roaming around in the dark." Grabbing his torch, he entered the passage, went from cubicle to cubicle. The remainder of his crew were there, all asleep but Rippy who was stirring in semiwakefulness. Dodging the rhomboidal object which trundled busily along the passage, he reached the armory, selected a small one-pound disruptor, placed it at the bottom of the ladder. Then he returned to his bunk, broadcast, "All set, Nilda," closed his eyes and tried to get back to the blonde.

Sleep refused to come. He found himself listening for Nilda coming to pick up the bomb though he knew he would not hear her. Although the three-inch port was on the blind side of the ship with respect to the distant gun, he felt impelled to glance through it every now and again. There were no more comments from Nilda or Clobo, and the others were deep in their slumbers. Silence lay over the outer world; there were no noises inside the ship apart from a steady hum and occasional clinks at its rear end.

After half an hour the trees facing the port lit up briefly in vivid crimson. The entire vessel gave a jolt. A terrible roar followed. The crew came awake with language more fluent than seemly.

"That was tricky," remarked Nilda. "I had to move faster

than the drop."

Four mental voices chorused sardonically: "Or you'd have ruined your make-up."

"Yes," agreed Nilda calmly. "Someone has to look decent."

Hector alone had the ability to make the answering noise telepathically.

Gloomily posing by the edge of the crater, and secretly impressed by its size as seen in the light of the new day, Sector Marshal Bvandt said to a land-force captain, "O.K.., what's your story?"

"We stood guard in a ring, two body-lengths apart, all through the night. The whole of the ground between us remained under such close observation that nothing could possibly have slipped through unseen."

"So it appears," commented Bvandt nastily. He scuffed some dirt with three of his feet, watched it slide down the great hole.

"Nothing passed," insisted the captain. "We had constant watch on every inch of ground around the ring. We maintained that watch even after the explosion and right up to dawn."

"Yet this disaster occurred behind you. You were between it and the ship. Something must have caused it—some *thing!*"

"I cannot explain it. I can only say that no alien passed through the ring of guards." He was very positive about it.

"Humph!" Openly dissatisfied, Bvandt turned his attention to a wounded trooper waiting nearby. "Well?"

"They had got the gun and its ammunition-trailer this far." Four of his eight eyes bent to stare into the crater. "I was following at short distance. All was dark and quiet. There was nothing unusual that I could see or hear, no noise, no warning. Then all of a sudden this happened." He used a shaky extensible to point at the hole. "I was lifted off my feet and flung against a tree."

"Nobody knows anything," spat Bvandt, kicking more dirt. "A gun, a trailer, two captains and sixty men go to blazes in one midnight blast—and nobody knows anything." He scowled at the land-forced captain. "Did the alien vessel remain silent, undisturbed, all through this?"

"No." The captain fidgeted.

"Come on then, you fool, speak the rest! I am able to

understand speech!"

"Immediately after darkness had fallen we heard the vessel's door open and close as if something had emerged, but there were no noises on the ladder, and in the darkness we could see nothing—if anything did come out. In any case, no attempt was made to penetrate our ring or even to approach it. Then toward midnight, and shortly before the explosion, the door opened and shut again. There were faint sounds up and down the ladder as if what was making them had come out and gone in almost without pause."

"That," declared Bvandt with much ire, "is too revealing for words. It tells me practically everything I wish to know."

"I am glad of that," assured the captain, stupidly pleased.

"Get out of my sight!" Bvandt waved furious extensibles at him.

"We have scanners," remarked Vteish thoughtfully. "We have apparatus that can scan mechanically by night and day. What a pity we don't utilize it here."

"You are not ahead of me," Bvandt snapped. "You are several days behind. I considered the matter en route. Scanning equipment cannot be extracted from the ships, neither can it be operated without power supplied by the ships, neither can we bring the ships any nearer than they are."

"I seem to have heard of self-contained transportables," ventured Vteish, glancing at him. "Small ones with their own generators."

"You talk like an imbecile. Firstly, I cannot produce by magic a transportable we do not possess. A couple of sets are being brought by ships not due for many days. It is beyond even my power to accelerate them."

"Of course."

"Secondly," he continued testily, "I doubt the usefulness of these scanners when they do arrive. Whatever can blow up a big gun obviously can blow up a transportable viewer. Thirdly, it is evident that this alien cylinder has some sort of unimaginable scanning apparatus superior to ours."

"In what way?"

"In what way?" echoed Bvandt, pointing all his eyes in dire appeal to the indifferent skies. "He asks me, 'In what way?' See here, Commander Vteish, we are upon the slope of a rise. The enemy vessel is over the other side. We cannot

see it from here. It is out of sight because we are unable to
view it through some thousands of tons of intervening dirt.
No scanner we possess, no scanner we can conceive is capable
of seeing straight through a hill." He nudged the other in
emphasis—"Apparently *they* can see through a hill. How else
could they know of the gun and strike at its precise position?"

"Possibly they have a contraption which employs sky-
reflection in a manner similar to our electro-communicators,"
suggested Vteish, striving to look profound. "In which case
hills and mountains would be no obstacles."

"Bunk! *Kaminnif!* You are back in your dream-plays!
Even if hills and mountains could be visually surmounted there
would be nothing to see but treetops. How is it possible to
devise anything so selective that it can dissolve the concealing
foliage to reveal what is beneath?"

"I would not venture to argue the possibility," said Vteish.
"I am content only to point." He pointed to the crater. "There
is the incontrovertible evidence that despite every technical
difficulty they can see and do see, through hills or through
foliage, by night as well as day."

"That's what I've been telling you all along," exploded
Bvandt. "You have argued right around in a circle. Do you
talk for the pleasure of your own voice?"

He was still fuming when a courier arrived, handed him
a message-cylinder which he unscrewed impatiently. Extracting the missive, he read it aloud.

"Have received your pictograph of biped other-life. Good
work!" Crumpling the paper, he tossed it into the crater.
"Headquarters calls it good work. For lack of their support
it has been mighty bad work so far."

"There is another," said the courier, offering a second
cylinder.

Bvandt grabbed it, read, "Have now received pictograph
of skew-shaped, multi-limbed, legless other-life, and cannot
reconcile this with record previously delivered. What is relationship? Clarify without delay." He glared at the courier
who edged away self-consciously. "Clarify without delay. Do
they think I am omnipotent?"

"I am only the courier," reminded the other.

A pictograph operator arrived before Bvandt could find
another avenue for expression. He had his box in one bunch

of extensibles, several glossy sheets in another. His expression was slightly befuddled.

"Well?" demanded Bvandt, glowering at him.

The operator gabbled nervously: "Last night we set boxes in trees on the order of Captain Hixl. They had back flashes and snare-lines attached. As expected, we get several records of tree-lizards." He held out the sheets. "We also got these. We might have got more if some boxes had not been destroyed by this explosion."

Snatching the sheets, Bvandt gave them the eight-eyed stare. Both his mouths worked around and his body humped with shock.

Three of the sheets showed different aspects of the same fantastic thing. It was sitting on a branch as if out to enjoy the air. It bore a perfunctory resemblance to the two-legged pipe-smoking creature first observed, for it had two legs, two jointed arms and somewhat similar form. But it was far smaller and, moreover, possessed a single tentacle which was curled around the branch on which it sat. Its tiny, impish face held a pair of tremendous eyes which stared from the picture like twin moons.

"By space!" swore Vteish, breathing close. "What an object!"

His breath jerked out in a sharp hiss as Bvandt shuffled the sheets to show the others. These depicted another, differently shaped but equally nightmarish thing also on a branch. It had a pair of three-fingered hands in lieu of legs, and no visible arms, tentacles or extensibles. Apart from the hands which gripped the branch it appeared limbless. Its body made one smooth curve on each side and the outlines of it were peculiarly fuzzy.

What got them most was the face, the awful face. Flat-topped, with demoniac horns at the sides, it had a great, menacing nose jutting between a couple of huge, glowing eyes still larger than those of the thing on the other sheets. Even in picture form those enormous optics fascinated them with the hypnotic quality of their cold, haughty, all-observing stare.

"Now we have *four* forms," mourned Bvandt, unable to tear his gaze away from those immense eyes. "You can see what is going to happen. I will transmit these to headquarters. In due time they will send acknowledgement." His voice changed to a mocking imitation of the stiff, officious tones beloved of bureaucrats. "Have received your pictographs of two more other-life forms. Reply without delay stating which of these is the master-type and define the relationship of the others."

"I do not know what answer can be given," Vteish confessed.

"No answer can be given—yet." Bvandt made an irritated gesture in the general direction of the alien vessel. "In the name of the eternal cosmos, why can't they make up their minds what shape and form they're going to take? In the name of the red sun, blue sun or any other sun, why can't they decide on one particular identity and stick to that,"

"Possibly their nature does not permit a decision," theorized Vteish after exercising his mind. "It is thinkable by me that they are all of the same type but, under some alien compulsion with which we are not familiar, are impelled to change shape from time to time. They may be creatures who can't help altering at certain moments, in response to certain impulses."

"Anything is thinkable by you," scoffed Bvandt. "Sometimes I wonder why you don't leave the service and become a constructor of dream-plays." He stared again at the great eyes of Clobo, the greater ones of Nilda. "We must solve this problem forthwith."

"How?"

"We have two choices. For one, we can make an assault in full strength from every direction, using every trooper and the ship's crews."

"That may cost us many lives," Vteish pointed out. "And if we fail there will be no replacements for at least four days. It will take us that long to conscript a force of local settlers; longer if we wait for the other ships."

"I have considered that," said Bvandt. "I prefer the alternative plan, though it is risky. We can take up a ship and use its armament to wreck the alien vessel or, at least, damage it sufficiently to ground it for keeps."

"By space!" exclaimed Vteish. "I wouldn't care to try that! The minimum velocity at which a ship is controllable means that you'd have to shoot in less than one-hundredth the blink of an eye. And hit the target. And fire while in a dive. And pull out in time to avoid plunging into the earth."

"I know, I know."

"Low level bombardment by spaceships is not possible because of the tremendous speeds involved."

"Many an impossibility has been achieved in a pinch," declared Bvandt.

Vteish said: "An ordinary air machine would be better."

"I agree. The idea is excellent, my dear commander. I congratulate you upon it. Please bring me an air machine."

"Perhaps the settlers—?"

"There are no air machines anywhere in the vicinity, none owned by any of the dirt-scrabblers. Do you expect all the amenities of civilization on this outpost world?" He sniffed his contempt. "There will not be one solitary air machine available until the main fleet arrives—and that will be several weeks behind the first comers." He sniffed again. "We must make do with what we've got precisely as these aliens are making do with what they've got. We'll bring a ship into action and hope for the best. When that fails, *if* it fails, I'll consider risking an assault and take a chance on losses."

"How about flying a bomb-carrying kite with an automatic release?" asked Vteish, picturing himself among the casualties to come.

Bvandt responded generously: "I will give the bomb if you will provide the kite and the necessary mechanism and clear away ten thousand infernal trees." Glancing upward, he added in different tones, "It has just occurred to me—what outlandish thing may be sitting up there now, hidden by the leaves, listening to us, glaring at us goggle-eyed?"

"Eh?" Startled, Vteish followed his gaze. So did several troopers. With a coldness upon them they ignored the many sky-gaps and studied the silent trees.

Their mistake lay in not looking higher, much higher.

Sammy the Sharpeye's mind cut through the ether saying: "One of their vessels is warming its main propulsors."

"I guessed it," answered Peter. "I can hear the dull roar of them from here." He paused while he thought it over. "Are there any of these eight-footed uglies hanging around me?"

"A ring of watchers," came Rippy's thought-form. "They're keeping at good distance, up in the trees, as if they're sort of nervous."

"Do you think they saw you boys go out?"

"A jump from a hole straight into deep brush doesn't tell much. You see something, you know it's something, but you don't know what. So you stick to the trees and say your prayers. Anyway they've not seen me since. Kim neither." Rippy sounded contemptuous.

"Kim!" called Peter.

No reply.

"What's the matter with Kim?"

"He's laconic," said Rippy. "Aren't you, Kim?"

"Speechless," corrected Hector, "with snitched food."

"There are times," snarled a menacing thought-form, heard for the first time in days, "when I am tempted to change my diet." Then, more sharply, "There's a dope on the ground, Rippy! Crawling toward you, dragging a box. Do you want him, or shall I take him?"

"This one's on me," said Rippy.

Sammy chipped in again with: "They are now closing all vents and trimming ship for a take-off, leaving troops on the ground. The bow armament turrets are projected. Looks like they've a notion to blow off somebody's britches."

"I'll check," said Peter calmly. Going to the control cabin, he switched the space-radio, sent out a call, listened. He repeated several times without result. "No Terran in this sector," he told Sammy. "So that means there's nobody to shoot up but us. Heck, that's going to be a chancy business with a spaceship, even one so slow as theirs are."

"Reckon they're going to risk it, all the same," replied Sammy. "I'm nicely set to copy Nilda's tactics, but a one-pounder won't get me much. These ships need something more."

"We'll give them more," decided Peter. "Get me the range and bearings."

Knowing that this would take Sammy a minute or two, he used the interval to broadcast a wordless but definite anxiety, an aching concern about a mechanical matter. The thing now listed by the pictographs as superior life-form number two promptly dropped what it was doing, clanked and buzzed along the passage, helped him load a robot bomb and slide it out upon its launching-rack. That done, the noisy one returned to his task.

"Relative to your longitudinal axis, I make it forty-seven

degrees leftward, exit side," Sammy informed. "Range: slightly over six miles—say six point two."

"I hate to do this because it tells too much," observed Peter. "So long as we remain in this jam we can't stop them learning something, but I don't feel like giving them more information than is necessary."

"You've about two minutes in which to relent, think up something better and bring it into action," Sammy commented. "The propulsors are reddening. They'll be boosting pretty soon."

"Ah, well, this is going to hurt them more than it hurts me." Shrugging resignedly, he tripped the trigger.

Twin rockets blasted, forced the winged projectile up to two thousand feet before their castings fell away. The intermittent jet-engine took over and the bomb speeded high above the treetops. Steadily it hammered into the distance with a noise like that of an asthmatic motorcycle.

Sitting on the empty launching rack, Peter swung his legs idly to and fro while his fingers rested on the key of the little transmitter standing nearby. The staccato noise of the jet had now died away in the distance. Even the trees seemed to be waiting, waiting.

"Now!" rasped Sammy.

Peter pressed the key, held it down. Resulting sound took a long time to come; when it did arrive it was muffled by mileage and trees to no more than a dull thump. Later, a thin, dark column of smoke snaked out of the landscape partway to the horizon.

"That," Sammy was saying, with grim satisfaction, "is what I call a number one big-time smiffelpitzer! Bang on the button! I could feel it even from here."

Nilda's tones hooted irritably: "Aren't you guys *ever* going to let me *sleep?*"

"Shut up!" ordered Sammy. "They were lying nose to tail about four hundred yards apart. The one which was warming up lost most of what it was warming. Nobody has come out of it, either. Maybe you've laid them for keeps."

"What of the other vessel?" Peter prompted.

"That's without a chunk of its bow. It could be repaired— in a month or two."

"It can't take off?"

"Definitely not," assured Sammy.

"Sle-e-eep!" wailed Clobo. "Ain't me and Nilda allowed any?"

"No more than I get when you two gabble all through the night," Sammy retorted.

"Lay off!" ordered Peter. "Let 'em have some peace and quiet for a while. Don't call me unless it's urgent."

He listened now. Sammy and the others remained obediently silent. With typical consideration he decided against winding in the launching rack, a process much lacking in slumbersome music. He felt a bit anxious about leaving it extended, for perforce the exit-trap had to remain open. But no matter.

Superior life-form number two responded to his momentary thought by clanking uproariously along the passage and winding in the rack. He did it right under Peter's nose, with great gusto, the maximum of noise, and complete indifference to the resulting flood of telepathic insults.

And that was that!

The most pungent portions of Sector Marshal Bvandt's speech were uttered with his eating-mouth. Moreover, he garbled the words and made simultaneous eating motions with his speaking-mouth. His whole performance set a new low in uninhibited vulgarity but was excusable on the grounds of sheer exasperation.

Having reached the end of his impressively extensive vocabulary, which included a description of the aliens as a cosmically misbegotten shower of *nifts,* he snarled at Vteish, "Now count 'em."

Vteish went around adding them up, came back, said: "One ship's crew intact, plus three survivors from the other. Also five land-force captains and four hundred six troopers."

"So!" said Bvandt. "So!" He jiggled his extensibles, humped himself and fumed. "So!"

"So what?" inquired Vteish, blundering badly.

That started Bvandt off again. He went a second time through his long list of choice vituperations, this time taking care to emphasize their especial application to supporting officers in general and one dream-play addict named Vteish in particular.

"Yes," agreed Vteish, when he had finished. He looked

abashed.

"Now," continued Bvandt, gaining control of himself with an effort, "I have noticed one peculiar feature of the enemy's tactics." He fixed three cold, contemptuous eyes on Vteish while the other five watched the trees. "I do not suppose that you have observed it."

"To what feature do you refer?"

"The enemy keeps to a one-blow technique." Bvandt carried on to explain it further. "There was one blow at our sniper, one at our six marksmen, one at the gun, one at these ships. Each succeeded because it was perfectly aimed and timed—but each was only one blow devised to suit a specific occasion. They have not yet demonstrated their ability to deliver two blows simultaneously, or three, or six." He stared meaningly at the other. "Perhaps because they are not able to."

"Ah!" said Vteish.

"Being alien, they have alien minds," Bvandt went on. "It is remotely possible that they lack the ability to concentrate on more than one thing at one time. A confrontation with several simultaneous threats might prove too much for them."

"Might," said Vteish dubiously.

"Do you hold the view that we should withdraw—and accept the consequences back at headquarters?" demanded Bvandt, quick to seize upon his skepticism.

"Oh, no, not at all," Vteish denied hurriedly.

"Then be good enough to display a visible measure of co-operation and enthusiasm. Remember that you are an officer. As such, you must set an inspiring example." He shifted his feet to strike an attitude more important. "As I do!"

"Yes."

"All right! For a start you can supervise the salvaging of the sideguns. Get them out of the ships, attach their ammunition-trailers and position them in a semicircle barely within range of the alien vessel."

"A semicircle?"

"Of course, you idiot! If we place them in a complete circle, we'll have them firing upon each other."

"What," persisted Vteish, "when the alien ship—which is the center of the circle—is barely within range?"

"I take no risk of range estimates and overshooting," Bvandt shouted. "We may have casualties enough." He gave himself time to cool down before he added: "The important thing is to spread the guns immediately they are out, and to keep them spread while making the approach. See that they are hauled to their stands while widely dispersed; they cannot then be put out of action with one selective blow." Glowering at the other, he snapped, "Get going!"

"Very well."

Bvandt turned to Captain Hixl. "You will remain here with the surviving crew. Take your orders from Commander Vteish and see that the crew digs out those guns in double-quick time." Then to Gordd. "You will command the land-force captains and their troops. Deploy them and make careful approach to the alien ship. Keep no closer together than is necessary to maintain contact. Select and guard a semicircle of sites for the guns which Vteish will bring. Hold them until he arrives. Beat off any attacks as best you can, and be careful to watch the trees." He got eight times an eyeful of the nearest tall growths before he repeated, "Watch the trees!"

"As you order." And with an air of ill-concealed fore-boding, Gordd departed with his small army. Bvandt roamed irritably around, watching the trees and ignoring the sky-gaps. Now and again he chivvied the crew as they sweated and strained to get out the guns.

One by one the heavy weapons were extracted, and lugged among the trees. There were twelve altogether. Bvandt would much have preferred to use the still larger and heavier bow-rifles, but these were fixtures impossible to remove without dockyard facilities. He had to be content with the two batteries of mobile side-guns.

The job was completed as dusk began to fall. Nothing un-toward happened—except the death of Gordd. A trooper brought the news. Encouraged by the aliens' seeming indiffer-ence, Gordd had attempted to get nearer their ship. He had crept cautiously forward, covered by two nervous troopers. He had been attacked in the deep brush by something swift and black and manifestly spawned of a ferocious world. The as-sailant had made violent, non-speech noises as it took Gordd apart.

"And what of the troopers covering him?" asked Bvandt, stabbing the messenger with his eight-eyed glare. "What did they do—sit around and chew leaves?"

"The black thing darted out too suddenly to permit a shot," explained the trooper. "It was upon Captain Gordd in a flash, became mixed up with him. Before the escort could intervene to separate them, they also were attacked."

"By what?"

"Another and different creature. It had a few points of resemblance to the black one but was not the same. It was more slender, more agile, and yellow-colored with curious markings. Its face was blunter, more terrible. It made no noises, and fought with an awful silence." He permitted himself a reminiscent shudder. "This yellow horror was faster moving than the black one, much faster. Indeed, it made motions so confusingly swift that the escort was ripped to pieces under our very eyes, and even the pictograph operators did not succeed in making a clear record of it."

"These creatures, the black one and the yellow one, did not correspond with other aliens already recorded?"

"No."

"Then that makes *six* types," observed Bvandt. He spoke to Vteish as the latter came up. "We have now discovered two more alien shapes. They've just slaughtered Gordd." He flourished his extensibles irefully. "How many *more* forms do they take? In the name of a thousand blue comets, why can't they make up their minds?"

Vteish pondered it before he suggested: "Might not their kind of life be shapeless?"

"What do you mean by that?"

"Now and again we hatch malformations," Vteish pointed out. "Some examples have been weird in the extreme, so much so that we have destroyed them on sight. But they were weird only in our estimation, not in their own! If malformations occurred frequently enough, they would become the norm. Infinite variety would be accepted as the natural course of events. The process would be self-sustaining, variations breeding further variations. No parents could forecast the shape and form of their offspring or expect those offspring to resemble themselves."

"*Kaminnif!*" snapped Bvandt. "We have other forms of life on our own worlds, tree lizards and water reptiles and insects. I can stretch my imagination far enough to conceive some nonexistent life-form able to progress through the air without engines, perhaps an ultra-light form with tremendously enlarged fins of a fish. But I just cannot accept the notion of different forms mating to produce other and more different forms, haphazardly, without law or order."

"Then how do you explain their great variety?" challenged Vteish. "So far, we have found no two alike."

"There is only one solution—they represent the inhabitants of several worlds. Each shape is the master-type of its own planet."

"If that were true it would mean that we're opposed not by one world but by an empire," protested Vteish.

"Why not? We have an empire. We cover twenty-four worlds. I see no reason why this mob of repulsive *nifts* should be confined to one. We do not know whether this vessel is small or large by their standards. If small, what do they call a big one? How many more outlandish shapes might be on *that*? How many worlds do they control—a thousand?"

"Not a thousand, surely!" said Vteish, finding this too much.

"We don't know." He slurged again, discontent rivaling anger. "We don't know anything of real importance. We have suffered losses and gained nothing worthy of the sacrifice. What makes their vessels so fast? How far through the cosmos do they spread? What is their power relative to ours? How many other strange entities have they got and what form do they take?" He made a spitting sound. "We are as ignorant as at the start."

"But we'll soon find out," Vteish promised.

"We better had! It will go ill with us if we fail. Are those guns positioned yet?"

"Almost."

"Then why do you hang around here? Go to them. Hustle them along. See that they open fire immediately they're ready. Maintain the bombardment until you are satisfied that the target is grounded forever—but don't wreck it completely. We want to learn things from it, valuable things."

"I will go at once." Suiting the action to the word, Vteish hastened between the trees.

Bvandt stared officiously at the trooper who had brought the news of Gordd. "Well, have you taken root like a vegetable? Or has someone granted you leave of absence?"

"No." Sullenly the trooper made off in the wake of Vteish.

Already it was dark. A few stars shone in the sky-gaps. The trees rustled in the cool night air. Something floated low over the trees, obscuring the stars in its passage and drifting silently on. It was like a wide-eyed ghost. Bvandt failed to notice it.

Humping across to the least damaged ship, Bvandt squatted within the shelter of its main port and waited for the fireworks. Hixl joined him. Together they brooded and waited—and watched the half-visible trees.

In due time the guns thundered raggedly. The whistle of their shells could be heard through the dark. Nearby trees quivered in response to the bursts. There was a long pause, then a second uproaring barrage. Shells screamed toward their mutual aiming point. The blasts caused a bright crimson flickering in the distance.

With much satisfaction, Bvandt said: "I guess that settles that!"

Hixl said nothing.

The penetrating thought-form of Sammy the Sharpeye came through with, "Their newest stunt is to extract their side-shooting mediums and drag 'em into the woods. They don't appear to be bothering with the bow heavies."

"Bringing them thisaways?" Peter asked. He was in the control cabin, rubbing his chin and listening, listening.

"Yes, of course."

"How many?"

"Ten so far. Wait a bit." He was quiet for a while, then said: "Plus two more. That's twelve. We should have mailed them another hoister."

"It's too late now," observed Peter. He grabbed the sides of his pilot-seat and hung on as the whole vessel suddenly floated a few feet upward and come down with a wallop. "Youps!"

"What's that for?" demanded Sammy.

"Results. We soared a yard."

"About time too," contributed Rippy's mind. "I get pretty sick of dumps like—" He broke off for a moment, returned excitedly. "Jeepers! Here's one of them practically crawling into my mouth. There are two more on his tail, holding handguns, and somewhat jumpy. How about it, Kim?"

"I'll take the two," Kim replied.

"Greedy!" defined Rippy. "All right, here goes!"

Both went silent, and Sammy came in again saying, "That pair of landbound lugs get fed too much. They don't know what to do with their surplus zip."

"Boys will be boys," Peter reminded. "What do you see now?"

"The guns have been dragged away, with plenty of ammo. I get occasional glimpses of them through the trees and they're spread over a couple of miles. The light is getting lousy—reckon it's time Nilda took over."

"Coming right now," Nilda chipped in.

"Three slurpers have lost interest," announced Rippy suddenly. "Pfaugh! What a mess they make." Pause. "Nice work, Kim."

Kim did not reply.

The boat floated again, remained poised ten feet from the ground. A shrill shriek like that of a whirling grinder-wheel came from the rear. It ceased abruptly. Someone started bouncing ball bearings on a pile of empty cans. The vessel remained steady at its new elevation.

"We are now in a state of suspense," Peter informed all and sundry.

"I know it," retorted Hector. "I've four full pans, two double boilers, one percolator and one pressure cooker all waiting for the drop."

The ship promptly dropped, not too hard, but hard enough. Hector bawled: "There, what did I tellya?"

Leaving the control cabin, Peter went along the passage, had a look in the antigrav chamber. All within was quiet and peaceful. There was no sign of the rhomboidal object.

Hopefully, he tried the fourth cubical along the passage, shoved open its door, had a glance through. Superior life-form number two was standing impassively in a corner, his various limbs folded or retracted, his air that of one patiently prepared to wait the crack of doom.

"Mechano has finished!" Peter transmitted the news like

a mental yelp. He did a little dance. "Back in the ship, all of you. Make it snappy!"

Clobo complained, "Just as I was going out. Oh, well—"

Regaining the control cabin, Peter fastened himself into the pilot-seat, fingered the familiar gadgets, stared anxiously through the armorglass and into the pall of darkness. He was not unduly worried about the hidden guns. He had the choice of six effective methods of dealing with those now that they were no longer shielded over the rise of land, the simplest being to cause a gentle but not soothing vibration in the molecules of their ammunition. The result would be drastic. He could arrange it right now if necessary, but was not sure of the necessity. Peter's tendency was to slaughter only in minimum terms suitable to the circumstances.

At the moment his only anxiety was for the missing members of the crew, and since they were strictly nonmechanical the noisiest *nift* reposed in his cabin and refused to do anything about the woe.

"Rippy in," suddenly reported that worthy.

"Sammy in," followed right after the other.

"They're ranging and aiming the guns but haven't yet loaded," informed Nilda, blandly ignoring the order to return. "We'll just about make it."

"Kim!" called Peter urgently. Bending forward in his seat, he stared hard into the dark. Nothing could be seen other than a faint haze of starlight over distant trees.

"Coming!" answered a harsh tone presently. Then, half a minute later, "Kim in."

"Now they've loaded!" screeched Nilda from somewhere far off in the gloom. "Take her up! Leave the lock open for me!"

Automatically, Peter shifted the antigrav control. The ship did a sharp, sickening rise to five hundred feet, hung there. An instant later great throbs of fire spurted in a half-circle from the trees. Unseen things whined shrilly through the night. A dozen gouts of crimson sprang from the ground immediately beneath.

"Nilda!"

"Keep your hair on—I'm coming."

He lifted two hundred feet higher, waited, fingers ready

at the controls, eyes gazing expectantly through the armor-glass. He did not see her approach but shortly she said: "Nilda in."

More fire spurted below. The closer sound of the missiles and spread of resultant bursts showed that the hidden guns had been elevated. With a brief, *"Tsk-tsk!"* he gave the antigrav full play. An hour later he cut them off, switched in the rockets. The world shrank behind.

The advance guard of four oncoming alien vessels sighted him half a million miles out, re-angled in pursuit. He did not bother to change course. Shifting the propulsor controls to the end notch, he watched the others gradually slide off his side-screen, reappear on his tail-screen and slowly diminish. By the time they had shrunk to barely discernible dots they had given up and turned back.

Setting a new course, he locked the automatic pilot onto it, checked its operation, unstrapped from his seat, stretched and yawned.

Hector's thought-form complained: "I've told you ten times that chow's ready. Dontcha want any?"

"Yes, sir! Give me a minute."

He watched the autopilot a little while before he left the cabin. There was laughter-impulses coming from the combined galley and messroom toward the tail. It was an easy guess that Clobo was putting on one of his ever-popular acts, probably his famous impression of Fleet Admiral Dickson going pop-eyed over his food. A good guy, Clobo, whose value lay mostly in his ability to entertain, to beat off space-boredom and maintain morale.

The same old wonder came to Peter as he closed the control cabin door, the marvel of a million long, long years, the frequently recurring realization that the hugeness of space is matched by the immensity of time.

For all had passed through the many eons. Some had leaped ahead, some lagged behind. But several of the laggers had put on last-moment spurts—because of late functioning of natural laws—and the impact upon their various kinds of the one kind called Man.

Until they had breasted the tape together.

For the hundredth or two-hundredth time he paused on his

way to the galley and studied the inscribed plate set in the wall. It read:

Patrol Boat *Letitia Reed*.

(Presented to the Associated Species by Waldo Reed).

Crew.	*Kind.*
Peter the Pilot.	Terraman.
Sammy the Sharpeye.	White-crested Eagle.
Hector the Hasher.	Venusape.
Rippy the Ranger.	Terradog.
Kim the Killer.	Hunting Cheetah.
Mechano the Mender.	Automaton.
Clobo the Clown.	Spectral Tarsier.
Nilda the Nightwatcher.	Great Horned Owl.

Grinning, Peter carefully left his mind wide open while he thought to himself, "Boy, what a bunch of bums we've got!" Then just as carefully he closed his mind while he added, "But I'd sooner lose my legs than any one of 'em!"

"For the eleventh time, you bum—" howled Hector.

"Coming!" He took his eyes off the plate and hurried to chow.

Second Genesis

T HROUGH THE FOREPORT THE VAULT OF THE NIGHT COULD
be seen with its vivid scattering of stars, the cross-
hairs being lined on a minor orb dead ahead. Yes, a
minor orb, small, red, of little importance relative to
the mighty host around and beyond it.

From end to end of space gleamed the mighty concourse
of suns—blue, white, golden and cherry-colored. Some were
giants burning in colossal solitude. Others huddled in groups
like fiery families. Many were more gregarious, flaming in
close-packed ranks to fling sparkling curtains across the dark,
or form glowing clouds of inconceivable dimensions, or rotate
themselves in mass to create titanic swirls beyond which lay
others and again still more.

Amid all this, one small red sun burning modestly as if
overawed by the vastness around it—maidenly shy and conscious of its own insignificance. But the cross-hairs kept on
it, selecting it for special attention, choosing it as the one true
beloved from a myriad of greater beauties. There was reason
for this special attention: its name was Sol—and that was
almost another word for home.

The man behind the cross-hairs, keeping the tiny ship
steady on its drive, was called Arthur Jerrold, a pilot-engineer
by profession, a near-suicide by choice. His light gray eyes
contrasted with his pure white hair. His features were a mass
of fine lines, a living map of where he'd been. He was thirty
years old, also two thousand and thirty years old.

It was that latter fact that filled him with anxiety and a
good deal of nostalgia as he looked at the sun called Sol. Three
years ago he had hurtled outward, leaving it behind his tail,
deserting it as one throws away his heart when others beckon

more enticingly. Now he was coming back, and Sol was some two thousand years older.

"Think carefully," they had warned him, "lest later you are racked with vain regrets. Within that ship you will be in a tiny artificial universe of your own; you will be in your own space, your own peculiar time. There is no other way to reach so far."

"I know."

"Nor will you meet another of your kind in some strange far-off field. This is one of those experiments that are not repeated until we have weighed and estimated the results of the first."

"Somebody has to do it first. I'm ready."

"When you return—if ever you do return—the world you knew may be well-nigh unrecognizable. You will be a relic of its past. Perhaps none will remember you even by hearsay. All those you once held dear will be so long gone that their names will have vanished from the book of life, and their resting-places will be beyond anyone's power to find. You will have been away *two thousand years.*"

"I'm ready, I tell you."

So they had fêted him and made much of him, and launched him amid a worldwide thunder of huzzahs. After that, he'd been on his own, just he and the ship, with Sol sinking and shrinking unseen behind the tail.

Now he was coming back. All he had to show for his Odyssey was his data on soundings of the great depths, a long, magnificent story of flaming orbs and whirling spheres, and the rise and fall of far-away civilizations and strange, almost incomprehensible barbarities.

Plus, of course, the countless seams on his face matched by the longitudinal scars on his ship. They were young and vigorous and full of intense vitality, he and the little ship; yet both were incredibly old, stamped with the mark of long years and great experiences.

Pluto was the outpost, the pointer down the starry lane. He swooped over it in a high arc and bulleted onward. Uranus was on the other side of Sol, and Neptune—far to his left; but Saturn was only slightly off his course, and Jupiter loomed almost straight in front. Maybe they were settled now, to what extent humans could settle them. Much can happen in twenty centuries.

For a moment he toyed with the notion of transferring the ship to normal time and making a swift circumnavigatory inspection of Saturn and Jupiter's satellites. It would be good to see outcroppings of slanty roofs and tall towers that identified the haunting-places of mankind.

But he resisted the temptation. To jump out of his own superfast time-rate would delay things unbearably. In the neighborhood of Mars would be the proper place to change over. He contented himself by curving over the big planets and again marveled at the way in which temporal ratios made them appear to whirl and move at tremendous rates. Even after three years of it, he was still amazed that he could discern any features of space at all, much less distortedly; for one hour on the ship was roughly one month on Earth. So relatively fast did the sands of time run out in the exterior universe that his course for Sol described a fine curve which compensated for the system's Vegadrift.

Jupiter swung grandly to the rear, it and its circling children seeming to move at some seven hundred times' their accustomed velocities. The Asteroid Belt had similar acceleration, its multitude of rocks and midget worlds appearing elongated by the sheer rapidity of their passing. Then Mars, the home world's next-door neighbor, pink and shining, like a lightship telling the far voyager of coming landfall.

Here was the point of readjustment. Jerrold braced himself and flipped a knife-switch. A terrible blackness momentarily encompassed his mind; a fragmentary but powerful nausea seized his body. It was as if a multi-million submicroscopic feet had stamped down hard to put the brakes on every vibrating molecule of his being. The effect was always the same, despite that he had used the switch times without number while scouting an army of distant suns. There was no getting hardened to it; one could only take the strain and wait for it to pass.

So it came, and tore at him, and went away, leaving him shaken but whole. Another line had been written upon his face. Another hair might have been whitened had it not already been silvery.

Now Mars was slowed to its old familiar pace. Its minutes were ship's minutes, its hours ship's hours. By contrast with former hugely zipped-up motions, the whole cosmos had suddenly become sedate. One could look forward and downward and see Phobos and Deimos circling the Red Planet like temple dancers rotating around a bland and silent god.

There were people on Mars that day two thousand years ago. Not many of them; just a small colony of metallurgists and mining engineers with their wives and families. A little redstone town with twenty streets, one oxygen plant and a widening ring of boreholes and quarries had formed their touch of Terrestrial civilization. They had called the place Lucansville after an agèd, toothless nosey-poke who had first discovered osmiridium in the Plains of Whispering.

In that long-gone day when the ship gleamed fitfully overhead before switching onto the endless trail, the folk of Lucansville had fired a dozen gigantic star-rockets in his honor. Shooting balls and wavering streamers and wide cascades of brilliant green had illuminated the heavens for half a minute—and that had been man's last farewell to man.

If the riches of Mars had held out, the boreholes reached new treasures, the quarries continued to surrender wealth, Lucansville might well be a metropolis by this time, a replica of the best that home had to offer. A place of wide avenues between splendid edifices. A city whose people could walk in pride, knowing their own mightiness.

He went down to see them.

They were not there.

The vessel went three times round, traveling low while gray eyes searched the landscape. From the Crown of the Snow King to the Crown of the Snow Queen, they were not there. From the Mountains of Desire to the Plains of Whispering, they were not there.

Only the red earth, the blue-green lichens, the eastering dust-clouds and an eerie inward voice murmuring: "Nothing, nothing, nothing."

Jerrold lifted the boat, pointed for Terra. He was both phlegmatic and hopeful. It had been so easy to expect too much of Mars despite that there had never been a lot to recommend it. Coldness, dust-devils, thin air and the need to carry oxygen flasks wherever one went. A brief whiff of reviving gas whenever the lungs became tired. A world of sniffers established to cope with odd veins of rare metals good for only as long as they lasted, and likely to give out at any time.

Lucansville had served its purpose, been abandoned and dissolved into the red dust. Once again Mars had lost its higher life and was left to float in the cosmic cold with its deserts, its dust and its mystery-pylons the origin of which no man knew. But Terra lay ahead.

It could be seen now as a thin white halo a fraction to one side of Sol. Near it, the smaller gleam of Luna. There was home. There was the world that had dreamed the ship, and planned it with clever brains, built it with cunning hands. There was the vital sphere that had provided the metals, the dielectrics, the instruments, the courage, determination, optimism, the very life-form that was its pilot.

Both of them, man and vessel, strained eagerly forward as the target grew larger. Art Jerrold felt an over-powering urgency while his damp hands mastered the controls and his gaze remained fascinatedly upon the halo. The ship seemed to sense it also. The engine purred with delight; the wake-flame grew long, steady and brilliant; the control-responses were prompt and willing.

Luna dropped beneath, then fled sidewise, crater-pitted and pale. Earth loomed up large, its continental outlines clearly defined as the ship sped round to the sunward side. Next, the vessel was skimming the fringes of atmosphere, dipping in, heating up, going out and dipping in again. This roller-coaster technique was the normal deceleratory process, providing neither the time nor the place for closer looks at the destination.

One and a half times round was sufficient. Velocity fell low enough to avoid a burn-up through thicker air. The boat went down, penetrating a thick layer of cloud and flattening out level with the expanse of whitecapped heaving sea.

This descent upon a world had been performed so often that Jerrold handled the controls subconsciously. He had done more of it than any man living, could swoop and draw close and examine a million square miles of terrain while the vessel seemed to fly itself in sentient coöperation. One could have a surfeit of worlds and—after the hundredth or two-hundredth—become cool, calculating, undisturbed, even somewhat lacking in the capacity for surprise.

But this was different. This was Terra. He had never felt so excited in his life.

The seas raced past. He kept wide-eyed watch ahead,

fingers moist and nervous, queer little thrills running up and
down his back. His mind was in turmoil.

*Here there are no deadly dart-beetles, no strangler-trees,
no wave-lattice life-forms like uncommunicative, incomprehend-
ing ghosts, no searing sun, no host of maddening moons. Here
the ship was made and I was born and a mighty audience
cheered us on our way. Here lurked the little school in the
woods, and the swimming-pool where Rudy stayed down seventy seconds and scared the wits out of us all.*

A deep frown corrugated his forehead, and he chewed
at his bottom lip. Of course, the school would not be here.
Nor Rudy either. Joe and Jean and Mimi and little low-voiced
Sue, they'd gone for keeps.

*It's hard to think they're gone—but I got fair warning.
Mustn't think of such things. I've only myself to blame.*

*There will be plenty of other folk around, some of them
remarkably like Rudy and Mimi and the rest. There will be
other little schools and candy-shops and warm, clanging smithys
where the sparks fly upward. Why the deuce do I think of
things like those? I'm thirty. I'm grown up. Be your age,
Jerrold!*

*All right: there will be bright little homes with windows
shining in the dark. And woodland walks scented with pine-
resin and herbs. I'll make new friends and settle down. Somewhere there will be a girl waiting for me, though she doesn't
realize it, and I don't either. We will know it only when we
meet each other. Perhaps later on . . .*

Four tiny islands broke the monotony of ocean, rushed
beneath, fled backward. He caught no more than the briefest
glimpse of unbroken surfaces of treetops, ragged rings of silver
beaches, outer rings of reefs and foaming breakers.

It would have been nice to land and breathe the air, pat
the earth, smell the leaves, admire the flowers, whistle at the
birds, shout and sing. A preliminary letting off of steam before
the final sit-down.

Nice, but it could not be done. Not enough room. The
slightest over-shoot would take him nose-first into a coral

barrier or plunge him into the deeps.

More islands in a long string suggestive of an underlying mountain range. All jungle-covered, green and moist, with the eternal seas nibbling at their edges.

They came and went far too quickly for him to gloat over the possibility of seeing a palm-roofed village, an upturned face, a waving hand.

All he could see were splashes of color, green surrounded by white and blue. Would there still be palm-roofed villages after two thousand years? Why not? At the time he went away, they had already existed through four thousand. Besides, in the most efficient and greatly developed world, they would preserve sanctuaries of simplicity.

Land and a great mountain! The ship gained altitude, engines humming, tubes drumming. Seas and trees and the big black mountain! Fiery-tailed, the vessel soared over a jagged peak, breaking into a cloud and coming out again.

It was not continental land; merely another and bigger island. Plenty large enough to have a main anchorage, a busy port and perhaps a dozen fishing villages.

No sign of active communities from what little he could see. At present velocity his minimum circle would have been radius of thirty miles: too great to permit a proper survey. The alternative was to reduce the circle by cutting down velocity, and he did not want to do that.

A metropolitan center of civilization was his goal, preferably one near to his original point of departure, near the places so long remembered though now forgotten by a world.

The eventual rise of a continental land-mass showed familiar outlines. Nearer, he became certain: it was the great wall of the Andes. There was a song in his heart as he let a side-tube blast, and the ship's nose swung round to point north.

Seas and islands for hundreds of miles, and then a neck of land with a wide gulf beyond. At this point the first spasm of uneasiness came over him. Clearly defined by the noonday sun, the isthmus below was that of southern Mexico. He looked at it as he arrowed across, and the song inside him faltered and died away.

The hills were brown, the valleys green with thin glistening streaks showing where rivers wound down to the sea. But something was wrong; something was not as it had been two thousand years ago and still should be today.

He was already over the gulf when he identified the missing feature: there were no checkered patterns on the surface of the earth. A uniform green crept along the valleys, enjoying the shelter of the hills and the moisture of the streams. Nothing broke it up into variegated squares and oblongs. No walls, no fences, no irrigation systems, no contrast of differently colored crops. No paths, no roads, no habitations of any kind. On the rim of the gulf should have stood the one-time city of Vera Cruz. It was gone, entirely gone.

At least, he thought it was gone. Lacking the navigational instruments of landbound vessels, Jerrold had to depend solely upon memory of past topography. He could be wrong—yet he remembered Vera Cruz with a wealth of detail. In the manner of his high-flying kind, he could picture it with fair accuracy, from above, as seen at a cloud-base.

Speed gave him little time to ponder that problem. He was across the gulf with the mainland rushing under the foreport just as his mind registered the worrying fact that he had seen no surface ships or air machines.

Land swept by. Bending forward, half out of his seat, he studied it anxiously. Miles of it, leagues of it, rolling by at tremendous pace. The ship went lower, so that it had to leap occasional hills, buttes and ridges. It jumped a mountain range, swung to follow a valley, traced a river to the sea, drummed across a harbor, over a headland and went back into deep country.

Like a hopelessly confused pigeon seeking the way to its loft, the boat scoured the territory in huge circles, zigzagged east-west and again north-south. At dusk it landed on a smooth plain, sliding toward the rim of the dying sun, cutting a long brown rut in the virgin green.

Jerrold came out and watched the sun go down without really seeing it. The feel of earth beneath his feet went unnoticed, completely devoid of its anticipated thrill. Neither did he perceive the waving grasses, the distant trees, the pink streamers in the sky. He was as one blinded by a vision of the impossible.

This was Terra, and yet not Terra, because there were no Terrans. Hereabouts, as nearly as he could tell, had been his launching-place, with seven towns just over the horizon, and a hundred roads radiating from them, and steel rails running from one to the other. Great stone towers and lattice masts and a spiderweb of power lines had marked the landscape, while countless air machines roared above. There had been fields of wheat and corn, barley and alfalfa, painting the scene in straight-edged jigsaw patterns.

Strong men in blue denims and women with sunbonnets had worked around here. You could stand and listen and hear for miles the sound of their voices, the clatter of their machines. Oaths and laughter—a voice calling to another across three fields. Smells of turned earth, warm crops, hot metal, engine oil and an occasional whiff of tobacco.

Now all were gone. The plain stretched undisturbed way back to the far hills. Grasses rustled in a breeze that bore no human sounds, no odors of life. Clouds drifted along with cold indifference. The sun went down at last, sucked away its streamers. Purple darkness encompassed the plain, the ship and the man—and there were no windows to light the way. . . .

With the morning Jerrold felt better. Lack of sleep encourages morbidity. Early to bed and long hours in the bunk made up in large part for what he had missed on the homeward trip. The sun smiled out of a clear blue sky. The grass was fresh with dew. Small birds chittered querulously outside the lock, urging him to get up and come out.

Emerging, he stretched his arms, combed his fingers through white hair. Thrilled anticipation came back, driving out remnants of disappointment and feelings of tragedy. After a meal he perked up enough to whistle a gay little tune as he walked around the ship and examined its outer condition.

The world is a big place; two thousand years is a considerable slice of history. Maybe they've discovered how to live without the bother of cultivating foodstuffs. Maybe they've reduced their numbers and clustered together some place else, enjoying companionship freed from the necessity of toil, independent of agriculture. Perhaps they've concentrated themselves in six, twelve or twenty super-cities, and are having one heck of a good time.

Satisfied that the boat stood in no need of repair, he went

inside, closed the lock and went up in further search of his kind.

He headed first for New York—but there was no such place: only two rivers parted by a woody island. London, Paris, Berlin, Madrid, Peking, Sydney, Los Angeles, Rio de Janeiro, all were empty names that had become as if they had never been. All over the world the good earth had become the property of vegetation, insects, birds and smaller animals. Of men there were none.

Eight times round the ship went, and found not a house, not a human. But here and there, in places part shielded from eroding elements, were vague signs that men had been within the scheme of things. Here and there were traces as baffling as the mystery-pylons of Mars.

From a great altitude could be detected faint square shadows in the sands where once the Pyramids had stood. Slight, almost imaginary criss-crossings of discoloration in the grass marked the one-time sites of London and Des Moines. At twenty thousand feet Jerrold felt sure he could define the avenues and streets of Cincinnati.

Seven areas in the world were scarred by groups of gigantic craters, old and overgrown, quite without radio-activity. First views of these irresistibly suggested a bloody holocaust that might have wiped out a large portion of humanity. The sight of the last such place made him think again.

There a cluster of twenty-eight craters linked two rivers, formed a string of reservoirs and effectively drained a huge area of marshland. This made him go back for a second look at the others. They were the same. Manifestly, all had been blasted with calculating care designed to effect some big improvement to adjacent terrain.

On a sheltered cliff-face in the south of France he discovered what was left of a once deeply carved message now dissolved to near-invisibility. It could be seen and read only from a very flat angle when the morning sun's rays struck across the surface.

Later, he found it again, in identical lettering, repeated in twelve places far distant from each other. Also more that looked as if they might have read the same had they not eroded beyond decipherability. He made a careful note of the message, warning, slogan or whatever it might be, intuitively feeling that once it had been displayed everywhere, without cease, all over the world.

It read: *WAR Q!*

Hope cannot live without nourishment. Raking a planet for what it has to offer was nothing new to Arthur Jerrold, but this time he was seeking his own. There were none to find, not one.

He made sure of this. He made doubly sure. He scoured the Earth from pole to pole, gave particular attention to remote hiding-places where possibly any remnants of a great disaster might yet linger, even sought evidence of flight underground. And after all that, he took the ship out to Luna, then to Venus, made another search of Mars and came back. A pathetic desperation had kept him going until in the end the flame of hope flickered and sank low.

Then and only then did he plant his little craft for keeps, and grimly review his own unique position.

The ship lay in a gentle valley where, so far as he could tell, the path had run down to the railroad crossing where he and Rudy and Sue had sat on the fence and waved at friendly engineers. That had been far back in memory's misty dawn. Two thousand years ago!

Now humanity was no more. One could be certain of that. They could not have transferred themselves elsewhere, not three thousand millions of them. Such a mighty exodus would take far longer than he had been away, even if an immense armada could shift them at the rate of a million a year.

He sat on a smooth, tilted rock, his back to the vessel that had served so well, his white hair stirred by a warm breeze. The gray eyes that had kept calm and steady in the face of a thousand dangers were still calm, undefeated, but immeasurably sad.

Something had happened beyond imagining. What, he did not know, could not discover. There weren't any clues, because it had occurred long, long ago; and the hand of time had obliterated causes and effects.

Or there was one possible clue, useless since it was untranslatable. Taking a slip of paper from his pocket, he pondered over the copy he had made.

WAR Q!

The only plausible guess he could offer was that some line-up of circumstances had precipitated a series of major conflicts ending with humanity's end. Possibly they had lettered the outbreaks alphabetically, the seventeenth one—Q—being the last. Maybe this was a slogan, part of the accompanying spate of propaganda designed to maintain the morale of people doomed to extinction.

He could not have been more wrong, but he was never to know it. Semantic modifications and linguistic changes over many centuries had turned him into a comparative illiterate, and he would never know that, either. The now-archaic language which he still used misled him hopelessly so that he could not recognize the clipped form and simplified spelling of the word BEWARE; neither could he identify a long-discarded capital letter as the stylized drawing of a hateful bacillus.

He could never know that humanity had left the stage of life non-explosively, more or less accidentally, and mostly as the unfortunate result of making something not theirs to create. Some experiments are for Man, some for Another.

So he sat on the stone, elbows on knees, chin on hand, lonely, sick at heart, bitter, resentful and yet strangely full of fight. Whatever had occurred, he decided, made no difference in the fact that he was the last man, the very last.

Ultimately there had to be a last man, anyway, but it could have happened more gloriously and at later date. It could have happened to someone changed beyond dreaming by countless millennia, so old that he was tired, content to sleep forever while the rest of humankind roamed among the stars. It need not have happened now, when the last man had come bearing gladsome news to a world that had always yearned for space.

His fists were tight, his knuckles white as he made decisions with grim disregard for the futility of battle.

All have gone but me. There are no others. But while I live, mankind still lives. I will build myself a rock house and give it a chimney. I will warm it with log fires, and the chimney will send smoke toward the skies, and the stars will peer down and know that man still lives. There will be one home, one window glowing through the night, one garden worshiping the sun by day—because man still lives.

Then, for the briefest moment, reaction set in, and he covered his eyes and murmured: "Oh, God! Oh, God!"

And when it had passed, he looked slowly along the grass and saw the mighty feet.

He could not gaze upward. If he had summoned every fiber of his being, he could not look up. The feet!

Nothing like these existed within two thousand years of space-travel. He knew that beyond doubt, for it was he of all men who had been to see. And he dared not let his eyes follow the feet upward to some colossal height and unbearable culmination. It would be more than human spirit could stand.

The feet could be sensed rather than seen. They stood before him, shapeless yet shaped, immaterial yet undeniably there, of no estimable size or proportions, compounded of the stuff of thought, and of mists and of far-away star-clouds. Their surfaces embodied multitudinous elusive, eye-twisting planes, almost as if while standing there they were simultaneously standing in a thousand other dimensions.

Jerrold had more than enough experience of lower, or equal or stupendously different life-forms to know when he was in the presence of a higher. The effect was hypnotic. The strength within him was not enough to save him from being paralyzed by a mighty awe—though still he had no fear, no fear at all. Man is not afraid, not even the last man.

The little house. A chimney giving forth smoke. I am the last, but I will show them. I will tell the stars.

"Sleep!" came on order into his mind, an irresistible order: "*Sleep*."

He slumped onto his back, his lidded eyes staring where they dared not look when open.

The feet moved a fraction, their countless planes shifting and angling into each other. Came a long-drawn sigh susurrating from the very limits of the space-time continuum. It expressed infinite patience.

"Nothing for it but to try again."

He took something from the sleeper's side, extended its cellular structure of blood and flesh and bone, shaped it, and breathed into it the breath of life.

Leaving the woman to await the man's awakening, the Stranger went away.

Also available from
Mandarin Paperbacks

ERIC FRANK RUSSELL

Next of Kin
WARNING

Upon the cover of this book the nominal publisher claims that this superb story was produced by Eric Frank Russell. It is a barefaced lie because his Eustace knows better.

Apart from the typing of it I had nothing whatever to do with this book. It was ghost-written for me by my next of kin. Or perhaps I should say it was kin-written for me by my next of ghost.

This character, the real author, deposes that his name is Eustace Postlethwaite and considers it a handicap to literary fame. All the same, he swears that this yarn will be printed because he has a fraternal influence with the real publisher, Eustace Bam, who is a shady relative of the nominal publisher.

I am given to understand that neither of these Eustaces would ever be seen dead with a Willy and that where the name appears herein it should be viewed as obscene.

Does this baffle you?
Do you crave enlightenment
Read on . . .

ERIC FRANK RUSSELL

Dreadful Sanctuary

When the seventeenth rocket to Mars, like its sixteen
predecessors, unaccountably explodes before reaching
its destination, at least one man decides to try and find
out what caused the explosion. That man is
John H. Armstrong, an inquisitive and sceptical
scientist who is directly concerned with the eighteenth
rocket, one that is going to have a human pilot. At first
sabotage seems incredible – who would gain from the
failures? But when another scientist dies while talking to
Armstrong and several influential senators seem
dedicated to preventing the rocket's completion, he
begins to smell a rat and hires a private investigator to
dig further. The results of their search are surprising, to
say the least.

Is there a sinister conspiracy to throw the world into
another global war?

Are there really people living on Earth who were born
on other planets?

Is there anything that Armstrong can do about it?

C. J. CHERRYH

The Pride of Chanur

The lordly Hani traders and their ancient enemies, the treacherous Kif, co-exist in uneasy peace at Meetpoint Station. Until the Outsider appears, and changes everything.

For this strange, haunted, smooth-skinned being holds the key to the future of the Compact, and, for the Hani, to future glory – or disastrous ruin.

All the qualities that won C. J. Cherryh her Hugo for Downbelow Station – pace, narrative, inventive scope – are present again on the grand scale in Pride of Chanur.

C. J. CHERRYH

Chanur's Homecoming
INTERSTELLAR WAR –
OR THE LAST HOPE FOR PEACE?

When those enigmatic entities called humans sent their
first exploration ship into Compact space, all the
traditional power alliances of the seven Compact races
were totally disrupted. And, giving shelter to Tully, the
only surviving human, Pyanfar Chanur and her hani
crew were pitched into the centre of a galactic
maelstrom, key players in a power game they scarcely
understood.

Now, with space stations destroyed by rival factions,
unwillingly "allied" with the most devious and
untrustworthy Kif, and forced to doubt their own long-
time champions, the Mahendo Sat, Pyanfar and her
space-going comrades had become the last desperate
hope of the entire Hani race! For, a one-planet race
among whom only the females were allowed into space,
the Hani were in the direct path of a running space
battle which might wipe the very memory of their world
from the galactic maps!

BEN BOVA

Kinsman

Wealthy and privileged, naive and idealistic, Chet
Kinsman is a young Air Force Astronaut who thinks
that the world's crises will never touch him. Until, in
secret orbital combat with a Russian cosmonaut,
Kinsman becomes the first person to commit murder in
space.

Haunted by guilt, grounded, unfit for active service, he
stubbornly clings to his belief in a high frontier. As
pollution, over-population and superpower hostility
push the world to the brink of disaster, only the moon
remains, humanity's last hope for survival and
Kinsman's ultimate goal.

But to win his goal Kinsman must sacrifice everything
in the corridors of power, blackmail his oldest friend,
and exploit the only woman he has ever loved . .

A Selected List of Current and Forthcoming Mandarin Science-Fiction

While every effort is made to keep prices low, it is sometimes necessary to increase prices at short notice. Mandarin Paperbacks reserves the right to show new retail prices on covers which may differ from those previously advertised in the text or elsewhere.

The prices shown below were correct at the time of going to press.

☐ 7493 0006 X	Exile's Gate	C. J. Cherryh	£3.99
☐ 7493 0007 8	The Chronicles of Morgaine	C. J. Cherryh	£4.99
☐ 7493 0021 3	Kinsman	Ben Bova	£3.50

Available June

☐ 7493 0041 8	Chanur's Homecoming	C. J. Cherryh	£3.50
☐ 7493 0068 X	Pride of Chanur	C. J. Cherryh	£2.99
☐ 7493 0037 X	Ravenmoon	Peter Tremayne	£3.50
☐ 7493 0038 8	Highway of Eternity	Clifford D. Simak	£2.99

All these books are available at your bookshop or newsagent, or can be ordered direct from the publisher. Just tick the titles you want and fill in the form below.

Mandarin Paperbacks, Cash Sales Department, PO Box 11, Falmouth, Cornwall TR10 9EN.

Please send cheque or postal order, no currency, for purchase price quoted and allow the following for postage and packing:

UK	55p for the first book, 22p for the second book and 14p for each additional book ordered to a maximum charge of £1.75.
BFPO and Eire	55p for the first book, 22p for the second book and 14p for each of the next seven books, thereafter 8p per book.
Overseas Customers	£1.00 for the first book plus 25p per copy for each additional book.

NAME (Block Letters) .... BARRHEAD ....

ADDRESS ....

....